MW01138216

Copyright 2012

Laurence E Dahners

ISBN: 978-1477673300
ASIN: B00897BJGK

Lieutenant

An Ell Donsaii story #3

———

Laurence E Dahners

Author's Note

This book is the third in the series, the "Ell Donsaii stories."

Though this book *can* "stand alone" it'll be *much* easier to understand if read as part of the series including

"Quicker (an Ell Donsaii story)" and
"Smarter (an Ell Donsaii story #2)"

I've minimized the repetition of explanations that would be redundant to the earlier books in order to provide a better reading experience for those of you who are reading the series.

Table of Contents

Lieutenant

Preprologue

Ell's father, Allan Donsaii, was an unusually gifted quarterback. Startlingly strong, and a phenomenally accurate passer, during his college career he finished two full seasons without any interceptions and two games with 100 percent completions. Unfortunately, he wasn't big enough to be drafted by the pros.

Extraordinarily quick, Ell's mother, Kristen Taylor captained her college soccer team and rarely played a game without a steal.

Allan and Kristen dated

more and more seriously through college, marrying at the end of their senior year. Their friends teased them that they'd only married in order to start their own sports dynasty.

Their daughter Ell got Kristen's quickness, magnified by Allan's surprising strength and highly accurate coordination.

She also has a new mutation that affects the myelin sheaths of her nerves. This mutation produces nerve transmission speeds nearly double those of normal neurons. With faster nerve impulse transmission, she has far quicker reflexes. Yet her new type of myelin sheath is also thinner, allowing more axons, and therefore more neurons, to be packed into the same sized skull. These two factors result in a brain with more neurons, though it isn't larger, and a faster processing speed, akin to a computer with a smaller, faster CPU architecture.

Most importantly, under the influence of adrenalin in a fight or flight situation, her nerves transmit even more rapidly than their normally remarkable speed.

Much more rapidly...

Lieutenant

Prologue

Steve dropped down from the pull up bar and picked up his jump rope. As a new techno beat thundered through his earphones, the rope began to whirr. Unfortunately, his mind wouldn't focus. As usual, money issues plagued him. He liked running security; it fit with his talents as a former Navy Seal. He loved being his own boss too, but work could be... irregular. Not just the fact that sometimes he had three offers to work on the same day and then none for a week, although that could make it hard to make ends meet. But, some of the jobs...

Sure, he'd been hired to protect celebrities as he'd expected when he went into the security business. But he'd *also* been hired to intimidate ex-boyfriends. On one occasion, he felt pretty sure he'd been hired *as* a boyfriend by a woman so irritatingly neurotic it was no wonder she didn't have a man of her own. Dismayingly, he'd been hired to protect shipments of material from one location in Boston to another and worried that the material wasn't exactly legal. However, his standard promise of complete confidentiality made it hard to ask or check. What he'd *like*, would be to hire on as full time security for one celebrity, but there weren't many such here in Boston. He wondered once again if he should move to New York or LA.

Or look for another line of work?

The music paused and his AI (Artificial Intelligence) spoke in his earphone, "Call for you regarding employment." There was a static in the audio.

Steve dropped the rope and, taking a couple of deep breaths, pulled the belt pack of his AI around front to wiggle the wire that went from the AI up to the headband mounting his earphones. Speaking to his AI he said, "Sound check?"

His AI said, "Check, one, two, three…"

The sound was clear again, "Okay, it's good, put them on… Hello?"

An alto voice came in his ear, "Mr. Jacobs?" She sounded young.

"Yes Ma'am."

"You've been recommended to me as someone who can be *completely* discreet and provide excellent security and protection."

Steve said, "Thank you," while once again worrying just why he might need to be completely discreet.

"I'm looking for someone to train me in self-defense and to lead a protection detail that would assist me if I were to be attacked. If you were to take the job, it'd almost certainly require you to move with me to a location away from the Boston area. Unfortunately, that location's at present undetermined. Would you consider such a job?"

"Uh, that could be pretty expensive?"

"I'd pay substantially more than your going rate."

He found his eyebrows were up, "Okay then, sure, I'm interested."

"Before we go into details I'd like to meet and have you give me a self-defense session. I will pay $500 for a one hour session whether or not I decide to hire you and whether or not you decide to come into my employ. Is that agreeable?"

"Sure…" He said wonderingly read he said

wonderingly he said, wonderingly.

They agreed to meet in two hours at the gym Steve usually trained at.

"How will I know who you are?" he asked.

"Five foot nine. Dark brown hair. Thin."

"Okay."

***

Amy buried her face in her hands, "Damn it John. They're *your* kids too!"

In her earphones John's voice said, "Maybe."

"Oh, come on! You want a DNA test?"

"Doesn't matter. I don't have the money."

"What? Did you lose your job?"

"I've... had expenses."

"Oh God, John," Amy said tremulously, "are you gambling again?"

Silence greeted Amy's question. Then her AI said, "Mr. Reston has disconnected."

Amy sobbed a few minutes longer, then got up to go and tell the apartment complex super that she couldn't make the rent... again. She'd ask him for another extension, but she didn't expect the request would be well received. He'd already given her several extensions and the last time she'd asked, he'd told her that he would *not* cut her any more slack.

She, Mikey and Janey were about to be homeless. If she wanted to keep her kids off the streets she'd have to try to get a second job working evenings at another casino and the kids would have to mind themselves. She hated the thought of leaving them unsupervised for hours on end, but it'd be several steps up the ladder from homeless.

***

Steve looked up as the gym door opened. A young brunette woman stood in the door. She was a little on the tall side, at least five eight, could be five nine. Wearing baggy sweats it was a little hard to tell how thin she was, but she wasn't fat by any means. She looked curiously around the gym. He glanced around himself, suddenly realizing how shabby his favorite gym probably looked to the kind of rich girl who could afford his services.

He wouldn't apologize; it was a working gym, not an effete health club. He got up and walked over. "Excuse me, ma'am, I'm Steve Jacobs." He got a better look at her up close, *My God, she's just a kid! Sixteen to twenty at most. And "wow" pretty. Probably a spoiled little rich kid,* he thought, *though she looks vaguely familiar, maybe she's one of the new movie stars?*

She stuck out her hand and said, "Hi," while her eyes ran over his muscular six foot two frame. Her assessment made him feel a little bit like a side of beef at the market.

Steve shook her hand, frustrated because she hadn't given her name. "Sorry, I don't recognize you?"

"Great! Please call me Anne for now. I'll hold my real name until we decide if we can work together."

Steve shrugged, thinking *that* was a silly request, since she must be well known if even *he* recognized her. He didn't follow celebrities at all. But he *could* just have his AI identify her.

At present there was no need to point that out to

the girl, but if she became a client, she'd need to understand it. He waved over to the side, "I've reserved this mat for us to go over self-defense as you asked.

Have you had any training before?" he asked as he walked out onto the mat.

She put her bag down and followed him. "A little... actually, just one session on how to respond to an attacker. A lot of it was on thought processes, like 'Scream—give them your money,' and, 'don't go with them to other locations.'"

"Okay, do you feel you have any strengths or weaknesses?"

She tilted her head, "I'm very quick, but have terrible endurance."

Steve grinned internally. *Everybody thinks they're fast – until they meet someone who really is.* He took justifiable pride in being faster than anyone he knew. He said, "For me to know where to begin, I should evaluate your current ability to resist an attack. Is it okay if I try to simply capture you and wrestle you to the mat? I promise to be careful to avoid hurting you. I won't strike you, only try to capture you."

She shrugged and said, "Okay."

Steve turned suddenly, throwing his arms around her. Before his arms could close, she'd simply *danced out of reach! Holy crap! How did she do that?* Embarrassed, but thinking that her escape had been some kind of weird accident, he lunged out in a dive for her waist, arms spread wide. To his utter astonishment she leapt into the air over his right arm, slapping her hand down on his shoulder as she went over him, then bouncing down behind him as he skidded face first onto the mat. Red faced with embarrassment, he lunged back to his feet, turning back to go after her, desperately wanting to show her that he *could* capture her. But then he stopped, shrugged, took a deep breath and said, "You're absolutely right. You *are* very quick. I'm fast… and you are *much* faster." He thought to himself, *I'm the fastest I've ever met and you just smoked me, so calling you "quick" is a major understatement*. "Your best and almost certainly successful strategy is simply to avoid being captured. I doubt I can do anything to improve your skill there, though I might be able to show you a few moves. Are there any kinds of situations that you imagine you wouldn't be able to simply avoid?"

She looked at him intently, then sighed, "I don't have to 'imagine.' In the past year I've been kidnapped twice. Once with drugs and once with a Taser. For certain reasons I've become even more of a target recently. I'd like to learn some strategies to avoid capture, as well as tactics I might use to disable my captors if I *am* captured. I'd also like to have a security team available at all times to rescue me in case I actually *am* captured by the SOBs."

Steve's brows rose. "Okay. But that'll be *very* expensive."

She shrugged as if the money didn't matter.

Rich bitch, he thought to himself. "Well, let me show you some disabling moves."

"Preferably ones that don't do permanent injury."

He grunted. "Pretty hard to disable someone without *some* risk of permanent injury. But let's have you try this." He demonstrated an open hand strike to the mid-face and nose that, properly executed, would set the nose on fire and water up the eyes.

She danced to his right and, before he could even start to put his guard up, she slapped him lightly in the mid-face, "Like this?"

Holy crap! Even though she had barely struck him, his nose stung and his eyes watered. She'd done it so quickly that he knew, with absolute certainty, that he wouldn't have been able to stop her. He grimaced, "Yeah, like that." He "snorked" his suddenly runny nose. Embarrassed, he said, "I can teach you more things but I'm ashamed to say that, with that much speed, you can probably protect yourself better than I can." He snorked again.

She put her hand over her mouth, "Oh, I'm so sorry. I hit you too hard didn't I? I thought I pulled it enough that it wouldn't hurt. I really, really apologize. I'll double your fee to $1000?"

Steve blinked, grinned at her and said, "I'm not really hurt. Pretty embarrassed though. Security experts aren't supposed to get beaten up by young girls. How old are you anyway?" Suddenly it clicked, "Oh Hell! You're Ell Donsaii aren't you?"

She nodded, an almost guilty look on her face. "Eighteen. I *knew* this wig wasn't a good enough disguise by itself."

"I'd sure like to have you tell me how you escaped those terrorists at the Olympics sometime. But, having seen your gymnastic moves, I guess it's no wonder you can defend yourself."

She shrugged again. "Can you show me some more moves? I promise not to actually hit you again."

Amazed to be teaching physical skills to an Olympic caliber gymnast like Ell Donsaii, Steve spent a half hour going over a variety of strikes and break-holds in slow motion. She replicated each at near full speed and precisely pulled every strike so that it didn't actually touch.

Steve cocked his head, "I should also advise you on how to avoid being a target. I notice that your AI headband's wirelessly communicating with your belt pack. You need to be aware that wireless headbands like that constantly emit radio signals in order to carry the video from the headband's cameras and the audio from your headband's microphones. Kidnappers can use those signals to track you if you escape a situation, so I'd suggest you use a wired headband," Steve lifted the wire that went from his headband to his own AI's belt pack, "even if they *are* kind of a pain."

Ell gave him a lopsided little grin as if she were in on some kind of joke that he didn't understand. "Okay, I think I'd like to hire you to lead a security detail for me. Let me tell you what I want and then you can think about whether you can provide it?" So they sat on the mat and spoke quietly about how he might provide protection. She didn't want visible bodyguards, on the assumption that she could protect herself from head-on attacks. She wanted him to hire a team that'd have members constantly on duty nearby, ready to rescue her if she *were* to be successfully captured. The team would take turns training with her, teaching her what each of them knew about self-defense. She said, "I'm in the Air Force and I expect to be assigned somewhere soon. It could be anywhere in the world. I think I'd be pretty safe while *on* a military base but I'd want your team standing by just off base and following me any time I left the base."

Steve cocked his head at her, "Are you sure you understand how expensive this'll be? You're talking salaries for 5-10 expensive people, plus travel and accommodation expenses. I'm sure you have some endorsement money from winning the Olympics, but we're talking around 1-2 million dollars a year if I hire really good people."

Ell looked at him coolly for a moment, "Hire really good people. My life's very important to me."

Steve thought he remembered seeing a news story about Ell Donsaii's poor childhood on the news feeds. Much as he respected her and as much as he'd like to work for her he couldn't afford to end up holding an empty bag financially. "I'd... need some assurances on the financial aspects..."

"Sure, my AI's just sent you a contract my lawyer drew up for me, or you can use one of your own, similar in substance. As you'll see it's backed with an escrow account holding a million dollars you can spend from if you agree to the job."

Steve's eyes widened at the casual way she could drop that kind of money into escrow, "Um, do you mind if I ask where the money came from? Stories about you from the Olympics implied you came from a modest background and I haven't actually seen any advertisements that capitalize on your gymnastic fame."

She laughed, "Less than modest background, I think. More like, edge of poverty. But sure, here, look at my back," she said lifting up the back of her sweatshirt, "no AI belt pack."

She looked at him with a question in her eyes.

Steve raised his eyebrows, "I don't understand. Going without an AI's crazy. The first thing the police or I would want to do if kidnappers took you, is download the audio, video and GPS record your AI'd stored on the net right before your capture. That way we could find out exactly where you'd been, who you'd been with and what'd been happening right before you were taken. You really should have an AI that stays connected to the net at all times."

"Yes, well that's where the money came from. I invented a communications device a few months ago. My headband *is* connected to an AI, but it's using one of my new communication devices. Since the communication device works great even over large distances I'm actually running my AI on a supercomputer back home in North Carolina instead of on a small belt pack CPU like everyone else."

"But that's *just* as big a problem. If that's the case, your headband is constantly punching out a radio signal to reach the net for transmission to the Carolinas. The constant signal it's using to transmit audio and video to the net's even more powerful and easier to track than one that just sends to your belt pack CPU. At least those compress the info and only intermittently transmit it to the net."

"Sorry, I didn't explain that very well. The communication device I invented *doesn't* depend on radio. Please trust me when I say that I am emitting no radio signals whatsoever. Well perhaps a little leakage from the electronics of the video cameras on my headband."

Steve looked at her dubiously, "Okay, if you say so."

He thought she could tell from his tone that he didn't believe it. She said, "Well, you'll have an opportunity to check it out for yourself if you hire on. I'll be wanting to fit you with PGR communications too."

"PGR?"

"Photon-gluon resonance. It's the basis of the communication device." She clarified, "Instead of radio."

"Okaaay," Steve said, wondering to himself if she

might be delusional.

But if she had enough money to put a million in escrow, did it matter?

Chapter One

The knob jiggled and the door began to open. Janey immediately started yelling, "MOM! Mikey won't let me use the big screen for my homework!"

Mikey leapt up from the couch and, pointing back at his little sister said, "She hasn't..." His voice stumbled to a stop when he saw his mother's tear streaked face. "What's the matter?" he said in a small voice. His mother'd been unhappy a lot the past few weeks, but he hadn't seen her cry.

Amy put down her purse and walked across the room to her children. "I... I'm so sorry kids." Their faces blurred behind her tears. "We're in trouble. Pretty bad trouble."

Mikey put his arms around her, "Mom?" he asked anxiously, "What happened?"

Amy had her right arm around Mikey as Janey crept under her left, "Your dad hasn't been able to make his child support payments for you guys for a long time now. And when Janey was sick, it cost so much money, and I missed so much work, we really got behind on our bills."

Mikey swallowed, not quite sure what the talk about money meant, but, from the trembling in his mother's voice, he felt sure it must mean something bad. "You can have *my* money Mom."

Amy sobbed and sank to the couch, pulling her

children to her. "Thank you honey, but we need a lot more money than you've got." She sniffed, "I do appreciate your offer though."

Janey said, "I'm sorry I got sick... Do we have to move in with a relative?" Janey had a classmate who'd moved in with her grandmother when her mother got sick. So, that possibility was something she could comprehend.

"Oh, Janey... Being sick wasn't your fault, don't blame yourself. I wish we *could* move in with a relative. But with Gramma and Grampa passed on, and me an only child, we don't really have a relative to take us in." Amy did have a cousin on her mother's side but she was pretty sure he was a drug dealer. She'd rather live on the street than move her children in with that guy.

"What *are* we going to do?" Mikey asked.

"I'm not sure yet honey, but we're going to have to move and we might have to live in our car for a little while. *Wherever* we go, we'll have to get rid of a lot of stuff. We can sell some of it, like the big screen you guys were fighting about. Selling the stuff will give us some money." She shrugged, "We won't have anyplace to keep those things anyway."

Ice ran in Mikey's veins. There was a rumor that one of the kids in his class was homeless. The other kids whispered, pointed, and sometimes they laughed. The kid had been popular last year, but now he hardly said anything.

"In our car?" Janey whispered, trying to imagine it.

***

Steve looked at Jamieson with some concern. The

rest of the team had been filled out with six guys Steve already knew. He'd hired two women, like Ms. Donsaii had requested, but even they'd been women Steve had already known and respected. However, Ms. Donsaii wanted to have a total of ten on the team with three members of the team dressed for action and immediately ready, though they could be napping. Three more were to be nearby, but available on call. The idea was to have three members immediately ready to come to her aid and three more available within thirty minutes. The remaining four could be completely off duty or on vacation. She felt confident she'd only be subject to kidnapping, not assassination, so she didn't want any actual bodyguards. She just wanted a team standing by to rescue her.

So far Ms. Donsaii'd met each of the members as Steve brought them in and she'd approved all of them. But they needed a tenth member and Steve had run out of people he knew well. Jamieson had also been a Navy Seal. He'd been recommended to Steve by an ex-military buddy of his. However, Jamieson seemed awfully cocky and… abrasive.

Maybe that'd be okay if it meant the team would have another highly capable member?

The entire team had gathered in a back room at Steve's gym and had been doing some hand to hand combat exercises while Donsaii interviewed Jamieson. She'd been talking to him a lot longer than she had when she'd interviewed the other team members.

~~~

Jamieson knew his ruggedly muscular looks melted most women. Dirty blond hair, handsome face, long ropy muscles, six foot one. His looks in combination with his SEAL credentials meant that he'd expected the interview to be a mere formality. Instead this child of a client had been busting his chops for thirty minutes now. Asking questions about how he'd handle various situations, then asking him to come up with less violent responses than he'd initially proposed. She had a pretty face, though he liked his women with more meat on their bones. He sighed, "Ma'am, you obviously don't know much about security. It isn't all sweetness and light. Sometimes you've got to break a few eggs."

She stood, "Okay, well, thank you for coming in Mr. Jamieson. We'll just have to keep looking." She turned and walked back over to the rest of her team.

"What! You're turning me down?" he followed her out onto the mat and sneered around at her existing team. "I could wipe the mat with any three of these people you've hired so far... I wouldn't even break a sweat."

She turned back to look at him, a bemused expression on her face, "That's as may be. Nonetheless, I prefer the team I have. I don't want someone with a cowboy attitude."

Jamieson leaned into her personal space, "That's so much bullshit! You're just a spoiled little rich kid who doesn't know what's good for her!"

Steve stepped over and reached out tentatively, a little concerned because Jamieson was younger than he and more recently in the service, stopping him might be difficult. However, eyes flashing, Donsaii put out a hand to wave him back. She said, "Spoiled huh? You're wanting to demonstrate your astonishing fighting skills?"

"Sure!"

She looked around, "Pugil sticks?"

Laurence E Dahners

"No problem."

~~~

A stack of pugil sticks with 2" diameter shafts stood in the corner. They were 50 inches long with heavily padded ends. Ell had trained on them briefly when she'd been at the Air Force Academy so she was familiar with their use. She went over, picked up a pair of them and threw one to Jamieson.

He said, "Okay, who am I taking on?"

"Me."

"What!?" He blinked, "I could break you in half with one of these!"

She smiled grimly. "I don't break very easily," she said giving her stick a little twirl. "The ring on the mat's our boundary, three solid strikes or push me out of the ring three times and you're the winner. I'll pay you $500 for your time." She waved the rest of her team off the mat.

Steve stepped closer to Ell and in a low voice said, "Ms. Donsaii? I don't think this is a good idea. Jamieson may not pull punches like he should."

She looked at him a moment, then said, "You may be right, but probably not for the reasons you think. However," she shrugged, "I think the team needs to be aware of my abilities—that knowledge might be important someday.

She seemed to relax, "On the other hand demonstrating them on Jamieson here is probably a stupid move." She tossed the stick to Mary and turned to Jamieson, "Sorry. I shouldn't have let you irritate me."

Jamieson muttered, but loud enough for everyone to hear, "Yeah, sure. I'd back off too, if I were you."

Ell's eyes flashed, "Mary? Toss that stick back." She held out her hand.

Mary looked at Steve, her eyes questioning. He shrugged, "She's the boss."

Ell said, "Steve, get us some headgear and gloves also, please?"

In a few minutes Ell was back in the ring with Jamieson. "You understand the rules? They aren't standard military. Push me out of the ring three times or three solid strikes, okay?"

Jamieson rolled his eyes, "No problem."

Ell took a deep breath and let herself slip slightly into the zone. "Steve? A one-minute bout. Blow the whistle?"

Looking uncomfortable, Steve blew the whistle.

Jamieson immediately charged Ell, stick held waist high and horizontal. He obviously intended to shove her out of the ring and be done with it.

Moving so fast the group hardly understood what'd happened, Ell dropped under the right end of Jamieson's pugil stick, shoving her stick between his feet to trip him, then bouncing up behind him and delivering a firm strike to his buttocks that sent him the rest of the way down onto his face and helped him slide on out of the ring.

Steve blinked as he blew the whistle again, "One out, one strike," he looked at his stopwatch, "eight seconds off the clock." The new members of Ell's team looked at each other, eyebrows raised. Even Steve, who'd had personal experience with Ell's quickness felt astonished all over again.

Jamieson leapt back to his feet, face red and looking like he wanted to kill someone.

Steve stepped over next to Ell and spoke quietly,

"You sure you want to continue? He's ready to rip your head off."

She nodded, her eyes fixed on her opponent, "You okay Jamieson?"

"Of course! I just tripped."

Ell realized that she might be too far into the zone if she'd moved fast enough Jamieson didn't even realize she'd purposefully snagged his feet. She took a deep breath and turned to Steve. "Whistle please."

Steve shrugged and blew the whistle. Jamieson stalked toward Ell, then lunged out, thrusting the pugil stick like a lance. Ell moved like a bullfighter, arching her body to let the thrust pass by on her left, then she touched Jamieson lightly on the back of the head with the pad on her stick. Steve blew the whistle again, "Second strike, eighteen seconds off the clock."

Jamieson shook his head like a bull in the arena, snorted once and hissed, "This is *bullshit!*" He stared fiercely at Ell.

With a concerned look on her face she asked, "You still okay?" Jamieson nodded vehemently, looking like he was ready to detonate. Ell turned to Steve "Whistle please?"

This time when the whistle sounded Jamieson stood in place, evidently having decided to take a defensive posture. He held his stick horizontally across his lower chest. Ell walked to him and stopped near the edge of his reach, watching his eyes. Suddenly, he swung the right end of his stick out at her.

This time instead of dodging she blocked the padded end of his stick with the central bar of her own. He swapped ends and punched out with the left. She blocked that one as well. A flurry of blows shot out with Ell blocking each of them precisely in the center of her stick as she slowly backed away. Feeling he had the upper hand, Jamieson pursued her, but she led him around the ring so he couldn't propel her out of it. Even in the superb condition Jamieson was in, the pace of his strikes slowed after a circuit of the ring—then there was a sudden thump. His headgear was twisted around so the earpiece covered his eyes.

Steve blew the whistle, "Three strikes, game over. Forty-three seconds off the clock."

Jamieson ripped off the crooked head gear and hurled it to the mat, "This is bullshit!"

He screamed it this time, stalking toward Steve, rage on his face. "I hit her a million times and you didn't blow the whistle. She grazes my headgear and you do?"

Ell stepped between Jamieson and Steve. Her face glacially still, she said, "You never hit *me*, Mr. Jamieson, only my pugil stick." She didn't mention how careful she'd been to "only" hit his headgear after what she'd done to one of her trainers at the Academy. "Review the video record from your AI if you'd like."

Jamieson glared at Ell, "I could have blown you off the mat any time I wanted, if I hadn't been afraid I'd break you in two! And if your boyfriend hadn't been blowing the whistle every time I got near you."

Ell put her hands up, calmingly. "Okay, Mr. Jamieson. I'll take your word for it. Now, if you'd leave us?" She raised an eyebrow politely.

"Not till I kick your boyfriend's ass," he roared, lunging around Ell toward Steve.

There was a loud "crack" as Ell slapped him in the mid-face. Jamieson dropped to the mat, then rolled over and sat up holding his nose and blinking rapidly. Blood seeped from beneath his hand and started dripping off his fingers.

Ell dropped to her knees in front of Jamieson. "I'm so sorry, I should never have let this go so far." She looked up, "Randy, please get the first aid kit." She turned back to Jamieson, "Do you know where you are?

Jamieson nodded blearily. "Da gym."

She held up three fingers, "How many?"

"Ffree," he said, a stunned look in his eyes.

Ell nodded, "Again, I apologize." May we look beneath your hand?" He lifted it for a moment. Ell said, "All the bleeding seems to be coming from your nose, there aren't any lacerations on the outside." She turned back to her team, "Barrett, can you take him to the ED to get him patched up and checked over?"

Barrett nodded, eyes wide.

"Thanks. Put it on my account."

After Jamieson'd been led blearily away and Ell had left for her apartment, the rest of the team sat and watched what had happened from the different viewpoints of each of their AI's video records. Even in slow motion it was hard to catch all the events. Randy turned to Steve, "Holy cripes Steve, what the Hell does she need us for? The girl's a one-woman demolition derby!"

Steve shrugged. "Chinese teams have successfully kidnapped her two times in the past year. Once they drugged her, once they Tasered her. She escaped both times, the first time without any help. Presumably they'll up their game next time. Their objective seems to be to get her out of the country. It's *our* job to be sure that they don't succeed.

"Why?! Surely they don't want to have her do gymnastics for them?"

"She's some kind of physics genius too. All the money she's using to hire us comes from an invention she made just back in November. She was dirt poor before that. The Chinese apparently want her to do physics research for them."

Mary said, "But Steve, she's spending money like it's water. Are you sure she's not going to run out and leave us in the lurch? What if this invention of hers doesn't pan out?"

Steve smiled, then lifted his shirt and turned around, saying, "Look Ma, no backpack for my AI." They all looked at him blankly. He tilted his head with a wry grin, "So, she's invented a chip, she calls it a PGR chip, that communicates wirelessly, without radio, over unlimited distances. The CPU for my AI is sitting at home on my desk. And, she's upgraded it to near supercomputer status. So I have a huge amount of processing power, but I'm not *carrying* anything except my headband. It has a chip that ties me into that high powered computer back in my house!"

"But what if someone blocks the signal?"

"Can't be blocked, intercepted, read or detected." Eyebrows rose. "*That's* why she has so much money. She mentioned to me that she donated a hundred and five million dollars to North Carolina State University. The girl *never even went to school there!* If she can *donate* that kind of money, I think she can probably afford our services for the foreseeable future." A serious look came over him, "But, every one of you remember. Her wealth is a secret and keeping that secret's really important to her. Do *not* breathe a word of it to anyone else. Remember that retirement fund she's set up for each of you? It's gone if you give up her secrets."

He looked around at the group. "Next on our agenda. She's been assigned to Nellis Air Force Base in

Nevada. We'll be moving to Las Vegas, so I hope none of you have a gambling problem. First though, at least some of us will need to follow her temporarily to Lackland Air Force Base in San Antonio. She's got to go through an abbreviated officer training course."

Chapter Two

Ell pulled off her brunette wig and fluffed her reddish blond hair as she drove up to the gate at Nellis. She was looking forward to this assignment with some anticipation. She wondered what the Air Force had in store for her. She assumed that they wanted to take advantage of their special access to her and upgrade their communications systems to PGR, especially their UAV (Unmanned Aerial Vehicle) fleet. Much of the fleet was based here at Nellis. Communicating with UAVs on the other side of the world through satellite radio transmissions would be crazy now that PGR was available. Before she'd had the idea for PGRs, Ell'd often worried about the possibility that opposing forces might find a way to interfere with, or worse, suborn communication with American UAVs. It only made sense that the Air Force would want to make use of its royalty free right to her PGR technology, something enemies couldn't possibly interfere with.

The Nellis gate AI queried hers and captured an image of her face. After a moment it lighted green. The guard waved her through and the AI in her new Ford Focus drove her to the Joint Unmanned Combat Air Systems office. In a few minutes she'd started cooling her heels outside the exec's office.

With nothing else to do she looked up at her HUD (Heads Up Display) and began re-examining some of her quantum dimensional equations, searching for her current holy grail, a method to achieve interstellar communications. Ell'd become convinced that the fact that no radio signals had been detected from other stars didn't mean that there *weren't* any advanced civilizations on the worlds surrounding them. Instead she thought it meant they just didn't use *radio* for communication. They probably used PGR or something like it and therefore didn't radiate in the radio band. She hoped she'd be able to find a method to communicate with such civilizations across interstellar distances. According to her theory, it'd be possible if entities at the two stars both had one member of a pair of entangled molecules in which Photon-Gluon Resonance could be elicited. Ell's equations didn't predict any limit to the distance over which PGR could communicate instantly.

There was however, the minor problem of delivering one member of such a pair of entangled molecules across the light years to another star. Ell had a gut feeling that such a molecule could somehow be delivered through the same tiny 5th dimension that the entangled molecules in her PGR devices used to instantly communicate with one another. But for the life of her, she couldn't see how that might actually be accomplished.

Deep in thought, her eyes had lost focus on her HUD when she heard her name.

"Lieutenant Donsaii?" said A1C Jobst, marveling at how nice looking the new "El Tee" was. "Colonel Ennis is ready to see you now." When she stood, Jobst was surprised to see she was as tall as he was. "Right this way Ma'am." He motioned down the hall. As he walked beside her he kept glancing over at her. She walked confidently and her uniform seemed to fit unusually well. He shrugged, her slender shape no doubt made her easy to fit.

Jobst stopped at a door labeled, "Lt. Colonel Ennis, Executive Officer." Jobst knocked on the frame of the open door and said, "Colonel Ennis, I have Lieutenant Donsaii here."

"Send her in."

Ell stepped into the office and came to attention. "Lieutenant Donsaii, reporting as ordered sir." She said, staring at the wall over the Colonel's head, expecting him to call her to "at ease."

He didn't. He said, "Dismissed, Airman," and turned back to Ell.

~~~

Ennis looked Ell up and down. She was really attractive, but looked like a teenager. Ennis hadn't ever seen a woman who looked this good in uniform. Suddenly he realized what must be making up a significant part of her appearance. "What's the maximum regulation height for women's heels in the Air Force uniform, Lieutenant?"

Ell's heart sank. Sounded like the Exec was a real ball buster. Oh well, she'd had a lot of experience with that kind of attitude as a Cadet. Ell continued to focus on the wall over Ennis' head. "Sir, the maximum height has been reduced to one and one half inches."

"How high are yours?"

"Sir, one inch."

"Bullshit!" He stood, "Let me see."

Ell made a right face and lifted her left foot up behind her so that the low heel of the shoe would be evident.

"Do you have lifts inside those shoes?" he asked dangerously.

"No sir. I *do* have unusually long legs."

He grunted and sat back down. "At ease."

Ell assumed parade rest and looked Ennis in the face. But she didn't say anything.

"How old are you anyway?"

Ell was a little surprised. Surely he would have her record readily available if she was being assigned to his squadron? "I'm eighteen, Sir."

"My God! I assumed you just *looked* young! How the hell'd you get those gold bars?"

"Sir, I graduated from the Academy at an unusually young age."

"What! The Air Force Academy?"

"Yes sir."

"When did the Academy start turning out children?"

"Sir, typically the youngest is aged twenty-one. I'm an unusual exception." She decided against mentioning that she'd actually been seventeen when she got her diploma. She was torn between a sense of relief to be somewhere that her reputation hadn't preceded her and an irrational irritation that he didn't know who she was. Inwardly she sighed. It seemed unlikely, after all, that the Air Force had made this assignment with an eye to using her special knowledge in outfitting the UAV fleet with PGR. Seemed more like the usual, "left hand not knowing what the right is doing" cluster that happens so often in large organizations.

Ennis threw his hands up, "What the Hell am I supposed to do with you?"

Assuming the question was rhetorical, Ell said nothing.

Ennis eyes went to her ribbons, seeing her Air Force

Lieutenant

service ribbon that everyone got , plus a Marksmanship ribbon. His eye's narrowed again. "What's the light blue ribbon?"

"Um, Sir, that's the Medal of Honor."

Ennis rocked back in his chair, feeling like someone had punched him in the gut. "What?" He said weakly.

"It's the Medal of Honor, Sir."

"I heard you the first time Lieutenant." His brow lowered. "Did you order that as a joke?" He said dangerously.

"No Sir." Ell said quietly. She was surprised. Hers had been the first Air Force Medal of Honor in fifteen years. It'd been in the Air Force Newsletter. She would've thought he'd of at least *heard* about it.

Suddenly recognition spread across his face. "Oh! You're that Olympic Cadet that stopped the terror attack?"

"Yes sir." Ell again said quietly, not at all sure how he was going to take this.

Conflicting emotions raced across Ennis' face, then he rose to his feet, came to attention and saluted.

With some surprise, because salutes are not normally rendered indoors, nor while "uncovered," Ell returned the salute. A salute is a gesture of respect, so she took it as such... she hoped?

"Pleased to have you on our team, Lieutenant. Please be seated." He gestured at one of the two chairs.

Ell sat, using the posture of seated attention she'd learned at the Academy.

Ennis looked up at the ceiling. Then he said, "Obviously I should have looked through your record prior to interviewing you Lieutenant. If I remember right, you're some kind of math whiz too?"

"Yes sir, I'm pretty good at math."

"And I suppose you must have pretty good reactions to be a gymnast?"

"Yes Sir."

"Is your vision bad? Not that fighter pilots aren't dinosaurs, but they still try to shoehorn the best physical specimens into that mold."

"Uh, No Sir. I have 20/20 vision. I suspect they didn't want to expend the resources training me as a pilot because I only have a two-and-a-half-year commitment."

"I thought you went to the Academy?"

"Yes Sir. But I only attended for two years, so I only accrued a two-and-a-half-year obligation."

"What? How'd you wind up a Lieutenant if you didn't graduate?"

"Sir, I did graduate. I achieved advanced placement in most of my classes when I arrived and completed the remaining requirements for graduation in two years."

Ennis sighed and rested his jaw on his fist as he looked at Ell with a bemused expression. "Somebody just tossed a grenade in my office."

Ell's brow furrowed, "Sir?"

"You. *You're* a grenade. If I don't figure out some way to utilize your talents *and* keep you out of trouble, you'll explode in my face and make a shambles of my career." He sighed, "Well, in *this* Command, we fly UAVs. Most of the flying is now done by enlisted, supervised by officers in small groups. If I assign you to logistics or maintenance like I'd planned, someone will accuse me of being uninspired. So, let's get you trained to fly UAVs yourself and plan to have you supervise such flights. Can't supervise the enlisted who fly UAVs if you don't know how to fly 'em yourself."

"No Sir."

Lieutenant

~~~

Over the next few hours Ell shuttled back and forth across the base, picking up supplies, talking to base housing, being introduced to the UAV pilot training squadron and having hundreds of terabytes of UAV training materials transferred to her AI.

~~~

At the end of the day she considered signing in at the Visiting Officer barracks, but didn't really want to. She had Allan summon her car and contact Steve. "Steve, what's the word on a place for me to stay?"

"Ma'am, we've tentatively rented an apartment for you that meets most of our criteria for a safe location. We've placed the change car in a parking lot near base. Your AI has the location. You can stay at the apartment we picked out tonight and, if you don't like it, we'll look elsewhere tomorrow."

Ell had tried to get her security team to stop calling her Ma'am, but Steve refused. In his book the boss should always be addressed with respect. Calling her Ma'am was a necessary part of reinforcing that attitude. She said, "Okay, I'm heading over to change cars now." Her Ford had just pulled up and she got in, quickly looking around to see if anyone was taking an interest in which car was hers. She flipped the switch to manual and punched the accelerator, just to feel the surge of power from the modified power train Steve'd had installed. With a sigh she flipped control back to the little Ford's AI and said, "Take me to the location Steve gave you."

Sedately, it did so, eventually pulling into a parking lot at a nearby shopping mall. The car took her out to a back corner of the lot where the cars were scattered around rather than packed in. Ell saw her small, old Chevy Colorado pickup and directed the AI to pull in about seven spaces away. She'd watched for tails and when she'd felt sure she was clear, she'd applied some makeup and taken off her uniform jacket, tie tab, Air Force Belt and name tag. All of this went into the compartment Steve had installed under the passenger's seat. This left her dressed in a fairly unremarkable light blue blouse and dark blue pants. She pushed the seat back down over the compartment and shrugged into a leather jacket. She picked up the brunette wig she'd taken out of the compartment before putting her clothes in and looked around to see if anyone was watching.

A little girl was staring at Ell out of the passenger window of the next car! Ell sighed and put her wig into her purse, then got out of the car. The girl sat in a minivan that had its back end completely stuffed with boxes and clothes. Half of the back seat was full too, but Ell could see a boy, somewhat older than the girl, sitting in the unfilled half of the back seat. The passenger window rolled down and the girl asked, "Are you Ell Donsaii?"

Internally, Ell cringed at the deceptively simple failure of all her efforts to make an identity change into someone who'd go unrecognized. Outwardly she smiled at the girl and said, "I am, and who are you?"

The girl quietly said, "I'm Janey Reston." She put a finger in the corner of her mouth, staring at Ell.

The boy in the backseat said something and Janey turned momentarily to him, "What's an autograph?"

Ell smiled at the two kids, then she took a pen and a card out of her purse. She wrote on the card, "To Janey Reston, from Ell Donsaii." and held it out to her. "That's an autograph."

The young girl took it goggle eyed, then looked up at Ell, "Thank you!"

Ell walked over to her truck and got in, telling the truck's AI to take her to the apartment Steve had picked up. She put the brunette wig on as the truck was turning out of the lot. She glanced around the applied her small nose prosthesis and some darker makeup while the truck drove to the apartment.

~~~

When she walked into the apartment complex she saw Barrett in the quadrangle, but carefully didn't wave or say anything. Instead she let Allan, her AI, direct her up to the 2nd floor apartment Steve had chosen. Allan unlocked the door for her. Entering, she found Steve and Mary sitting in the living room.

They looked up and Steve said, "There was a little hold up in the parking lot?"

"Yeah, cute kid recognized me and asked for my autograph."

Steve looked askance, "Even in your wig?"

Ell shrugged, "I was just about to put it on when I saw her watching me."

He looked up at the ceiling, "May be better to put it on while the car is moving?"

"No, I think the plan to do it in the fringes of a parking lot where there aren't many observers is sound. It was just a freak accident these kids were sitting in their car close to where I parked."

Steve grimaced then shrugged, "Okay. Can we show you around this apartment?"

"Sure."

It had three bedrooms, one for Ell, one for Ell's office

and one for storage. Because the complex was new Steve'd been able to tentatively rent the five apartments adjoining hers for Ell's security team, two to an apartment. If she agreed to the plan, he'd have interconnecting doors installed so the teams could get into her apartment unobserved. That way they could have meetings and still keep up an external appearance that Ell and the team didn't know each other. The complex had a pool and a workout room where they could keep in shape. There was a martial arts gym nearby where they could practice and get further training in hand-to-hand combat. The apartment was moderately close to Nellis, but not so close that it was known as a military apartment complex. There were a number of parking lots between the base and the apartment where Ell could change vehicles from her Donsaii military life to her disguised civilian one as Raquel Blandon. Steve had purchased another Ford Focus of the same model, color and year as the one that Ell drove onto base. It was in the shop having its powertrain upgraded. Same thing for a copy of her old Chevy Colorado pickup.

"Seems great to me Steve. Thanks for a job well done."

He shrugged, "I was worried you'd want a more upscale apartment complex, but I couldn't find anything that met the security and proximity needs."

Ell laughed, "I'm not an 'upscale' kinda girl." She looked around and laughed. "This is the nicest apartment I've ever had."

Steve turned to Mary, "Can you give us a minute?"

Mary got up and went into the kitchen, saying "I'm thinking I'll make some tacos, okay?"

"Thanks, that'd be great." Ell turned to Steve and

raised an eyebrow.

"Here's the deal," he said. "You need a personal assistant. Someone who can cook your meals when you're too busy. Someone to do your grocery shopping and otherwise hustle to do the little crap that'll clog up your life. Someone who can deal with payroll for your employees." He raised an eyebrow. "We, the security team, have been doing a lot of that stuff so far, and we don't mind, but it's going to degrade our efficiency at doing what you really want us doing—protecting you."

Ell sighed. "You're right of course. The only problem is finding time to find someone to fill the role."

Steve said, "See, you even need an assistant to find someone to assist you! But, if I've got your approval, I'll place some ads tomorrow."

~~~

After Steve left, Ell called her Mom and Gram, ate tacos with Mary and then went into her office. She was pleased to see the team had already set up a large screen display. She launched into her briefing materials on the UAV program, skimming rapidly through the astonishing amount of chaff to find the kernels of important stuff. Then she looked over the curriculum of the UAV classes she'd missed in the first three weeks and read the course materials for those lectures. Eventually she began running some flights on the included simulator and getting a feel for what some of the different UAVs could do.

~~~

After Ell's usual three hours sleep, she got up and grabbed a couple bananas and three breakfast bars. When she pulled out of the parking lot another car pulled out of an adjoining lot. She checked with Allan and found that Randy and Dan were in her trailing car. She parked the truck at a little different location in the parking lot and looked over at the Focus. With surprise she recognized that the minivan full of boxes and clothes was still parked next to her car. She slowly pulled off the brunette wig and put it in her purse then ran fingers through her short reddish blond hair. As she walked slowly over to her Ford she wondered if, despite the kids, it could be some kind of "set up" to trap her? Ell told Allan to have Randy and Dan drive on into the lot instead of staying outside like they'd planned.

Ell walked closer and, to her amazement saw Janey sound asleep in the reclined passenger seat. Her brother looked to be asleep in the back seat. No one was in the driver's seat. *These children couldn't have spent the night here could they? Where are their parents?*

Just then a woman walked up to the driver's side of the car. She was pretty, about Ell's height though not as slender. She was a brunette like Ell's "Raquel" identity. The woman set a bag with the McDonald's logo down on top of the car and quietly said, "Are you really Ell Donsaii?"

Ell nodded.

"Thanks for signing that autograph for Janey last night. It really made her day." The woman's voice sounded a little choked and Ell saw a tear roll down her cheek.

"Uh, sure. What are you guys doing here so early in the morning?" Ell had a feeling of dread, certain she knew the answer to her own question.

"We, uh, we've... had a run of bad luck. We were evicted from our apartment on Saturday and we're having to live in our car until I can get our finances straightened out." Her shoulders sagged and a tear slipped down the other cheek.

Ell looked around, no one else was nearby. She walked over to the woman and touched her on the shoulder, crouching a little to look up into her down-turned eyes. "What happened?"

"Ah, cripes, what didn't happen? Mike and Janey's dad, he... he's a deadbeat, though I don't want *them* to know that. Janey got sick and I missed a lot of work staying with her in the hospital. My job fired me, my health insurance expired, suddenly we're in a lot of debt to the hospital, my credit cards are maxed... I took a job dealing blackjack at a casino, but it hasn't been catching me back up. I got three months behind on our rent... and my new boss is a jerk..." She stumbled to a stop with a sob. "Sorry." She pulled a napkin out of the McDonald's bag and wiped her cheek. "These aren't *your* problems." She gave Ell a tremble lipped grin. "I've got to feed these kids and get them to school." She opened the car door.

Ell held the door open for her. "Hey, I might have a tip for a better job Ms. Reston. What are your skills?"

She gave a bitter laugh, "I was an executive assistant for one of the casino managers. *I* thought I was indispensable. Turns out it was my job that was indispensable. My boss threw me over pronto when I couldn't be there at his beck and call every instant. 'Got to have someone I can count on Amy.'" She used a nasal twang for the last line.

Ell looked up and saw Randy and Dan parked about four spaces down and across, Randy watching Ell with his eyebrows raised. Ell shook her head at him, then turned back to the woman who'd slid into her driver's seat. Ell lifted the McDonald's bag off the roof and handed it down to her. "Ms. Reston, can you port me your resume? I happen to know someone who's looking for an assistant?"

Reston took the bag, sniffed and said "Okay."

Allan spoke in Ell's ear, confirming that he'd received the resume from Reston's AI. Ell quietly closed the car door and, as Reston shook Janey awake, she walked around to her Focus.

In transit to the base Ell took off her leather jacket and, except for the coat, put the components of her uniform on. During the ride, Allan spoke in her ear, summarizing the contents of Amy Reston's resume. "Grew up in Las Vegas, college with a BA in history, worked as an administrative assistant, then an executive assistant... now a blackjack dealer."

"Allan," Ell said, "do a web search to confirm the material in her resume and find out about her erstwhile husband. If it all checks out, ask Steve to consider her for my personal assistant job."

~~~

Ell made it to the UAV flight training center ten minutes early and sat down at one of the simulators to confirm that all the controls were as they'd been laid out in her briefing displays. Other people filtered in, mostly enlisted, but a few other officers, they stood in the middle of the room talking quietly amongst themselves. The door opened and someone barked, "Room, ten-hut!"

Ell rose to her feet and stood at attention with the rest of the trainees. Out of the corner of her eye she saw a Major stalk into the room. "At ease. We're supposed to have a new El Tee being inserted sideways into our group three weeks late?" He looked around.

Ell put her hand up, "Sir, that would likely be me."

He lifted an eyebrow, "That 'likely' would. Well, you're three weeks of class work behind the rest of the group and you're going to have all kinds of Hell playing catch-up, but we can't spend time nurse-maiding you. Today we're doing some actual flying simulations which you won't even have a *chance* with, not having attended the classes. So you observe Lieutenant Sasson, he's leading the pack and may be willing to waste *some* of his precious time explaining a few things to you. You'll have to do your best to catch up by studying nights and weekends though, 'cause I warn you, lots of folks that start this course *on time* have to repeat it. I recommended they assign you elsewhere until the next class starts, but my recommendation was denied because someone, somewhere *way* above my pay grade, is 'sure you can catch up.'"

Quietly, Ell said, "Yes, sir."

He turned to the class as a whole. "Okay, today we're going to run some simulations with the same RQ-7 reconnaissance drone you were running Friday. Take offs and landings from Kadena AFB on Okinawa. We'll throw something new at you this time. Saddle up."

~~~

Sasson had rolled his eyes when Major Axen assigned the newbie to him. He intended to graduate "top of class" and spoon-feeding a late entrant could only hurt him. At first other trainees blocked his view of her, but he could see enough to know she was wearing her dress uniform instead of her BDUs. He groaned internally, she had to be a complete neophyte, just out of officer training school. At the command to "saddle up" he just walked over to his usual simulator. It was her problem to find him, not his to baby-sit her every step.

As he'd brought up the day's feed on the simulator he felt her standing behind him. He didn't look around, but did say, "Watch what I do and try to learn. Don't ask too many questions."

A quiet "Yes, sir," came over his shoulder.

Glancing down as he sought one of his controller pedals, Sasson saw with amazement that she'd assumed a stance of parade rest with her feet separated about 12 inches. He thought about telling her to pull up a chair, but then thought, *if she's so much of a stick she's going to stand there at parade rest, I'll let her do it.* He did an electronic preflight check on the bird and then touched his mike, asking the simulated on-site crew chief at Kadena AFB to go through the local preflight check with him.

With the preflight complete, he began engine ignition, then rolled out to the runway.

~~~

Standing behind Sasson, Ell'd been pleased to be able to follow the preflight as it'd been outlined in the manual, but she hadn't seen Sasson check the weather. In view of the Major's admonition that they'd "throw something new" at them she wondered if he'd forgotten. Or had he somehow checked it on a screen without her noticing? Her eyes flashed from screen to screen looking for a weather report that she'd missed. Ell subvocalized to Allan, asking if he could access the weather report on the simulator. Allan reported, "Yes, I've put it on your HUD." Ell glanced away from what Sasson was doing and saw the crosswinds were about

20% higher than the RQ-7 was rated for.

Major Axen chose that moment to check in. "Lieutenant, something on your HUD more important than what Lieutenant Sasson is doing?"

Ell said, "No Sir." Her eyes were already back down on Sasson's screens anyway. She wondered if she should point the crosswinds out to Sasson. *Would the major, or Sasson himself, want her to help? Or did Sasson know something about handling high crosswinds she didn't?* The major stood watching Sasson as he rolled up to the end of the runway, *was he waiting for Sasson to get in trouble?* Unable to stand by if Sasson had simply overlooked the winds, Ell finally bent down near Sasson's ear to whisper, "Sir. Just making sure you're aware of the crosswind situation?"

Sasson hissed, "Don't bother me during take-off!" The RQ-7 started rolling forward and the horizon began to shudder. Sasson said, "Damn it!" gripping the flight stick with white knuckles. The left wing lifted up and Sasson slammed the flight stick to the left to try to keep the right wing tip from dragging. The horizon leveled momentarily, but the runway began to slide to the left. Sasson pumped in rudder, then the left wingtip rose again and after a momentary pause, went on over the top. The image of the airfield flipped upside down and filled with flames.

Sasson leapt to his feet, saying, "Damn it!" He brought his face close to Ell's, "Do *not* ask questions during takeoff!" He was startled to realize she was pretty. He had a moment's chagrin, thinking to himself that he definitely would've been nicer if he'd gotten a better look at her.

~~~

Ell thought if Sasson'd had a hat, he'd have thrown it on the ground and stomped it. At attention, she kept her face bland and simply said, "Yes, sir.. I'm sorry sir."

Sasson turned to the Major. "Sorry sir. I shouldn't have let her distract me."

The Major looked back and forth from one to the other, and then he said, "Lt. Sasson, what'd she ask you?"

"Sir, I *do not* know. I was focused on my take off." He muttered, "Evidently, not focused enough."

The Major turned to Ell. "Lt...."

Ell said, "Donsaii, Sir."

"Donsaii. What did you ask Lt. Sasson?"

Ell wondered if answering was a betrayal and paused a moment.

"Donsaii? I'm waiting." the major said dangerously.

"Sir, I asked if he was aware of the crosswind situation."

Sasson's eyes widened and darted to Ell then down to the simulator as he realized what'd just crashed his simulated plane.

Axen had developed an amused expression and reached up to rub his moustache. "Donsaii? As in the Olympic Donsaii'"

Quietly Ell said, "Yes sir."

"And you knew those crosswinds were higher than what the RQ-7's rated for, didn't you?" His eyes glanced down at the row of medals above Ell's left breast pocket.

Another brief pause, then Ell resignedly said, "Yes Sir."

Sasson's heart sank. Then to his astonishment the Major came to attention and gave Donsaii a sharp regulation salute. She saluted back. Next Axen turned to Sasson and murmured, "I suggest, Lieutenant, that the next time someone offers a suggestion regarding your flight conduct or preparation, you take such suggestions under serious consideration. Do you understand what you just did, to, in theory, destroy eight million dollars' worth of aircraft?"

At attention himself, Sasson said, "Yes sir!"

Axen turned back to Ell, "Perhaps we should see what you can do with a simulator yourself?"

"I would like that Sir."

As Axen led Ell over to an unused simulator station, Sasson wondered just what the Hell had caused a Major to salute a Lieutenant? Indoors!

***

Axen waved his beer vaguely at Ennis, "So then she sits down at the simulator I assigned her, boots it like she'd been doing it all her life, preflights, notes the weather is beyond limits, asks for a determination as to whether the mission was critical enough to risk attempting to take off anyway? Instead of the usual, "Wait until weather improves" I get my AI to send her a message to take off anyway and she does!"

Ennis grinned, "So'd she crash and burn with the best of them?"

"No! She got that RQ-7 off the ground! There were some wild wobbles, but this was her *first* flight! You know only one in ten trainees get their plane successfully in the air on their first flight, even in dead air?"

Ennis studied Axen with narrowed eyes. "Luck?"

"Oh *Hell* no! That flight was picture perfect.

Landing? Nearly flawless. I asked her if she'd had any flight experience. She says, 'Yes Sir, I reviewed the briefing materials on the UAV program Colonel Ennis gave me. I made some runs on the embedded simulator last night.'" Axen pitched his voice a little higher to imitate Ell.

Ennis' brows rose, "She picked that pack up yesterday afternoon!"

"You're tellin' me! It has *terabytes* of information in it. Mostly useless of course, but how could she even sort through all of it in one night? And that embedded simulator she practiced on is only *vaguely* like flying the actual simulators. Commercial joysticks don't have all the controls, and the embedded software isn't even programmed for the second joystick."

Ennis took another sip of his beer, "Could she have engaged the AI and had it do most of the flying?"

Axen leaned forward, "First thing I thought of! AI's supposed to be disengaged to make them learn how the plane really works, but I checked to be sure. No AI. 'Read the manual.' One evening's practice on the desktop simulator and she flies better than most of our graduates. Hell, even the AI's only occasionally able to get off the ground in that much crosswind."

Ennis reached out and clinked his glass against Axen's. "And I was ready to rip her a new one yesterday morning."

"What for?"

"I thought she was wearing non regulation heels, turns out she just has 'unusually long legs.'"

Axen grinned, "Look good too, don't they?"

Ennis rolled his eyes, "You didn't hear that from me."

"So, what the Hell are we gonna do with her?"

"Let her do her job, my man. Let her do her job. Train her up, graduate her early if she can do it, which I assume she can, and turn her back over to me. We could use someone brilliant doing our China surveillance out of Kadena. I don't like the way they've been acting over there."

Axen leaned back. "Tell you what. I'll bet she *deserved* that Medal of Honor."

Ennis raised his glass in silent agreement.

***

When Ell left base that evening Allan took her to a different parking lot to get her truck—which the security team had moved. She asked Allan what'd happened to Amy Reston and her children.

"Steve's waiting to talk to you about her."

When Ell got to the apartment Steve waited at the dining table. "Hi, how was your first real day?"

"Kinda fun. Just flying simulators, but even they're pretty cool. What do you think about Ms. Reston?"

"I don't like it. You know she's homeless?"

"All the more reason she needs the job."

"I'm not sure you should hire people according to *their* need? Besides, she made good money in her previous job. She's just spent it all, then got laid off."

"Wasn't her daughter sick?"

"Well, yeah."

"Did you find any other issues?"

Steve narrowed his eyes a moment, then shrugged and shook his head, "No."

"I'm pretty sure I want to hire her. She's experienced as an executive assistant. If you don't have a substantive objection I want to interview her. Can you make contact?"

He twisted his lip, then shrugged. "Sure."

***

Amy was walking Janey and Mike into the mall food court when her AI said, "You have a call from a Mr. Steve Jacobs about a job interview."

Amy said, "Put him on. Hello?"

A baritone voice said, "Hello Ms. Reston. My employer's interested in interviewing you for a job as a personal and executive assistant. Would you be interested?"

"Certainly. Are you with one of the agencies?"

"Uh, no Ma'am." Steve realized she must have applications in through some employment agencies. "This contact is a result of your conversation with Ms. Donsaii this morning."

"Oh!" Amy hadn't expected anything to come from that encounter. "When do you want me to interview? I'm working the graveyard shift at a casino right now so I could come in most times except when I'm picking up or dropping off my kids for school."

"How about right now?

"Oh my goodness! I'm not dressed for it." Amy began a panicked thought process, considering how she could get cleaned up and dressed in the Mall bathrooms. "And I'm just taking my kids out to eat dinner. Could it wait just a little while?"

"Much more important to this employer than how you're dressed at present, is how you adapt to a situation. We'd like to meet you wherever you're having dinner."

"*With* my kids?"

"Yes."

"Okaaay, I *can* adapt. We're at the Meadows Mall food court."

"We should be there in 10 minutes or so. We'll buy dinner if you'll wait for us."

Amy set Mike and Janey down. "Hey kids. A man's coming here to interview me for a job."

They looked up at her with uncertainty.

"I don't know if the job is better than the one I have, but if it is, it could help us get a place to live. Do you understand how important that is?"

Eyes wide, they both nodded slowly. Janey's finger nervously slipped back into the corner of her mouth.

"We're going to wait until they get here to eat because the man said they'd buy our dinner and that'll help us a little with our money problems. Can you be calm and quiet while they're here? That could help me get this job."

"Yes Mom." Mikey said. Janey nodded again, eyes wide with apprehension that she might mess up something this important.

Amy said, "Don't worry too much about this kids. All you need to do is use the good manners I've taught you and stay seated. If you feel like you just can't sit still, ask nicely for permission to go play on the Mall playground, Okay?"

About fifteen minutes later a muscular dark skinned man strode up to the table and said in a Boston accent, "Hello Ms. Reston, Mike, Janey." He nodded to each of them in turn.

Amy was impressed that he'd taken time to learn the names of her children. She'd had her AI play back his name from when he introduced himself on the call, so she said, "Hello Mr. Jacobs. Is this table Okay?"

"Yes it'll be fine." He said, sitting down, "But I have a request and need your kids help."

Amy's heart froze; did he intend to use her children for something? "Uhhh…"

Recognizing her concern, Steve quickly said, "It's just that Ms. Donsaii's with me but she's wearing a disguise so people won't recognize her." He squatted down and turned to face the kids. "Do you kids think you can keep quiet and not say anything to draw attention to her so she can keep her privacy? Otherwise, a bunch of people will be wanting autographs and pictures with her."

"Oh…" Amy frowned, "I think we can. Let me take a moment to explain this to the kids okay?" After Steve nodded, Amy spent some time talking to Mike and especially Janey about what privacy meant. When Ell, wearing a brown wig and dark makeup, walked up and sat down, Amy was gratified to see her kids staring wide-eyed at her, but sitting quietly without saying anything.

Ell said, "Let's go get some food. I'm buying. Steve, if you'll defend the table I'll bring you back whatever you want?"

Steve asked for a cheeseburger, fries and Coke and the rest of them took off to wander around the offerings in the food court. Ell walked around with the kids and appeared to be just as delighted as they were to be picking out her own food. Ell had Allan electronically pay for whatever any of them ordered. Soon she walked back to the table with a tray carrying her food and Steve's. The kids were torn between their desire to chatter in excitement, and their recollection of their Mom's admonition to keep quiet. Amy anxiously waited to hear about the possible job. At Ell's suggestion, the kids sat at the next table where they could be more themselves while the grownups talked, though the kids kept darting glances over at them.

Ell turned to Amy, "Actually, I'm the one who needs an assistant."

Startled, Amy thought to herself that Ell almost looked young enough to need a babysitter. She'd been in the Olympics a year and a half ago—wasn't she in college now? "What do you need assistance with?" She tried to keep her face bland. *And who's paying me to assist you? And* who's *in charge?*

"Well, there are a surprising number of things I need help with. I'm actually serving a military obligation as a second lieutenant in the Air Force which requires a lot of my time. I have a problem in that Chinese nationals have been trying to kidnap me. That's led to me hiring Steve here as the leader of a security team that protects me. I've got some research endeavors I'd like to undertake in my spare time. Essentially, I don't want to spend my time doing the payroll for my security team, shopping, cooking, cleaning, laundry, ordering and receiving supplies for my research…" She sighed, "I want to be able to focus on the things I want to do and leave the rest of my life to someone else."

Amy tilted her head, "As a business executive assistant, I've done some of those things and," she lifted an eyebrow, "as a *mother* I've done some of the others." She paused, "I believe that I could adapt to learn others like payroll, though I'd think that a good AI could do most of that kind of number crunching?"

Ell said, "An AI could, but I don't even want to have to *talk to* my AI about handling the payroll." Ell asked a lot of questions then, posing "what if" situations and "if this happened would you be willing to..." questions. She obliquely determined Amy's capabilities from her answers. Finally, she said, "I'd like to offer you the job if you don't have concerns. You should at least be worried about the danger the Chinese pose. So far it seems that they only to want to capture me, not do me harm. They apparently hope to have me work for them, but they may be willing to accept some collateral damage to you or perhaps even your children. I sincerely hope they've given up after several failed tries, but I can't know that. I *also* hope that, if they haven't, Steve's security team will be able to protect us, but we'll never be sure whether they could stop such an attack."

Amy studied Ell's face, "Pardon me for asking, but how can you *afford* this? I know Lieutenants aren't paid all that much. I don't want to quit the job I've got and then find out that you can't actually pay me."

"You're right to be concerned. I have some royalties from an invention..."

Steve snorted at this statement. "'Some' royalties!" he chuckled.

Ell continued, "And, I'll put two hundred fifty thousand dollars in an escrow account that you'll be able to check the balance of yourself." She muttered to her AI, "My AI's sent yours a link, you can check it now if you like?"

Amy found it hard to believe when she glanced up at her HUD and saw confirmation that an account had been established with a quarter million dollars. She looked back at Ell, "Okay. That's pretty convincing."

Ell said, "That account would be payable to you if something were to happen to me. Hopefully it'd tide you over until you found another job. As one of your benefits I'll provide a place to live for you and your children at the same apartment complex I live in. I'll double the salary you're currently paid as a dealer and, as my executive assistant, you'll be in charge of establishing an excellent benefits package for my staff—yourself and your family included."

Amy rocked back in her chair, staring at Ell. "How... How old are you?" she asked, absolutely certain that Ell's young appearance just didn't jibe with the maturity of her words.

Ell's pale green eyes were steady, "Eighteen."

Amy swallowed, then blinked. She turned to Steve, "She's paying you and your team? Regularly?"

Steve nodded gravely.

After a long pause, Amy said, "When would you want me to start?"

"Tomorrow."

"But... I have to give two-weeks' notice."

"I'm pleased you want to comply with any agreement you have with your previous employer. I'll reimburse them for six weeks of your salary. That way they can pay overtime to have other dealers fill in for the unexpected loss of your services and still come out ahead."

A tear ran down Amy's cheek. "Thank you." she said in a small voice.

Janey'd been carefully watching her mother. At sight of the tear she jumped up, ran around the table and slipped under her mother's arm, placing her arms around Amy's waist, "Mommy?"

"It's okay, honey. I'm happy, not sad."

Chapter Three

The officer strode up to the group and came to attention. "General Wang?"

The general turned to him, "Well?"

"Sir, the launch was successful."

The general turned back to the civilians he had been speaking to. "Two more launches and we'll be ready, in one stroke, to destroy *every one* of the Americans' surveillance and military communication satellites that cross our part of the world."

The entire group turned to look at one man. Expressionlessly, he said, "And when the satellite strike is ready, will you also have readied your tactical plan to recover our wayward province?"

The general gave a sharp nod.

***

Ell opened the door to her apartment. Steve and Amy sat at the dining room table with a pizza and a salad. Amy said, "Sorry I don't have a home cooked meal for you today, I've been trying to catch up with everything else and didn't get to the store."

Ell said, "An occasional home cooked meal would be nice, but I don't care where you get it, as long as it's good." She picked up a slice, "I love pizza. Did you make any progress?"

"Oh yes, with a lot of things. I found some heavy, vibration isolated tables for your lab and got them delivered. I've found some of the lab equipment you said you wanted and sent the specs to your AI for approval before ordering. I took an online payroll refresher course and bought a payroll module for my AI. The kids and I moved into the apartment you rented for us." She swallowed and spoke a little hoarsely, "Thank you very much."

Ell's eyes narrowed. "You seem tense. Is there a problem?" She dished up some salad.

Amy took a deep breath. "Yes, but I'll take care of it."

"Good. But I want to know about it. If it *might* impinge on me, I don't want to be ignorant."

Amy's eyes dropped to the table. She shrugged, "It's my old boss. I think I mentioned he's a jerk?"

Ell nodded.

"He used to touch me and say rude things and it'd been escalating. But when I told him I was quitting, he got angry and started making threats."

Ell's eyes frosted, "What kind of threats?"

"That I'd regret doing this. He implied that I owed him favors for hiring me and that he still intended to collect them."

Ell's gaze tracked over to Steve, "Can you protect her? I assume someone from the ready team can go with her whenever I'm on base and otherwise protected?"

Steve nodded.

"Make sure her AI is upgraded to match everyone else's so she can call on you immediately if she needs it?"

"Ahead of you there, Ma'am. We already had a spare AI setup we gave her. I've had her order a few more."

Eyes on the floor, Amy almost whispered, "I'm afraid he might have connections. It might be better if I just gave in to his sick little game to get him off my case."

Steve's eyes narrowed, "You mean underworld connections?"

Without looking up Amy nodded, afraid that revealing this might lose her the job but feeling somehow that she had to be honest with this young woman.

Tightly, Ell said, "I don't believe we should let loathsome scum destroy our lives. Steve, when you're not protecting me or Amy, I'd like you and the team to consider how we can take this guy down, legally, if he gives us trouble. Allan?" Ell's eyes flicked up like many people's did when talking to their AI, "Begin an investigation into this man's financial and other net accessible data." She turned to Amy, "What's his name?"

No one would want a computational engine with the power of the supercomputer currently powering Ell's AI to sift through their life looking for "irregularities."

"Felton Bonapute," Amy whispered as a mixture of relief and new anxiety flooded over her.

They discussed plans and possible responses to this new problem for a while, then Ell retired to her office-cum-lab. She'd read extensively beyond the current UAV curriculum and spent a lot of time on the software simulator she'd been provided. She was now quite a way ahead of the rest of her UAV class, so she once again had some time to spend on her physics research. The last of her equipment had arrived so she wanted to start the first of the experiments she'd planned.

Her new research related to the connection that quantum entangled particles had through the tiny fifth dimension she'd worked out the new math for. According to a new solution she'd run using her math, a group of entangled particles, arranged in a circle and energized properly, might hold open a passage between them that entered into that fifth dimension. She hoped she could push some molecules through such an opening and have them travel through the fifth dimension to reappear back in our universe some distance away.

According to her calculations, the molecule's reappearance could be a *long way* from where she'd pushed them into the fifth dimension.

She'd ordered newer and more powerful versions of the same equipment she'd used as a grad student at NCSU to entangle molecules as well as a micromanipulator setup to allow her to position the entangled molecules. Working on setting it all up kept her happily occupied until 3 AM when she forced herself to get some sleep. She had to get up at 6:15 the next morning to make it out to Nellis on time.

***

Axen knocked on Colonel Ennis' door. Ennis leaned back at his desk, "Come in Major, but don't bring me any damned problems."

Axen grinned, "I have a combination 'Golly gee whiz wonderful' and 'Uh-oh, what do we do about that.'"

Ennis rolled his eyes, "Okay, I'll bite, what is it this time?"

"Your favorite El Tee."

Ennis just raised his eyebrows and motioned for Axen to go on.

"She's gone from starting three weeks behind the rest of the class, to so far ahead she must be bored, though she hides it well. Honestly, I feel sure she could pass the final exam today, even though we aren't even to the halfway point in the curriculum. Probably get a record breaking score on it too."

"So? Graduate her and send her back to me."

"I'm worried about the demoralizing effect that all have on everyone else in the course. I think, for their sake, I should keep her at least a little longer."

Ennis pursed his lips. "Okaaay, but try to keep her challenged somehow. Maybe she could rewrite some of the more obtuse course material? Or, remember she's a math genius, could she reprogram any of the software? Fix some of the glitches?"

Axen tilted his head in consideration, "Those *are* some good ideas. I'll talk to her about them."

***

As Ell ate her hamburger, Amy brought her up to date. "I've arranged for the rest of your hundred and five-million-dollar donation to be sent to North Carolina State, you just have to tell Allan to approve the transfer."

Ell nodded as she chewed. As soon as she swallowed she looked up and said, "Approved."

"The NCSU Physics department sent you some one page applications for funding from some of their physics professors and grad students like you requested. You were going to approve or disapprove them? I've forwarded them to Allan."

"Okay."

"Your portal experiment seemed to run fine for eight hours today, but there wasn't any increase in pressure in the recipient chamber."

Ell's shoulders slumped. She'd been so sure that *this* experiment would move a few molecules... Hmm, she thought, *maybe a few molecules had moved, just not enough to detect by measuring a pressure change? I need a different method to detect movement of molecules.*

Amy watched Ell's eyes glaze over. Oh well, she'd learned to save any news about Ell's research for last. Once Ell got to thinking about physics, she seldom paid much attention to the rest of what Amy had to say. Amy put the dishes in the dishwasher and left through the inter-apartment doors that Steve's team had installed. They let her get back to the one she shared with her kids without being seen doing so.

As she walked into her own apartment, her AI gave her a list of the eight physics projects from NCSU that Ell had approved and two that she'd disapproved. To Amy's surprise Ell'd approved an application from Ell's old professor, Albert Johnson. The one Ell had hated. Amy noted, however, it was marked "pending completion of interpersonal counseling." For a moment Amy wondered if she'd even read them—in the short time she'd had them it didn't seem likely—then Amy noticed that there were brief notes on the two rejections specifying the issues that kept them from being approved. Amy shook her head, *My God, the girl reads fast!*

***

On Saturday Ell headed over to Master Mark Moody's Martial Arts, or "4MA" as it was colloquially known. Several of her security team were already there for their weekly training sessions and three were outside in a car on call. 4MA was located a block from Ell's apartment complex and she'd committed to taking sessions once a week. Ell'd insisted Amy take lessons and Amy had said it didn't make sense for Ell not to take them too. Amy's kids were taking a class for little ones on Saturday afternoons.

This Saturday morning would be Ell's first session and she looked forward to the exercise. She hadn't been getting in a lot of physical activity lately. To keep her brunette wig from getting displaced Ell wore a tight stocking cap over it. She'd arranged the hat and wig so some strands of brown hair stuck out to match her "Raquel" identity. She'd done the identity up completely with skin bronzers and dark pencil on her light eyebrows.

Steve looked at her. "I thought you were doing this as "Ell Donsaii?"

"No, I don't want to be seen anywhere near the apartment in that identity. Besides, if I'm in that identity everyone'll act weird."

"The first time you get thrown, it'll knock that prosthetic off of your nose."

"I just won't let anything hit my nose."

"What? You're going to be getting thrown around!"

Ell stared at him a moment, "Steve, I *can* keep things from hitting my nose."

Steve stared back for a moment, then shrugged, "I guess you probably can."

Lieutenant

~~~

Their instructor in the beginning class was Moody's wife Millie, a tiny Asian lady. Crinkles appeared around her eyes as she looked around the group. "So. This class for people who have had some jujutsu, but not much, yes?" Nods came back to her and she said, "Okay, we begin with falls. If you are to learn martial arts, you must learn to fall down without getting hurt, yes?" Ell carefully positioned herself on the other side of the group from Amy to maintain the fiction that they didn't know each other. It was helpful to the security team for both of them to attend the same class so the team didn't have to cover each of them at different times. However, she didn't want it to appear they had any relationship besides their assignment to the same class.

***

Watching Ell wolf down lasagna, Amy wished she could eat like that. She said, "Ell, before we talk about your research, Janey has a question she'd like to ask?"

Ell said, "Sure," putting another forkful of lasagna in her mouth. She turned questioning eyes on Janey, who'd been sitting patiently on the couch.

Janey kicked her legs, "Mom! *You* ask her."

Ell looked at Amy, but Amy was focused on her daughter. "Janey, you've got to learn to ask politely for the things you want. You won't always have me ask for you."

Janey kicked her feet back and forth a moment longer, then said, "Ms. Donsaii? Would you come to my class for show and tell?"

Ell grinned crookedly. "You want *me* to be your show

and tell?"

Janey nodded emphatically.

Ell laughed, "Sure. But remember, at work, and in your classroom, I'm Ell Donsaii. Here at the apartment, and any time you see me in my brown wig I'm not Ell Donsaii. Who am I then?"

"Raquel Blandon."

"Okay, and when I come to your class, you won't say anything about me, as Ell Donsaii, living close to you, correct?"

"Yes, Ms. Blandon."

Ell grinned at her. "Just in case you might forget, we'll talk about it again right before I come to your classroom, okay?"

"Okay!" an excited Janey exclaimed.

Amy said, "Okay, Janey. Good job. Now you need to wait until Ell and I are done talking. After that I'll take you home."

Amy and Ell discussed how to arrange the date and time for her show and tell. Finally Amy said. "I think you might be excited when you look at your new experiment. Looking in the microscope I think I might be seeing a teensy, tiny bit of blue where the port's supposed to be."

Ell's eyes widened and she leapt up from the table to run into her office. Amy thought she looked like a little girl who'd just been told she could open a Christmas present early. Feeling like a mother chastising her child Amy called after her, "You didn't finish your beans!"

~~~

Ell excitedly stared at the screen of the microscope. Its objective was focused where she'd calculated the other end of the portal should be. The primary or near portal, with its ring of entangled particles was centered in a pressurized chamber full of methylene blue. The secondary or far portal was supposed to be centered in the drop of water beneath the microscope. If she'd really created a portal from one location to the other using the 5th dimension predicted by her math, and the portal was large enough to pass methylene blue molecules with a molecular weight of 320, she should be seeing some bluish discoloration as the blue leaked through the portal into the drop of water.

Amy stepped into the room. "What do you think?"

Excitedly Ell said, "I think I see a little bit of blue too. Could it be diffusing away from the port into the drop and turning the whole drop faintly blue?" She leaned to the side, "Do you think the light leaking out of the sides of the drop looks a little blue?"

Amy looked dubiously at the light leaking out of the side of the drop under the microscope, "Maybe? I don't remember what it looked like when we started."

Ell said, "Allan, bring up an image of the microscope when we set it up. Put it on the big screen next to a current image." A moment later side by side images of the microscope yesterday and that evening appeared on the wall screen. The two women looked at it, "What do you think?"

Amy shrugged, but Allan spoke in Ell's ear, "Your AI's camera's not calibrated for such work, but the chroma of the pixels in the image *is* slightly bluer on the current image."

Ell pumped her fist excitedly, "Yes!" She explained what Allan had said to Amy.

Amy said, "So what's it mean?"

Ell said, "It means we'll let this experiment run until tomorrow to see if we get even more blue. We want to be sure!" When she turned to talk to Amy, she saw Janey standing in the door. Ell leapt to her feet in enthusiasm, picked up the seven year old and spun her around in a little dance. Janey grinned and started dancing exuberantly with Ell, despite not understanding the root cause.

When Ell put Janey down, Amy rolled her eyes, "Now, one of my children has gotten the other too excited to do her homework!" She gave Ell a mock frown as she shepherded Janey out the door.

Ell was still bouncing on her toes when Allan said, "You have a call from Roger Emmerit."

As she waved "bye" to Amy and Janey Ell buoyantly said, "Put him on! Roger! You gettin' any physics done back there at NCSU?"

"A little. My paper got accepted at the APS meeting in Las Vegas."

"Really! That's great! Did you know I'm at Nellis Air Force Base in Las Vegas?"

"Um, yeah. That might have had *something* to do with my submitting the paper to that particular meeting."

"Aw, shucks, you really know how to impress a girl! When will you be out here?"

"Five weeks, will you be in town?"

Ell's heart bounced a little at the sound of hope in Roger's voice, "Sure! And, I'd be delighted to buy a broke ass grad student dinner. What's the exact date?"

They spoke a few more minutes about the details, and then broke the connection. Ell danced excitedly around the room a little more, then went back to reexamine her experimental setup.

Lieutenant

***

Millie smiled at her class, "Okay, now you know how to fall. So, this week, we begin some throws. First we line you up by size, eh? Tall ones over at this end, short at that end." She worked her way through the line until she was satisfied with their alignment then had them count off in twos.

~~~

To her relief, despite being the same height, Amy and Ell managed not to stand next to each other. Ell found herself paired with a slender redheaded man, slightly taller than herself. "Hello, I'm Raquel." She put out her hand.

~~~

They shook, "Gary," he said, wondering what it was going to be like throwing a girl. *Lord, she's pretty! But so slender! What if I hurt her?*

~~~

Millie brought one of the smaller women out and demonstrated an O Goshi throw in slow motion, then had the woman throw her, demonstrating the landing. Soon her pupils were throwing one another as she went around giving critiques. "Raquel! You mus' not treat Gary like expensive dish! Throw him, throw him!"

Gary found himself flying through the air. Then it was his turn. "You okay with this?" he asked, thinking again that she was so slender she'd surely be easily injured.

She grinned at him. "Sure, do your worst, Gar'." He heaved her over his right hip, dismayed when she landed with a loud thump.

~~~

Millie's eyes narrowed as she watched. *Raquel lands perfectly, but she slaps her hand very hard. As if she wants to make it seem she's coming down harder than she really is,* Millie thought. After a moment she shrugged, no rule against that.

***

Bemused, Ennis said, "She did what?"

Axen said, "Fixed nine bugs in the flight control software. I only *knew* about four of them. Issues where we've worked around a problem for so long that no one really thinks about them as bugs anymore. But it turns out that part of the problem with crosswind takeoffs has been a software bug that has a feedback loop in it that doesn't damp aileron control properly. Now I can easily get the simulator's AI to take off in crosswinds above tolerance. We'll have to try it on a real bird to see if it works outside of software, but she says it will… and I believe her." He snorted, "She did all this during lecture time over a period of three days. All while, of course, answering any questions the instructor posed her in class. And, while she was working on the software she was still scoring higher by far than her classmates on both the tests and the simulated flights."

Ennis leaned back in his chair, hands behind his head, looking at the ceiling. "Damn," he mused quietly, "I wonder what else we could get her to fix?"

***

Ell looked at the drop of water under the microscope on her experimental setup. It still had that very faint blue appearance, but it didn't seem any bluer than it had the day before. Allan confirmed its chroma hadn't changed. Her shoulders sagged and she started disassembling the setup. As she took the cover off the electronics her nose suddenly twitched at a burned smell. *Yes!* The power supply had a blackened spot on it. She leaned back, musing. *Could the power requirement for a molecular sized hole be higher than I calculated? Or was it just a bad power supply?*

Amy came in the room behind her, "Time to go out and celebrate?"

"No," Ell said morosely.

Amy took in the slumped shoulders as well as the screws and covers lying on the table. Ell'd been pretty frustrated about her research before the recent breakthrough. Amy hated to see her down again. "Okay. It's time to go out for some Friday night R and R then."

Ell cast a squinty eye back up over her shoulder at Amy. "I don't feel like going out," she said in a grumpy tone.

"How would you know? You never go out. My assessment is that you're a girl in serious need of a social life."

Ell hunched her shoulders sulkily and peered back down at the power supply, thinking that she did miss her Friday nights at West 87. "What'd you have in mind?" she asked without looking up.

"My favorite local band is playing at "Tres Locos" and, thanks to a kindly employer, I can afford a babysitter again!"

Ell scratched at the charred area on the power

supply. "I don't have anything to wear!"

"Yes you do, I'd suggest those snug Western jeans and boots of yours."

Ell frowned, "I don't *have* any Western jeans or boots."

"Yes you do. Move away from the machine Ma'am, nothing to see there. Look at this instead."

Ell slowly looked around, Amy grinned as she held up jeans in one hand and boots in the other. Ell frowned, "You think your clothes will fit me?"

"You'd *better* not be sayin' my clothes would be baggy on you! I *bought* these for you. They're a size 2 like the rest of your pants."

"Hmmm," Ell arched an eyebrow, "did I authorize clothing expenditures?"

"Yep." Amy grinned, "It's right there under 'whatever you gotta buy to keep me happy.'"

"Humph, okay. I guess I could use some socializing, what time do we leave?"

"As soon as you're ready, Tres Locos has great Mexican food too."

"Okay," she glanced upward, "Allan, order a replacement power supply train, see if you can boost all the tolerances by 100%."

Ell spent a few minutes doing the Raquel Blandon look in full. The wig, skin bronzer, darker makeup, pencil to cover her light eyebrows, a beauty mark on her cheek and her nose prosthetic. She didn't look anything like Ell when she was done, but the nose prosthetic wasn't big enough to make her truly unattractive like her old "Ellen" prosthetic had.

Tres Locos turned out to be laid out in a huge building with a band on a stage at one end and a large dance floor around the band. The floor was surrounded by tables. There were various stalls around the walls of the huge room selling food, drink and mementoes. Amy got a beer and tacos, while Ell picked out a grande burrito and a Coke.

~~~

Cody watched the slender brunette with the long legs walk around Tres Locos choosing her food and then walk with her friend over to a table. She moved with a smoothly fluid grace. To himself he thought, *That girl's a dancer.*

~~~

Ell pulled out a chair at a table near the edge, but Amy said, "Oh, no! We've got to sit near the dance floor," she raised an eyebrow, "so the boys'll know we want to dance."

"We do?" Ell asked, not sure whether she queried the table location, or their desire to dance. She'd only danced a few times in her life, and those times were slow dances with people she knew pretty well. She really didn't feel like she even knew *how* to dance.

"We do." Amy responded definitively, without making it clear whether she spoke of the location or the dancing either.

While they ate their Mexican food, a band warmed up on the stage, then began playing. The music was fast, bluesy and fun. Ell found her foot tapping to the beat. Out on the dance floor a few people wandered out and began dancing in a variety of styles. A small group of five was doing some kind of line dance. One couple whirled around the floor and several other couples seemed to be freestyling whatever movements they felt like. She wondered what in the world she'd do if someone actually came and asked her to dance? She'd be terribly embarrassed if he expected to whirl around the floor like the one couple—Ell had no idea how to do such a dance.

Ell had wolfed her burrito down and sat entranced, watching the dance floor. When Amy finished her tacos, she cleared the food off their table and carried it to a bin. Returning she saw a handsome young man bend down near Ell and ask her something. Ell drew back, looking panicked and shaking her head. The young man stood, shrugged and moved on. Amy sat back down and said over the music, "What just happened there?"

"He wanted to dance!" Ell said in astonishment.

Well, *of course* he did. This is a *dance* place. You're sitting near the *dance* floor. Why aren't you out there dancing with him right now?"

Ell looked stricken, "I don't know how!"

Amy laughed, "Well then, just tell the young man that he'll need to teach you. He would have loved that."

"He *would* not!"

"Raquel, Raquel. He'd much rather have taught you to dance than been shot down *asking* you to dance." Amy leaned closer, "I'll let you in on a little secret. Most of these guys don't really know how to dance either. They're just here to meet girls." She leaned back and raised her eyebrows as if she had just revealed a shocking secret. "Especially pretty ones like you."

Ell looked embarrassed again. "I hadn't thought of how it would seem to him if I said 'No.' I'm sorry."

"Well don't tell *me* you're sorry, go tell the guy. He's standing over there with his buddy trying to pretend his feelings aren't hurt."

Ell buried her face in her hands, "Oh, I *can't* do that!"

Amy thought she saw a blush leaking out around Ell's hands despite her skin bronzer. "Hah! Momma Amy's gonna to take care of you. First, we're going to go join that line dance, then later you can apologize to the poor guy who asked you to dance." She tugged on Ell's arm until she got up. They walked across the floor to the small group of line dancers. They made it nine line dancers.

Ell found herself at the end of a line. The group had three men and, with Ell and Amy, six women. The steps they were making looked complicated, but were actually relatively simple and repetitive. Ell, with her phenomenal mind-body coordination, quickly learned them and danced along. She noticed the more accomplished girls putting extra twitches and shimmies into their routines. Ell copied those as well. Amy, still struggling to get the steps right, shouted over at her, "I thought you didn't know how to dance?"

Embarrassed, Ell shrugged, "I learn pretty fast." Looking out over the dance floor she saw the dark haired guy who'd asked her to dance whirling around the floor with another woman. They were doing a very complex swing dance that involved a lot of turning and spinning, all the while keeping their hands in contact with one another. He even whirled the girl into the air once. It looked like a lot of fun. Since Ell's mind wasn't really on the line dance she focused on what exactly the swing dancing couple were doing.

The music slowed and the line dancers broke up to sit. Ell noticed that the young man took his dance partner back to her seat and went back to where his friend still stood. She walked back to her own table with Amy who turned to her, "Now it's time to apologize to that guy you shot down and ask him to dance."

Ell stuck out her lower lip and lowered her head, "Don' wanna!" she said mulishly. Then she looked up from under lowered brows. Her eyes crinkled as she said, "But I will if you insist."

"Yep, Momma Amy says it's the polite thing to do."

Ell stood and started walking towards the man, her heart in her throat. When she was about half way there his blond friend nudged him and pointed her out with a wave of his beer bottle. They both turned to watch her approach. The dark haired one lifted one eyebrow as she got close. Ell stopped in front of them, finding herself momentarily struck dumb. Finally, she choked out, "My friend Amy," with a thumb she pointed back over her shoulder, "says it was rude of me to turn down a dance. So, I've come to apologize and ask if you would dance with me after all?" She smiled tentatively at him.

~~~

Cody'd admired her walking towards him, hoping she'd changed her mind about dancing. Girls often came up to him wanting to dance after they'd seen him dance with Connie. Connie and he studied dance together at UNLV and liked going out to bars to, as they called it, "slum with the dance impaired". It was fun to dance with regular folks who struggled to keep up, then occasionally throw in a dance with Connie to show them what they could aspire to. With a serious look on his face he said, "No."

Ell's face fell and she turned, red faced, to make a walk of shame back to her seat.

"Wait! I was kidding! I just wanted you to feel all turned down like I did. Of course I'll dance with you. I'd love to."

Ell turned back and flashed him a blinding smile.

"Thanks!" She tilted her head ruefully. "I guess I deserved that."

"Naw, you didn't. I was being a jerk. My name's Cody, what's yours?" He studied her face, thinking she was pretty cute.

"E… Raquel, I really don't know how to dance. That's why I turned you down before. Would you teach me?"

"Hah! I watched you line dancing, you've got some nice moves."

"But I don't know how to do anything else."

He shrugged, "Sure, all you've gotta do is follow. Keep your elbows bent ninety degrees so I can push and pull you and then I'll just sweep you around the floor like a broom."

Ell widened her eyes, "Oh, *could* you? That's *just* what I was hoping for." Her eyes rolled.

He grinned, "Ah, a spunky one!" They reached the floor as a slow song finished and another fast one started. His left hand took her right and he started a gentle push pull with the beat. She immediately picked it up. His right hand pointed down at his feet, indicating the simple shuffle he was doing to keep time. Cody's brows rose as she immediately picked up the step he was doing, shuffling an exact reciprocal to his.

~~~

Ell looked up at Cody and was pleased to see that he didn't look too bored. Delightedly she saw Amy walking out to the dance floor with Cody's older blond friend.

Cody took her left hand and, with a quick pull of his left, twirled her in to a "cuddle" in his right arm. Smoothly, he began moving her around the floor, their hips swinging together. He twirled her out, then back in to cuddle in his left arm. Her eyebrows rose, this looked hard, but the moves she'd watched him do with the other girl were actually pretty easy. She thought to herself that it must be Cody's strong lead that made it that way.

~~~

Cody's eyebrows drew together, *she'd lied! She does know how to dance!* Normally, when dancing with someone new, even if they "knew how to dance," he had to show them each move several times. They often fought his lead, trying to do something else, whereas this girl just effortlessly followed his lead on every move he threw at her! He decided to push her limits. He spun her out and back in, then turned himself to the inside, then began more and more complex turns and whirls.

~~~

Ell followed easily. She'd seen each of the moves he was taking her through when he'd been dancing with Connie. She found them simple enough to copy, especially with Cody strongly leading her through each of the different turns.

~~~

Mixed emotions of irritation that she'd fooled him and pure joy at how well she danced flooded over Cody. He decided to push her as hard as he could.

~~~

Ell found the effortless swinging rhythm of the dancing and turning to be exhilarating, though she knew her poor endurance would leave her exhausted if they kept up such a pace! She hoped to herself that Cody didn't have any moves that she hadn't gotten to watch him do with the other girl.

Suddenly, Cody doubled timed his footwork. Ell matched him and then he double timed the speed of the turns, pulling her through the twirling movements rapid fire. Ell found it breathtaking. Having already danced the moves with him at the lower speed, they were easy to follow, even at the greatly increased speed. She thumped in against his side, whirled away, then back in, then spun, then began going under and over in a spinning, flashing pretzel turn that went on and on.

He spun her away from him and began dancing solo, feet pounding and hands clapping occasionally. Ell matched him, throwing in her own shimmies and twirls from the line dance earlier. In sudden exuberance Ell did a backflip as the music thundered to a stop.

Ell clapped a hand to her mouth. The other dancers had all stopped to watch them, people at the tables were standing to get a better view, the band stared and the fiddler saluted them with his bow. Cody threw a leg and arm out in a theatrical bow to her. In embarrassment, Ell realized that, in the elation of the dance, she'd tremendously over-performed. Hands to her heated cheeks, Ell turned and ran from the floor, shouldering through the crowd and fast-walking to the bathroom.

Hiding in a stall with her feet up, Ell heard Amy calling her name. "Ell, where are you?"

"Here," she said faintly.

"*Why'd* you run off the floor?!" Amy asked, pulling on the door to the stall.

Ell unlatched it to let her in. "Embarrassed. I shouldn't have danced like that!"

"What do you mean? Why not! Not that I had any idea you could, of course. I thought you said you didn't know *how* to dance."

"I don't! It's just that Cody leads... Really well."

Amy snorted, "Girl, I guarantee, no matter how well a man leads, I'd never, *ever*, be able to dance like that."

"Yeah, well, I'm pretty good at athletics and pick stuff up really quick. But performing like that doesn't exactly help me fade into the woodwork like I'm supposed to."

Amy tilted her head, "Huh... I guess you'd have to be 'pretty good at athletics' to win all those Olympic gold medals. But you're *embarrassed* about that dance?"

Ell bit her lip and nodded.

Amy grinned, "Sometimes I forget you're only eighteen. If I'd danced like that, I'd *still* be out there taking bows. Well what do you think, are you ready to go back out and face the world?"

"Can't we just sneak out and go home?"

Amy rolled her eyes. "Come on, I guarantee all those folks think they just witnessed something cool, done by someone who'd practiced forever. There's nothing to be embarrassed about." She held out her hand.

Reluctantly Ell took it and they headed back out into Tres Locos. As they stepped out of the women's bathroom, Cody hitched up away from the wall where he'd been leaning. "Raquel, are you okay?"

Ell nodded, though she kept her eyes on the floor and her cheeks warmed again. She wondered to herself why she felt so awkward in situations like this. Her training from the Academy stood her in good stead when dealing with people in her usual circumstances. She could handle her superiors and subordinates in the Air Force. But when the situation called for her to interact with strange men in what *might* become a romantic encounter she suddenly became shy.

Lieutenant

~~~

Cody said, "I'm not sure what just happened there? You sure fooled me with that, 'don't know how to dance line though.' Where'd you learn?"

Ell said something, but he couldn't hear it over the music. He leaned closer, "What?"

Ell said, "I'm a gymnast. I really don't know much about dance, but I can follow pretty well." She hoped that would satisfy him.

"You can't fool me." Cody said with some exasperation, "I study dance at UNLV and I have *never* danced with someone who could follow like you. The way you were able to pick up on everything I did... it, it was like we'd been dancing together for *months*!"

Ell didn't say anything and after a long pause Cody said, "Can we dance again?"

Suddenly Connie showed up on Cody's other side. "Come on Cody; let's show your little friend how it's *really* done." She tugged at his elbow. Connie'd been stunned at the graceful style the slender brunette had displayed dancing with Cody, then shocked and hurt by the way everyone stared at *them*. The crowd hadn't even paused to watch Connie dance with Cody earlier. She'd realized that Cody and the girl hadn't done anything all that hard, they'd just done it *very* well. Connie wanted to show everyone in the bar what *she* and Cody could do.

Cody allowed himself to be led away, but not before calling back to Ell, "Raquel, wait for me till after this dance. Please?"

Ell shrugged, then leaned back against the wall where Cody'd been leaning before. Amy gave an exasperated snort and walked back out to her beer. After a moment Ell slowly followed.

The band was playing another fast song and with a whirl Connie burst out onto the floor, then trailed her hand back to Cody, starting a routine they'd perfected for a dance contest a few months ago. They swung around the floor whirling through flips, Charlestons, lifts and other aerials, finishing in a pose that brought the bar to its feet clapping. They took a bow and walked back off the floor toward Amy and Ell's table. As they approached Ell stopped clapping and raised her glass of Coke in a salute to them.

Connie sashayed past, acknowledging Ell only with a muttered, "Top *that*, bitch!"

At first Ell's temper flashed with the intent to do exactly what Connie had requested, top her dance with one leavened with gymnastic moves, but she relentlessly tamped down her anger. She'd caused too many problems in the past, putting obnoxious people in their places. This time she felt determined to just let it slide.

Cody came back to Ell's table, "Ignore Connie! She can be a real ass. She's just jealous of how well you danced when we didn't even have any experience together."

Ell shrugged, then offered a crooked smile, "Connie's a great dancer. Give her my compliments."

"Would you dance again?"

"Take out my friend Amy here. She could use a turn around the floor with a really great dancer."

He got a yearning look, "You could probably do even better on a second dance; don't you want to really show Connie what you can do?"

"Nope!" Ell grinned, "I want you to show Amy what it's like dancing with a great dancer." She gave him a little shove.

He laughed and held out a hand to Amy. She took it with a grin. Soon they were out on the floor, creditably swing dancing, though without the grace and athleticism that Cody and Ell had displayed.

Ell and Amy stayed at the bar a little longer. Amy was asked to dance several more times, but Ell refused to dance with Cody anymore, having decided she didn't want to ruin his relationship with Connie. Cody insisted they were only dance partners at the school, not lovers, but Ell stood firm, "That's an important relationship. You shouldn't screw it up."

No one else asked Ell to dance and she wondered why. Later, Amy explained it without being asked. "Though they won't admit it, guys are surprisingly delicate creatures. You've got three issues that're keeping them from asking you to dance." She held up fingers as she ticked them off, "They think you're too good looking; they've seen you shooting Cody down; and, they think you dance so well you'll laugh at them for asking. They aren't going to ask you to dance for fear of being humiliated on the basis of any of those three counts. We're going to have to go to a different bar before you'll get asked to dance again."

"Aw," Ell stuck out her lower lip again, "Just when I decided I *liked* dancing."

"You really do need a social life you know? Something besides going out dancing with me. How 'bout Gary?"

"Gary?"

"Yes, Gary. The young redheaded guy that almost always manages to pair himself with you at 4MA. You know he has the hots for you don't you?"

Ell rolled her eyes, "You ready to head home?"

"Okay." As they walked out of Tres Locos, they

carefully ignored Barrett and Dan from Ell's security detail. The guys were sitting at a table near the door. Ell hoped they hadn't been too bored.

Chapter Four

Roger, Ell's lab partner from her physics grad student days sat in the bar across the street from his hotel, waiting for Ell. He looked at his watch again. She was only ten minutes late, but it made him nervous. Somehow, he still found it hard to believe that *Ell Donsaii* would actually take the time to go out to dinner with him. Deep inside he half expected a call saying she couldn't come. Or maybe she'd just stand him up?

He took another sip of his beer, determined to make it last, and looked around the bar. His eyes lingered a moment on the shapely legs of a pretty girl sitting at the bar then roamed on around. When he looked back that way he realized that the girl with the short skirt and the really nice legs was staring at him. *Why?* he wondered, then realized. *It's Las Vegas, she's probably a hooker?* Trying not to make it seem like he was staring, he glanced back at her. *Oh my God. She's smiling at me!* Roger looked out the window a moment, hoping he'd see Ell coming his way. *Ell!* He looked back at the girl; she grinned even bigger, then got up and walked his way.

"I wondered how long it would take you to figure it out!"

He rolled his eyes, "Why are you in disguise?"

She made a face like she was hurt, "I thought you *liked* me this way? Though I couldn't bring myself to put the fat pants back on, even for you."

Roger got up and gave her a hug, *Oof, she feels good! And she's hugging me back, hard!* "Well I'm so disappointed!" he whispered in her ear, "I like my Ells with some back on them." He held her back out at arm's length and grinned at her. *She's wearing some skin bronzer and another nose prosthesis, smaller than the one she wore as "Ellen." And I think that's a wig, though a really nice one. She looks pretty, not like when she's "Ell," but still pretty damn cute.*

Ell slapped him lightly on the shoulder, "You'd *better* like me as I am, Roger Emmerit!" She mock glared at him.

"Yes Ma'am." he grinned back.

"Well Allan made us reservations at seven and you spent so much time figuring out who I am that we're going to be late. Let's get moving."

"Help me drink my beer?"

"I'll have a sip, but I can afford to buy you another. Make you my kept man."

"Yes Ma'am." he grinned again.

As they walked to the restaurant Roger asked, "Really, why *are* you still in disguise?"

Ell shrugged, "Because the Chinese might still be after me. Better safe than sorry and all that."

"You can't work at Nellis in disguise can you?"

"I don't think a bunch of Chinese Nationals are going to try to kidnap me on a United States Air Force base. I only wear my disguise when I'm off base."

The restaurant turned out to be quite elegant. As they were seated Roger said, "Wow, we're moving up in the world!"

Ell shrugged, "Believe it or not, even though I've had some money in the bank for a while now, this is the first hoity-toity restaurant I've gone to. What should we order? Your family's the one in the restaurant business."

Roger raised his eyebrows as he looked over the menu. "We may be in the restaurant business, but we don't serve stuff like this."

Eventually they both ordered Filet Mignon and, to the waiter's most evident dismay, French fries. Roger watched in awe as Ell finished a salad, the steak, all her fries and then ordered a Bananas Foster. She looked at him, "What are you having for dessert?"

"Jeez, I'm stuffed, you go ahead. What's Bananas Foster?"

She grinned, "I don't know, but I like bananas and I like dessert, so I'm counting on it making me happy," she patted her tummy.

~~~

After their dinner they slowly walked back toward Roger's hotel. Ell felt pleased that he'd managed to take her hand like he used to back at NC State. As they passed a bar with live music Roger said, "Hey, you want to go in and listen a while?"

She smiled at him. "Sure." They went in and listened until the band took a break then meandered the rest of the way back to his hotel, hand in hand. In the lobby they paused uncomfortably, Ell worrying that he'd invite her up to his room. Then worrying that he wouldn't.

Roger dithered over the same question, then— remembering their old game—said, "If I invited you up to my room, could you restrain yourself from taking advantage of me?"

She pursed her lips and tapped her chin as if in deep

thought, then grinned up at him, "Okay, I promise." She lifted an eyebrow, "Though it'll be difficult."

Up in the room she strode to the window and threw open the curtains, "Wow, nice view!"

Roger came up behind her and put his hands on her shoulders, "Best view of the building next door that money can buy. But, if you lean waaay to the right you can see a thin sliver of the bright lights of Las Vegas."

Ell snickered and leaned back against him, "Oh well, I didn't come up for the view of the city."

Roger leaned down and blew gently on her neck.

Ell squirmed, "You're giving me goose bumps!" She turned in his arms...

***

Incredulously, Roger watched Ell finish her second pecan waffle.

"These are really good!" she said and twinkled up at him. "Sure you don't want another one?"

"Hah! If I ate the way you do, I'd have to buy adjacent seats on the plane back to Raleigh." He looked at her pensively, "When are you going to be back in North Carolina?"

She shrugged, "I'm not sure, sometime in the next 6 months. I'm hoping I'll be there for Christmas or Thanksgiving, but everyone wants those dates off and I'm a really junior officer, so," she made a face, "probably not."

He took her hand, "You'll let me know when you're there?"

She flashed him a brilliant smile, "You bet, I've gotta get my regular dose of Roger!"

Lieutenant

***

"Sir I'm concerned."

"Well, I am too Varnet. But the Chinese have concentrated troops in Fujian province before."

"Yes sir. But those times have been when they've been rattling sabers about Taiwan."

"So you think we should be more worried because they *haven't* been making those kinds of noises this time?"

"Sir, if you actually want to win a fight, you don't telegraph your first punch."

"You can hardly help but telegraph your punch when we're watching every move you make with umpty zillion satellites."

"Sir, we don't really have that many satellites. And the Chinese have had killer satellites since way back in 2007."

"They couldn't take out *all* our satellites!"

"Sir, we don't know that. They've launched a lot of satellites in the past few years."

"How would they rationalize taking out our satellites?"

The younger man shrugged, "They want their privacy? They could just take out the ones that pass over them."

"But we have polar orbit satellites that are only over them sometimes."

He shrugged again, "They might take those out as they go over?"

Stimson said, "Varnet, I know you're paid to be a pessimist, but you're ruining my whole week. What can we do about this? Send over more reconnaissance UAVs?"

"Our UAVs are controlled and transmit their data back by satellite link."

"Oh Gods! Surely they can transmit by other means?"

"Yeah, but first we'd have to get control consoles and UAV pilots onto boats over there. Close enough to the action that they could fly the birds without satellite communication. Then the UAVs would have to return from a flight so they could have line of sight communications with base in order to send their pictures back. Or they could land and download their data directly. Then the info could be sent by undersea fiberoptic cable."

Stimson closed his eyes and pinched his nose. "To repeat, what can we do about this?"

"Sir, I don't know."

"Well, we're paying you to figure it out! Get on it. I want estimates on the likelihood they could take out all our satellites and what we could do to prevent it."

Varnet stood and shambled out of Stimson's office without saying anything else. The older man shook his head, *How could someone that smart be such a slob?*

***

Gary studied "Raquel" as she swayed gently side to side. Sparring with her made him nervous because he kept worrying he might hurt her. He must have thrown her dozens of times by now and, though she landed hard, she always bounced right back up. However, her slender build made him feel like she'd break in two.

He'd been getting more and more attracted to her, so he knew he'd feel terrible if she got hurt. When she hit the mat it made more noise than anyone else he threw, but she seemed less bothered by coming down hard than the other students. On the other hand, when she threw, him his landings seemed softer than when he sparred with the others. He didn't understand why, but it almost felt like she tugged him up at the last moment to soften his landing or something. Gary snatched at her wrist. *Yes!! Got it!* He pivoted, pulling her across his hip and, putting his body into it, he tossed her. *She seems so light!* He tried to follow with an immobilizing arm hold, but her wrist broke free of his grip as she landed and she bounced back to her feet to begin swaying again!

Behind him Millie said, "Raquel, do not always be defensive, you *mus'* do some throws yourself if you want to *know* this art."

Raquel nodded, danced a step to his left, then suddenly Gary found himself in the air and descending to the mat. Damn! *I'm off balance!* Before he landed as clumsily as he'd feared, his gi tugged. He suddenly straightened to land flat, slapping the mat with his left arm. *Did I twist* myself *in midair to land like a cat—or did her hand catch in my gi and* accidentally *straighten me—or did* she *use my gi to turn me so I'd land safely on purpose?*

Gary tried to bounce back to his feet like Raquel did; it wasn't as easy as she made it look.

~~~

Millie studied them a few moments longer. Raquel seemed to do so much better whenever Millie watched her. So unusual! Other students became nervous and clumsy when they knew they were being watched. When Millie watched out of the corner of her eye, pretending to watch other students, Raquel was tentative, easily caught and thrown and, when she did throw another student, she never threw them with any authority. Millie shook her head and moved on. She wondered how this puzzling girl would do when they began strikes next week.

~~~

When class was over Gary steeled his nerve as they put equipment away, "Raquel?"

She seemed focused on something else, but when he got close and paused, she said, "Yeah Gar'?"

He hated it when other people messed with his name, but somehow it seemed nice when Raquel did it. "Um... I've been wondering if you'd like to go next door for pizza... I'm kinda hungry." He looked at her out of the corner of his eye. She'd tilted her head curiously. "It's no big deal if you can't." He shrugged, trying to look nonchalant.

"I'm kinda in the middle of a big project..." she cut her eyes over to Amy, one of the other girls in the class. Amy, Gary saw, was frowning at Raquel and shaking her head.

Gary put his hands up, waving them weakly, "Hey, no big deal, some other..."

Raquel cut in, "But, I've got to eat *sometime* right?" She smiled brightly at him, "Sure, let's go. Just let me... let me change out of my gi." She turned away and whispered to her AI for a moment.

Gary wondered who she'd talked to.

~~~

Lieutenant

Gary and Ell walked into Fast Eddie's Pizza and looked around for a table. It was only 5:30, so the place wasn't very busy. However, they weren't the only students from 4MA eating there.

Steve was already in the restaurant, as were Mary and Randy, though they were all pretending they didn't know each other.

Gary started to sit down at a table out in the middle but Ell pointed at an empty table with her chin, "Can we sit over there by the wall?"

The young waitress brought them menus and took orders. A Coke for Ell and a diet Mountain Dew for Gary. An awkward pause followed as they looked at the menus. This was as far as Gary's plans had gotten, so he found himself somewhat tongue-tied. Ell asked, "What kind of pizza do you like?"

Gary cursed himself, he should have asked her! "Uh, I like pepperoni, sausage, Canadian bacon..."

"Ah, a meatza kinda guy, huh?"

He shrugged.

"Black olives?"

"Sure."

"Pepperoni and black olive to share?"

"Okay."

~~~

Ell's eyes twinkled. After her own share of awkward episodes dealing with the opposite sex, it was a relief to see him embarrassed and having more trouble than she was with this little date. She put the menu down, "So, what do you do for a living, Gar'?"

Gary's relief that she'd taken up the management of their conversation was almost palpable. "I'm still a student." He shrugged with a little pride. "A grad student in Chemistry at UNLV."

"Ooh, that's tough!"

He shrugged again, "Yeah, but I'm getting by."

The waitress stopped by with their drinks. To Gary's surprise Ell ordered a large pepperoni and black olive pizza for just the two of them. She sat back and patted her stomach, "I'm starving!" She turned her eyes back to Gary, "What's the topic of your research?"

"Um, my professor... and I... work on long carbon nanotubes. He's sure we can make truly long nanotubes with his new synthesis system." His eyes flashed to Ell, "Uh, carbon nanotubes are single molecule thick sheets of carbon molecules rolled up into tubes like straws. They're really..." He paused at the twinkle in her eyes.

She patted him lightly on the back of his hand, "I know what nanotubes are—tubular sheets of graphene with incredible tensile strength. Did you think you were eating pizza with a complete bimbo?" She grinned, "How are you doing it? If it's not a secret?"

"We start with a field of nanotubes created by ordinary methods. They're standing on end with the open ends of the nanotubes exposed. Then we establish certain conditions of heat, pressure, catalyst molecules and vaporized carbon. Those are the secrets, but with the correct settings, voila, the nanotubes get longer. So far, not long enough, we're still measuring in meters, but, if we find the right conditions, we hope we can just spin them out forever!"

"Wow! That *would* be really cool. Maybe long enough to use for a space elevator?"

"Yeah," he grinned conspiratorially, "riding up a skyhook I had a hand in building. That's my secret hope."

"That's so cool!" She touched the back of his hand

and he felt a tingle where her fingers rested.

"What do you do for fun?"

"I like to go out to clubs sometimes. I'm a real music aficionado." He looked embarrassed, "Believe it or not, I like to swing dance, though I'm not the greatest."

Raquel clapped her hands, "Cool! A friend of mine took me to Tres Locos once and I learned little about swing dancing. We should go together sometime!"

"Okay, when?"

She grinned and leaned across the table toward him. She whispered, "It's Saturday, how about tonight?"

"I thought you had a big project?"

She quirked an eyebrow, "Not a project that can't wait on some dancing."

"Then sure! Should I pick you up?"

"Oh, no. You don't want to come to my ghetto. I'll meet you at Tres Locos, say nine?"

He shrugged, feeling a little disappointed, "Okay."

The waitress arrived with the pizza and Gary dished a slice for Raquel, then another for him. The waitress said, "Will there be anything else?"

Raquel smiled at her and said, "Jar of parmesan please?"

After the waitress left, Gary held up his Mountain Dew, "To 4MA."

With a serious look Raquel held her Coke up. "To 4MA... and long nanotubes," she intoned, then touched her cup to his.

Gary asked, "So, what do you do for a living?" suddenly his stomach clenched. She looked awfully young. It would be horrifying if she said "Go to high school." *Why didn't I ask that question back while we were in the dojo?*

She swallowed a huge bite of pizza and arched an

eyebrow, "I'm just a spoiled little rich girl. But I'm happy to be buying a starving grad student some pizza."

"Um," he squinched his face, "how old are you?"

Ell grinned at him. She leaned forward and whispered, "Fifteen."

He blanched.

She took pity on him and, with a little smirk said, "Sorry, I shouldn't have said that—actually I'm twenty-one. I could tell you thought I might be too young though." Though she was actually eighteen, her "Raquel" ID did *say* twenty-one.

Gary took a deep breath and said, "That was *despicable*!" He grinned at her, astonished at the way she was wolfing down pizza. How could she eat like that, yet be so thin?

***

Ell walked into Tres Locos a little early and looked around. Her eyes slid over Barrett and Mary without stopping and she claimed a table near, but not right by the dance floor. A waitress came by and she ordered a Coke, then leaned back to listen to the warm up band and wait for Gary. She watched a pretty large group of line dancers do their thing and carefully noted the routine they were using. Someone tapped her shoulder.

Ell looked up, expecting to see Gary. Instead, a dark haired guy she didn't recognize held his hand out, "Dance." He said. It was a statement, not a question. His breath smelled heavily of beer.

Ell said, "Sorry, I'm waiting for a friend."

"Dance while you wait!"

Ell thought it wouldn't be all that bad to dance while

she waited, but somehow it seemed like it'd be rude to Gary. Besides, she didn't like this guy's attitude. She shook her head.

The guy actually grabbed her wrist and tugged, saying, "Come on, you're here alone, sitting near the dance floor. Don't be such a bitch!"

Ell glanced over at Barrett. He'd gotten out of his seat, but she shook her head minutely and he subsided.

Ell was considering a number of possible responses to the man who had his hand on her when she heard Gary's voice, "The lady said she didn't want to dance."

Without letting go of Ell's wrist, or looking at Gary, the man said in a low, menacing tone, "Back off, asswipe!" Ell realized with dismay that the man was quite a bit bigger than Gary.

Gary grabbed the man's wrist in one hand and his shirtfront in the other. The man let go of Ell's wrist and—cocking his fist back—said, "Butt out!" He threw a punch.

Gary—as if he did it every day—dodged the wild swing. As the guy's fist flew past, he stepped in and executed the "O Goshi" throw they'd learned at 4MA. The man sailed over Gary's hip and landed clumsily on his side. He cried out. Gary suddenly looked ashen, "Hey, man, are you okay?"

Bouncers materialized around them as the man on the floor grated out, "I'm fine. Back off *shithead!*"

One of the bouncers helped the man to his feet and escorted him to the door over his protests. The other bouncer looked at them a moment then said, "Normally we'd throw both of you out, but I saw the guy hassling the young lady and was just too far away to stop him myself." He waved a finger at Gary, "But, don't be gettin' in any more fights, okay?"

~~~

After the bouncer left, Gary slumped down into the seat next to Ell. "Whew! I'm taking jujutsu for confidence and exercise. I didn't expect to ever use it!"

Ell gave him an admiring look, "Wow! Thanks for coming to my rescue!" She beamed sunnily at him.

His heart soared.

"Had he been bugging you for very long? I thought I was meeting you at nine."

"No, I got here a few minutes early and I'd just claimed this table. Can I get my white knight a beer?" She waved at a passing waitress.

"Sure!" he winked, "I think it's the least you can do for my saving your life."

~~~

After half of his beer had disappeared, Gary nudged her, "You ready to dance?"

She got up and led the way to the floor. Gary enjoyed the walk out to the floor. She had on snug jeans and little western boots which made the trip quite inspiring.

~~~

They began making some circuits around the floor. Though nothing like Cody, who Ell'd learned to dance with, Gary was a pretty good dancer and Ell enjoyed herself immensely.

After they sat down, Ell saw Cody over near the edge of the tables, he raised his beer in her direction and she gave him a little wave. Gary asked, "A friend?"

Ell shook her head, "He's the guy that taught me to dance one night here at Tres Locos. Just a nice guy, taking pity on a poor girl with two left feet."

Gary snorted, "He must be a great teacher if you learned to dance this well in one night."

"I guess so," Ell said. She lifted an eyebrow, "You ready to dance again? Or are you just gonna lay around in that chair and drink beer?"

Gary grinned, "Ready, ma'am. Anytime you say, ma'am. Let's get out there now, ma'am."

After another session on the dance floor, Ell excused herself to visit the bathroom. When she came out Cody leaned up off the wall, "Raquel." He nodded his head at her. "Are you and that guy serious, or could I take you out for a real dance? Kinda show him what he could aspire to, so to speak?"

Ell grinned at him, "He's a very sweet guy Cody, and you've got no call to be tryin' to make him feel bad."

"Maybe just a little bit?"

"No. But one of these nights when I'm here with Amy, you can show me what we can really do, okay?"

He looked enthusiastic, "It's a date!"

When she got back to the table, Gary asked with some concern, "You sure he's not an old boyfriend or something?"

"Nah, just a dancin' friend. Don't you go getting all serious on me." They danced a few more times. When it came time to leave, Gary settled for a polite kiss on the cheek in the parking lot before Ell got in her little pickup.

***

Ell finished placing the last of a tiny ring of carbon nanotubes with entangled tips in a circle around the spot on the platinum coated surface. The circle constituted what she planned to be her "port." She sat back up rolling her shoulders to ease their stiffness. Reaching to one side she opened the valve to let liquid nitrogen start running through the plate the nanotubes were on. The cold should fix them in place. She clamped the cover on the chamber they were in and opened another valve to pressurize it. Once the pressure had reached two atmospheres she closed the valve and watched the gauge to make sure it was stable—indicating no leak.

She'd pressurized the empty chamber a couple of days ago and it'd held pressure until this evening, thus indicating that it didn't leak. She hoped her nanotubes would form a port as her calculations said they might, allowing gas to leak out of the chamber through the port. The port would be extremely small so it might take a while to detect the loss of pressure. Unlike her previous experiments, this time she wasn't trying to see if the material leaking out of the chamber was showing up in the correct location. She'd realized that, just like when she'd done the experiments with which she'd discovered photon-gluon resonance, she could do her experiment one part at a time.

So first, could she create a port that simply let material leak out of a chamber. Where the gas actually *went* wasn't that important, at least for now.

Confident that the chamber didn't have a gross leak she energized the platinum plate. She put her finger on her newer, bigger power supply to be sure it wasn't about to burn out like the first one. It was warm, but didn't seem to be getting hot.

Ell looked at the gauge, *Nope it hasn't dropped yet.* Well, it was half past two in the morning, she'd check it again when she got up. She had Allan turn out the room lights as she walked to the door. Just before exiting the room she glanced back at the glowing lights of her setup.

What the Hell! There were tiny sparks falling from underneath the table! "Damn it!" Ell muttered, *Did this power supply burn out too?* She stepped back over to the table in the dimness, expecting to see the power supply glowing or something. Everything was dark, she noted with puzzlement. She stepped back and crouched to look under the table. A line of sparks still trailed down from the table, straight down, seemingly unaffected by any air currents. She blew at them, but the puff of air didn't affect them. In fact the sparks didn't seem to be falling, just appearing, then winking out at different levels, all in a line! And, they weren't appearing under the power supply, it was over to the right.

Ell crouched lower to peer up at the bottom of the table. The line of sparks went right up to the bottom of the table. The light was too dim to see the hole they were coming out of. She noted the location and stood up, it looked like the sparks were coming from directly under the chamber she'd just spent all that time setting up. She had Allan turn the lights back on. Everything looked okay with the apparatus on the top of the table. She sniffed, *Nothing smells like it's burning.* She crouched to look under the table, but if the sparks were still there, they were hard to see in the brighter light. The bottom of the table looked okay, but it was pretty dim under there. After a brief search, Ell found the flashlight she kept in one of the drawers. She shone it up under the table.

She couldn't see a hole the sparks could be coming out of.

A chill ran over her. She picked up a pencil then had Allan switch off the lights. Ell knelt again and looked up under the table at the sparks. She put the pencil into the line of sparks, but they weren't deflected or changed below the pencil! Slowly she reached up and drew a small circle around the spot on the bottom of the table that the sparks seemed to be emanating from. Then she had Allan turn the light on again. Crouching, she peered up under the table. The area inside the circle she'd drawn was unmarked! There really wasn't a hole there for sparks to fall out of! Using the pencil as a measuring stick she placed the tip of it at the center of the circle and then gripped the pencil with two fingers at the edge of the table. She knelt back up and moved the pencil to the top of the table sliding it back. *Yes, the sparks are coming from* directly *beneath the chamber!* Slowly Ell sagged back from her kneeling position, to her buttocks... then to her back where she lay, staring unseeing at the ceiling as her mind raced with implications.

~~~

A couple of hours later, as she still lay unseeing on the floor, Allan spoke in her ear, "You have less than two hours before you must leave for work, I recommend that you get some sleep."

Ell shook herself and got off the floor to go into her bed, but it was another thirty minutes before she fell asleep.

~~~

The fact that she'd already completed the reading for the entire course helped out during the next day in class. Instead of listening, Ell spent the time running her equations through her mind and pondering the meaning of the sparks she'd seen last night.

She'd had so little sleep she expected to have trouble staying awake. However, she felt so excited that dozing off wasn't a problem. The only problem was that she couldn't keep her mind on the UAV class.

The alignment of the line of sparks just below the port she was trying to create strongly suggested the sparks were related to the port. Ell now hypothesized that the port actually might be working. She thought that as molecules squeezed through the port in the fifth dimension and appeared back into Ell's observable universe, an energy leakage could result in the emission of visible light that would appear to be a spark.

Wait! she thought, *It could also be that when the port opens, a flash of light results. If the flash is tiny, it'll look like a spark.*

After she considered she also realized that the distance traveled in this universe when a port opened through the fifth dimension could vary enormously depending on the conditions in the port at the moment it opened. After all, an atomic distance in the fifth dimension could equal a significant macroscopic distance in this universe, so minor voltage and current fluctuations could result in the other terminus of the portal being either much farther from, or much closer to, the near terminus of the port than calculated.

Ports could be opening and closing every time the voltage changes a tiny bit, she thought. *And that could cause a spark every time.*

Setting up the experiment, Ell had calculated conditions to open a port across a ten mm distance in this universe, intending that the port would open outside the chamber itself and into the empty space above the table, but below where she'd positioned the chamber. But now she realized that microscopic fluctuations in the field could open the port anywhere from microns to meters away. She worried that some of the sparks from the portal openings had appeared in the apartment below hers.

***

Back home in her apartment Ell walked straight past Amy who sat waiting with her dinner. She stepped into her office/lab leaving the light off and looking for the sparks in the dim light coming from the curtain covered window. There weren't any visible. She wondered, *Maybe there's too much light?* Amy called out, "You've got to eat, your damned experiment can wait *that* long!" Ell stepped over to check the pressure gauge—it read a little lower. *Is that enough lower to truly indicate that some molecules actually escaped from the chamber through the port? Or could it be a leak? Or just inaccuracy in the gauge?*

Ell picked up a sheet of paper and sat down to look under the table. Locating the circle she'd marked the night before with the pencil she wrapped the paper around the other side of it to block light and leaned in close. *No sparks!* She sighed as her shoulders sagged. Moments later she had the cover off the power supply, *Burned out again!* She had Allan order a large, stand-alone power supply that could provide voltages and currents far higher than anything she'd been using and went back out to eat dinner. She raised an eyebrow at the exasperated looking Amy, "You're turning into a nagging wife!"

Lieutenant

Amy snickered, "You're *making* me into one!"

Chapter Five

The car'd been parked across from the Nellis entrance for two days, a small but powerful video camera mounted next to the visor and focused on the exit. In a van across the parking lot a man watched a screen displaying the take from that camera. He said into his mike, "There she is! Blue Ford Focus, turning right, pulling into traffic… now." One of the chase cars, a nondescript Chevrolet, pulled out into traffic a block behind Ell. As she drove down the road, the other chase car, which had been parked down the road the other direction in case she turned left, pulled out and fell in three blocks behind her.

***

Ell knocked on the door of the classroom and a few moments later it opened to reveal a short, plump, red headed young woman. She grinned up at Ell with a sparkle in her eye. "Oh, thank you so much for coming in Ms. Donsaii. Oops, I mean Lieutenant. The kids will love meeting you. I'm Diane Smithers." As Ell stepped into the room Ms. Smithers turned to the kids in her class who were all staring at the newcomer. "Kids, I know it's not time for Show and Tell right now and normally we aren't allowed to bring anything living to

Show and Tell either, but today we're making an exception. Janey, would you like to come up to the front?"

Janey got out of her seat and shyly walked up to stand beside Ell. Like she often did when she was nervous, she had the tip of a finger in the corner of her mouth.

Ms. Smithers said, "Okay, Janey's brought a very special person in for her sharing and, as always with Show and Tell, you can ask questions and try to guess what's special about this person.

Hands shot up around the room and Ms. Smithers pointed to a boy near the front, "Jimmy?"

"She's a lieutenant!" Jimmy volunteered excitedly.

Ms. Smithers raised a questioning eyebrow at Ell. Ell leaned forward and said, "Yes, I am. These bars on my shoulders," she leaned farther forward so they could see the embroidered bars on the shoulders of her BDUs, "mean I'm a lieutenant, a rank in the military. I'm in the Air Force."

Hands continued to wave excitedly and "Sally" was called on. "I'll bet she's a pilot." the girl said excitedly.

Ell looked down at Janey who said, "Yes, she flies planes, but she does it by remote control rather than riding around in them. That's not what's so cool about her though."

A number of excited questions followed, many showing that child's particular interests such as, "Does she ride horses?" and "Does she shoot rockets from her plane?" But eventually a little girl in the front row who'd been studying Ell's face since she entered shot her hand up. Without waiting to be called on the girl burst out, "She's Ell Donsaii!"

Excitedly, Janey said, "Yes!" Some of the kids were

thrilled, though many, who hadn't heard of Ell's performances in the Olympics nearly two years ago—a lifetime for kids at the age of seven—were puzzled.

Janey excitedly explained who Ell was to the kids who'd never heard of her and then Ms. Smithers showed a couple of video clips of Ell in the Olympics.

Ell did a couple of aerial cartwheels for the kids. Ms. Smithers let the kids ask a few more questions and finally Ell leapt up into the air, did a back flip, saluted the class and left out the door.

She didn't pay attention to the Asian man who was walking into the school as she walked out.

The man walked in, made a circuit of the hall and walked out, whispering through his AI, "Yes, it's *definitely* her. Track that car!"

***

 Ell heard a knock on the door between her apartment and Steve's. "Yes?"

Steve's voice said, "It's me. Can I come in?"

"Sure." Ell had Allan release the lock and saw the door open.

Steve said, "Bad news. The parking lot team found a tracker on your Ford."

Ell sighed, she'd *so* hoped that the Chinese had given up on her. "Not on the truck though?"

"No, the truck was clean and, believe me, we went over it with a fine toothed comb. But we can't use that parking lot anymore. And, we've got to assume they might track your Focus to another lot and follow you home. You'll have to try to be even more vigilant about watching for tails."

Lieutenant

***

The younger man said, "After she left the school, we tracked her vehicle back to the Air Force Base. Later, her car left the base and parked in a parking lot. The tracking device we put on her car was destroyed shortly after stopping in the parking lot and the car was moved elsewhere. At a distance we were able to follow the adhesive trackers we put on her car seat. They must have successfully attached to her clothing. We followed them to an apartment complex. We can't pick up a signal at present, presumably because they're inside the building somewhere. The adhesive trackers are very small and their she signal's very weak.

"We've checked and none of the apartments are rented in her name. We don't know what part of her clothing the trackers attached to, so we have no idea when she might wear that item again, nor the likelihood of the tracker being destroyed in the wash. We only have a day or two until the tracker goes dead anyway. However, we're ready to follow her if and when she does leave with a clothing tracker. We'll also try to track her car coming and going from the base again, but I don't think we should attach another tracker to her car because the first one was detected and removed so quickly. She must be very suspicious because of the previous attempts that've been made to gain her cooperation."

"Okay," Zhou said, "have men standing by this apartment complex at all times. They should check *each* person leaving the building with telescopic imaging. Don't just wait for the tracker's signal to leave the complex."

***

Inside the van the smaller man said, "Someone leaving the building." He manipulated a joystick, centering the woman in the field of the camera in the small car parked in the apartment complex parking lot. He zoomed in, "Right height, but she's brunette." He started to zoom back out and center the complex in the lens again.

Suddenly, the heavy set man sat up and said, "One of the adhesive tracking beads just responded to a query!" He glanced up and spoke to his AI, "Get Mr. Zhou!" To the smaller man he said, "It's the bead that was on the headrest. It must be attached to a hat because these Americans wash their hair so often, it'd be gone from there by now." He fiddled with the controls of the panel in front of him, "A moment to triangulate, yes, the tracker bead's on this side of the building, has anyone *else* left the building?"

"No, just that brunette. She's on the sidewalk heading away from us. No hat."

"Maybe she's wearing a wig! The tracker could be in the hair. Have Dog team follow her! Yes the bead's moving away too! Tell Dragon team to stand by."

Zhou joined the conversation then, ordering the surveillance van to stay where it was, but confirming that Dog and Dragon should follow the brunette. He told them to wake up the other two ready teams and have them come to the apartment complex.

Shortly, Dog and Dragon had followed the brunette to a small shopping center where she entered a martial arts dojo. The two members of Dog team went around to the back of the dojo to cover the rear exit. Dragon team parked in the lot out front, two members staying in the car and Xu walking into the dojo on the pretext of asking about lessons. Twenty minutes later Zhou arrived with Snake and Tiger teams, three per vehicle. They parked farther away. Xu came back out of the dojo and walked to the car where Zhou sat, getting in the back seat with him. "Well?"

Xu shrugged. "There are many brunette women in there. I think one is thin enough to be Donsaii, but they're all wearing gis so it's hard to tell."

~~~

Zhou called for the surveillance van to bring its sensors over and had it park directly in front of the dojo, but it still couldn't pick up the tracking bead while—or if—it was inside the building. Zhou's eye began to twitch irregularly as anxiety and frustration made his tick resurface. He decided they had to wait for her to leave and tried to settle back to wait, but it was hard to be patient. It'd taken forever just to find out she'd been assigned to Nellis AFB. His supervisors were calling frequently, asking for updates and riding him for more progress. Yesterday he'd noticed a small patch of hair missing on one side of his head. He reminded himself that he had a much bigger team than the two previous groups who'd failed to capture this girl. *But, fail they had, and my team has had so much trouble just finding her...*

***

Gary unobtrusively made his way over to stand near "Raquel" at the beginning of the class. He stayed near her as they made strikes on some stationary targets. When Millie called for them to pair up, he turned to her and raised an eyebrow, gratified when she nodded. The longer the class went on, the more attraction he felt for the pretty young woman. Going out dancing with her had certainly whetted his appetite for more. He trotted over to pick up a pair of the padded hand targets.

At Millie's direction Gary held up one of the padded targets for Raquel to strike. Graceful as always, she launched a blow, *wow she's quick!* She struck the target with a loud "thwap!" Gary's hand stung like it'd been spanked with a ruler! Astonished, he pulled his hand out of the strap on the target and shook out his fingers. He looked the padded target over. *There's two inches of padding on this damned thing! I didn't think she could hurt me through all that!* He saw Raquel grimace; *She must have hurt her hand too.*

Millie's head had tracked around at the loud sound, thinking something bad had happened. She saw Gary and Raquel rubbing their hands, but neither really looked hurt. She wondered momentarily what those two had done now, but then was distracted back to the students in front of her, *big men trying to hit things hard, without finesse!* She shook her head in amusement.

The rest of the practice passed without incident, Gary, surprised that none of Raquel's other strikes hurt, wondered just what had happened on the first one? When the class finished, he said, "How 'bout another pizza?"

Raquel grinned back at him, "How 'bout? I'm hungry. I'll just go change."

Lieutenant

***

Zhou's eye tic got worse as students started leaving the dojo in fits and starts. "Which one? Which one?!"

Xu said, "I don't think she's come out yet..."

"Are you sure?" Xu shrugged. Some of the students wore their gis, some had changed. Some walked out to cars, several small groups went into the pizza place next door. Some walked away on the sidewalk, but they didn't look the right height, nor thin.

Xu sat up sharply, "I think that's her. With the redheaded man, see how slender she is? Maybe he's her brother?"

Zhou exploded, striking Xu hard on the shoulder "She *doesn't* have a brother! Did you even look at the briefing materials?!"

Xu ducked his head, "Sorry, sorry, yes, you're right, no brother, she's an only child, I'm sorry."

After a bit, a message came from the surveillance van. "She left the dojo and went into the pizza place." There was a long pause in which no one said anything, Zhou crossed his arms and settled down to wait.

~~~

Gary followed Ell to the same table against the wall where they'd sat before. They ordered a Coke and Diet Mountain Dew from the waitress. Ell grinned at him, "Wanna live on the wild side? We could try a sausage and artichoke pizza?"

"Hmmm, that's kinda out there for me," he grinned, "but you only live once. Let's go for it."

Gary'd intended to learn more about Raquel, but she

immediately steered the conversation back to him. She learned that he'd grown up in Reno; that his Dad was a mechanical engineer and his Mom a software programmer. Then she pumped him for information about the nanotubes he and his professor were creating, wanting to know how long the longest nanotubes were that they'd made so far. She wanted to know their conformation, how pure and on and on. Her fascination in him and his research kept him talking, only occasionally thinking of how little he was learning about her.

***

Suddenly Zhou couldn't take it any longer. He undid his seatbelt, "We'll go have pizza too!"

***

Steve sat at the counter watching the outside and making his coffee and slice of ham pizza last. His eyes narrowed. The four men who'd just been sitting in a car in the parking lot suddenly stirred. All the doors opened and four Asian appearing men got out and started walking toward Fast Eddie's Pizza. Steve looked over at Mary and Randy, sitting at a table for two near Ell, intending to draw their attention to the Asians, but they'd already started glancing that way. Ell and her young man were sitting at another table for two, Ell with her back to the wall as Steve had taught her. Steve saw her eyes flick to the window, taking in the men walking toward the parlor. A grimace flashed across her face.

Steve looked carefully at the Asians as they entered. They were a badly mismatched group. Two in Levis, one in a coverall and an older man wearing a sports coat. They didn't *look* like they belonged together. They didn't look like the kind of people who'd be sitting together in a car in a parking lot. They didn't look like the kind of guys who'd be going out to dinner at a pizza place. And, every last one of them glanced over towards Ell's end of the room when they came in.

Not very good craft if they were who Steve thought they were. He whispered to his AI to contact the rest of Ell's security detail and get them on their way over to the little shopping center, even the ones who were off duty and asleep. They'd only have nine of their ten team members because Barrett was on vacation. Steve's mind raced. The safest thing would be to go over, get Ell and leave, but he wasn't sure Ell'd like that. He'd come to know her pretty well and she *wasn't* timid. He thought she'd rather deal with these guys now, rather than worry about them popping up again later.

On the other hand, what if the Chinese had their own reinforcements? He whispered to his AI to pass a message to Ell, "I think the Chinese are here to try to pick you up. The rest of our team's on its way here. Consider that there are must be more of the Chinese than the four who just came in the door. Nod if you want me to come pick you up and get you out of here *now*. Shake your head if you want to take them on now so they won't be able to come after you again in the future."

Ell gave a little head shake and so Steve started sizing up their prospects for dealing with these guys.

~~~

The waitress showed up with Ell and Gary's pizza. As she was putting it on a stand in front of him, Gary realized that a group of four Asian guys were sitting down at the table right behind him. *That's weird,* he thought, *there are plenty of empty tables.*

~~~

Zhou'd seated himself opposite the brunette woman and now he tried to examine her without staring. *That might be a wig, but it's hard to tell with the stocking cap over it. Her skin was definitely darker than Donsaii's though. And her nose was wrong, a little too big,* he thought, though he wasn't exactly sure what was different. He looked around the restaurant, wondering if they could have chosen the wrong girl, but none of the other women were slender enough… or young enough. His eyes narrowed, her knuckles were pinker than the rest of her hand! Perhaps as if a dark stain had been rubbed off by striking things in her karate class.

It *was* her! He looked around the room again, thinking how best to arrange her abduction. This was *not* a good place, there were too many people. He sat back, *we'll just follow her when she leaves,* he decided. The waitress came to take their orders and he ordered a single medium cheese pizza for the four of them, hoping to be done eating as soon as the girl and her friend finished. That way they could leave without it seeming so obvious they were following her.

~~~

Ell grimaced inside. For a little while she thought she might've convinced the Chinese men that they were following the wrong girl. She had Allan watching him through her AI video cameras though and the AI said, "The older Asian man focused on your hands briefly and seems to be satisfied about something." Ell looked down at her knuckles and saw where the bronzer had broken down over her knuckles during their training strikes.

She sighed, wondering if the Chinese guys would *ever* stop coming after her. *Okay,* she thought, *looking around. They probably won't make a grab for me in such a public place, but I'd like them to do it here where there are plenty of witnesses. We won't get them thrown out of the country because we* have suspicions *they have ill intentions. Probably couldn't even get the police to give them a good once over. But I don't want them to come after me here in the main area of the restaurant where Gary or some of the other witnesses might get hurt.* She reached into her pocket and got out her pepper spray, moving it into her waistband while staring the older Chinese man directly in the eye. Gary'd been talking to her, but she hadn't heard what he said. She looked at him with a little frown, "Sorry Gary, gotta run to the little girls' room." She got up and made her way toward the back of the restaurant.

~~~

Gary watched Raquel walk gracefully away from the table. The shorts she had on emphasized her legs. *Wow, she looks* amazing *out of a gi!* He looked down at the table—she'd again eaten half of a large pizza while he'd only eaten three slices and felt stuffed. *Damn! Where's she put it all?*

~~~

When Donsaii stared him in the eye, Zhou realized

that she was as much as saying, "I know who you are." Startled, he felt like she was saying she *dared* him to do something. Then she got up and walked toward the back of the restaurant. *Is she leaving?!* He looked to the back of the restaurant and saw an exit sign. Just before he leapt to his feet in a panic, she turned into the women's restroom. *But what if she climbs out a bathroom window, or comes back out of the bathroom but turns immediately left and goes out the exit?* He had his AI tell the team out back to watch for her.

~~~

Steve heard Ell's voice in his earphone. "Steve, I want these guys to come after me here in the restaurant so we'll have the restaurant's video record for the police, as well as plenty of witnesses and our own AI video records. We need evidence of their intent so the State Department will ship 'em back home instead of leaving them here to regroup. *But*, I want them to come after me back here in the back of the restaurant near the restrooms so there'll be less chance any innocent people might get hurt. My plan's to stay here in the bathroom long enough that they get fidgety and do something foolish. Can you forward your video to me so I'll know what they're doing?"

"Sure," Steve subvocalized, "but what if they have lethal weapons? Someone could *still* get seriously hurt. Like you!"

Allan put the video from Steve's AI on Ell's HUD. She studied it while she thought about it. The Chinese guys hadn't moved, but the fidgety older one was looking back toward the bathroom more and more often. "I don't know. Do you think if they pull out guns I should just go with them until they get me into a less crowded environment?"

"No! That's not a good option either! Let me think—by the way, the other teams tell me there's a couple of Asian looking guys sitting in a car out back, and five more in two cars out the front of the restaurant."

Suddenly the older Chinese man got up and motioned to the other three. They also rose. The four men started toward the back of the restaurant. Steve's time to "think about it" had just run out.

~~~

Gary sat, chin in hand, musing over his good fortune to be having pizza with such a pretty girl. *Would she go for a boyfriend-girlfriend relationship?* he wondered. Belatedly, he realized that she'd been gone to the bathroom for a long time. He turned to look back toward the restrooms. He was surprised to see the four Asian guys from the table behind him, all standing up and heading to the bathroom together. He frowned, *what kind of guys do that?* They all stopped and stood arguing in whispers just outside the bathrooms.

~~~

Ell watched the feed from Steve's AI on her HUD and saw the men approach the bathrooms. She got her Taser out of her purse and took it off safe. She put the business end into the open end of her purse, curling her right ring and small finger around the handle and holding the purse over the barrel with her thumb and long fingers. Her index finger was just off of the trigger. She looked up at the ceiling for a moment. *Am I doing the right thing? Am I crazy to think I can take all four of these guys, even when I'm in the zone?* Ell sighed and wished she could be sure of what she was doing. *But I* don't *want to be dragged off like those other times!* Shrugging, she took the pepper spray out of her waistband and palmed it in her left hand. The men stopped outside the bathroom and argued with one another.

She reached for the doorknob…

~~~

Steve tensed and turned toward the bathrooms himself, lifting his satchel into his lap and reaching inside to grasp his SIG Sauer. He hoped he wouldn't have to bring it out, there'd be *so* many issues with the police afterwards. He looked at Mary who'd gotten out of her chair and begun walking across the room as if she were going to the bathroom too. Randy glanced out the windows of the restaurant then turned his attention back to the Asian men…

~~~

Gary watched the four Asian men in puzzlement, wondering what they were doing, then worrying again about what was wrong with Raquel. He started to get up. Then the door to the ladies' bathroom opened and Raquel stepped out. Instead of coming back to their table she took a power stance facing the Asian men with her feet slightly apart. She stared at the four men, her eyes flashing with anger. She didn't look anything like the pleasant Raquel Gary knew from class! Or the Raquel he'd gone dancing with! She didn't look pretty and slender, she looked… she looked frightening!

~~~

Ell said, "What do you want?!" to the older Chinese man. She let herself fall into her zone and the world slowed down around her.

Lieutenant

Lifting the lapel of his sports coat to show her the pistol in his shoulder holster, the older man nodded meaningfully. "You come with us." He waved with his right hand toward the rear exit door next to the bathrooms. To Ell this brief communication seemed like it took minutes, which gave her more time to agonize over whether she was doing the right thing.

The man in the coverall reached out for her elbow.

Ell lifted the pepper spray with her left hand while allowing her little purse to drop off the barrel of the Taser. She curled her index finger tighter around its trigger as she raised the weapon...

~~~

Gary saw Raquel say something to one of the men and then the little group of Asian men began to contract around her. He watched with astonishment as Raquel's hands blurred up and around.

A hissing, popping noise came from the back of the restaurant, perhaps from her?

The man on her left cried out and leapt back, hands to his face.

The three men on her right fell, each quivering as if poleaxed. Their falls to the floor decelerated strangely. Just before they hit, Gary realized Raquel's right hand had a grip on the sleeves of the two men on her right and her left hand had grasped the shirt front of the one on her left. She was leaning back hard to slow the impact of their heads with the floor. The one in the middle got away from her some, his head hitting hard enough to bounce a little.

Gary belatedly noticed a black device skittering across the floor from where the incident had occurred. It looked like a plastic pistol!

A black man leapt up from the counter, stopped briefly, then came forward to take the elbow of the fourth Asian man. That one was still on his feet, crouched over, moaning, his hands over his eyes. The muscular African American led the sobbing Asian man into the men's bathroom.

A woman who'd already been on her way to the bathroom continued to the group of Asian men where they lay on the floor. She pulled some stuff out of her purse. She tossed something to Raquel and knelt by one of the men, picking up his wrist and twisting something around it!?

Gary shook his head and blinked as if that might make what had happened clear. Then he stood, walking uncertainly toward Raquel. His eyes widened, *Raquel and that woman are putting handcuffs on the Asian men!* Raquel's eyes were focused out the windows of the restaurant while she applied them. She glanced up at Gary and said, "Sorry Gar'."

"What just happened?!"

She frowned and looked down at the men. Her speech was very rapid and hard to follow, but he thought she said "These guys came here to kidnap me."

Incredulously he said, "Kidnap you?! How do you know?!"

She looked up at Gary then down at the older man. She reached down, flipped back the lapel of his coat, then, using two fingers, she extracted a handgun from the shoulder harness there. Though Ell felt like she had done this slowly, to Gary it appeared to be so quickly done as to be a completely reckless way to handle a firearm. She looked up at Gary and raised her eyebrows. She set the gun behind her on the floor then leaned back over the man, quickly and efficiently patting him down. She did the same for the man in the coveralls, removing a gun from one of his pockets as well. The other woman did the same for the man she'd cuffed. The men were starting to moan and move around. From the smell, at least one of them had voided his bowels. Ell pulled darts out of each of the three men and tossed the darts into the corner. *Ah,* he thought, *that pistol like device must've been a Taser.*

Raquel frowned and said, "Take cover Gar', more of them are coming in the door."

~~~

Ell's stomach roiled. It felt like the situation was escalating out of control. The Asians approaching the door were all carrying handguns out and exposed. They looked agitated. As excited as they looked, she thought they were bound to shoot someone, by accident, even if not on purpose. Getting everyone else down and herself out in plain sight seemed like the best way to focus the Asians on her and perhaps keep them from shooting a bystander out of frustration.

She stood and barked in a loud command voice, "Everybody down!" She waved at the door, "Guns!"

~~~

Startled, Gary looked over at the door. Three Asian men were coming in the door and two more were running down the sidewalk toward the door. All of them were carrying pistols in their hands! More people were sprinting across the parking lot toward them! Raquel knelt and picked something up off the floor, then took several strides out in front of where the men lay on the floor. Over her shoulder she said, "Gar', get behind the counter!" The command voice she used brooked no argument. To his surprise he found himself meekly following her order and kneeling behind the counter, then wondering why. He glanced around. The other patrons of the restaurant were already cowering on the floor.

The first Asian man in the door waved his gun, shouting something in a foreign language. The second one, also waving a gun and apparently translating, said, "Put-a you han's up! Not move!"

Ell raised her hands up in the air and locked them together over her head. Watching her, Gary realized she had something between the front hand and the back one, Ah, the pepper spray! Looking her over carefully he realized that she had her Taser again, mostly hidden in the waistband of her shorts! The handle of her Taser looked like an asthma inhaler.

The other people timidly crouching on the floor of the restaurant were lifting their hands so Gary did too.

Raquel slowly shuffled backward and the new men followed her toward the back of the restaurant, repeatedly shouting at her to stop moving. Her heels bumped into one of the Asians lying on the floor and she stopped. The men's bathroom door behind her opened and the fourth Asian man from before shuffled out, ankles cuffed together, hands cuffed behind his back, eyes puffy and red, tears running down his cheeks and snot dripping down his upper lip. The muscular dark skinned man who'd taken him into the bathroom came out behind him. This resulted in more shouting from the Asian men with threats to "shoot on sight" or maybe "shoot dawn sigh?" Or "don sai?" Was that some kind of Chinese language threat? Slowly the black man knelt, then laid down on the floor in response to their threats and waving guns.

The apparent leader of the Asians stepped up and slapped Raquel. Hard! It left a bright red hand print on her cheek. "You do a like-a you told!" She glared at him, but didn't move, not even to touch her cheek. "Keep-a you han's up!"

One of the three men near Raquel knelt near her feet with a bundle of cable ties. He pulled one out and put it around her right ankle, zipping it shut. He did the same with the left ankle, then used a third cable tie to connect the two.

Gary desperately wondered what he could possibly do. Having guns, the Asian men seemed to have all the cards. 4MA taught cooperation with gun wielding assailants until a better opportunity presented itself— but surely there must be something he could do to *promote* that better opportunity?

The head Asian guy pulled out his own bundle of cable ties. He stepped up closer to Raquel and barked, "Give a you han', now!" He waved the cable ties peremptorily.

Gary's heart pounded. *They're going to have Raquel trussed up so they can just carry her out of here!*

As Raquel slowly lowered her hands, her eyes darted around the room. Gary looked around too. Two of the Asians were still there with the head guy. One had a restraining hand on Raquel's shoulder, the other knelt, holding on to the cable ties between her ankles. The other two of the five remaining Asians were over by the door of the pizzeria, pointing their guns at some men outside who apparently wanted to get in.

Gary swung his eyes back to Raquel. As her hands came down to horizontal and were just in front of the Asian's leader a blast of pepper spray shot out into his face. Her left hand grasped the barrel of his gun, turning it up to the ceiling. Gary heard two pops. My God, she'd done it again! Gary hadn't even seen her right hand snake down to her waistband, but the two pops must have come from her Taser because the other two Asian men near her were quivering as they fell to the floor. The gun of the pepper sprayed man who'd been in front of Raquel slipped from his fingers into her hands as he dropped to his knees in agony, hands over his face. Raquel reversed the pistol and fired twice toward the door. Her intimidating command voice whipcracked across the restaurant, "Do. Not. Move!"

Gary tore his eyes away from her and looked at the last two Asians who were over by the door. Plaster fragments from the ceiling were showering down onto them and they were slowly raising their hands. Raquel's voice barked again, "Drop. Your. Guns!"

They did.

~~~

Gary's memories from that point seemed disjointed. The men who'd been outside the restaurant came in and helped restrain the rest of the Asians.

The African American man came over and cut the cable ties off Raquel's ankles.

Someone guided the second pepper sprayed man into the bathroom to wash his face.

Two more Asians were brought in the back door, also wearing plastic handcuffs.

All the people who were stabilizing the situation appeared very deferential to Raquel, acting as if she were some kind of VIP.

The police arrived and took statements, downloading everyone's video records of the events including Gary's.

Even the police, who appeared to be asking Raquel hard questions at first, seemed to become more and more respectful of her. They gathered around to watch some of the downloaded video on a screen, repeatedly glancing up at Raquel. At first they looked startled, then developed awed expressions. The black man showed the police some kind of ID and talked to them quietly for quite a while.

The restaurant owner angrily approached Raquel, but after speaking to her briefly, walked away looking like someone who'd just won the lottery.

~~~

Eventually the police took the cuffed Asians out to a paddy wagon and started letting the restaurant patrons go home. Raquel picked her way back across the room to where Gary sat in her chair, back to the wall, fiddling with the cold remnants of their pizza. Well the fourth slice from his half of it anyway. She sat across from him looking exhausted. She stared at him for a while, as if at a loss for words. Finally she said, "Again, Gary, my apologies."

Gary blinked, "For what?"

She tilted her head, "For getting you dragged into my mess."

"Hey, *they're* the bad guys, not you. Who *are* they anyway? Some kind of Asian mafia?"

"No... they're... Chinese Nationals."

"And... what? They were going to hold you for ransom? They came all the way here from China just to kidnap you? And why the Hell are you taking self-defense at 4MA when you can take out a whole group of guys like that?!"

Raquel put her hands up in a fending off gesture. "I

don't suppose there's any way we can just go back to being Gary and Raquel, a couple of friends who work out at 4MA and share an occasional pizza?"

Gary stared at her as he slowly raised an eyebrow. "I don't think *friends* have secrets like this between them, do they?"

Raquel shrugged, grimaced then looked back up at him. "So can you keep a secret for your friend?"

He stared at her a moment and then shrugged, "Sure."

She tilted her head, "My name's not Raquel."

He snorted, "Big surprise."

She put out her hand, "Ell."

As he took her hand, his eyes clouded for a moment. He gave it a perfunctory shake. His eyes regained focus, "Donsaii? Those guys were yelling your name? 'Shoot Donsaii'?"

She nodded.

"You don't look like her," he said suspiciously.

She quirked a lopsided grin, "Disguise."

He studied her a moment, then seeming to accept the disguise statement said, "You're the one that stopped the terrorists at the Olympics?"

She shrugged.

He sagged back in his chair, "Holy shit!" he muttered. He looked back up, "But who are all these *other* people? And why are the Chinese after you? I thought *those* terrorists were Arabs?"

"My security detail. I wrote a physics paper and the Chinese government apparently thinks it can make me develop some products for them based on the principles in the paper."

Gary's eyebrows rose, "Oh yeah, I heard about that paper when it came out. Caused quite a stir..." He clapped a hand over his mouth. Eyes wide, he said, "Crap, and I was explaining nanotubes to you like you were some kind of rube!"

Her eyes twinkled, "It was kinda sweet, actually." She reached a hand out to him, "Raquel?"

He grinned back and took her hand, "Albert."

She lifted an eyebrow, "Albert?"

"Einstein... *my* secret identity," he whispered with one eyebrow raised as if revealing a great confidence.

This time Ell snorted, "Well, 'Mr. Einstein,' would you like to walk me home?"

"Sure!" On the sidewalk he turned to her, "The owner of the restaurant seemed pretty pissed. How'd you calm *him* down so fast?"

"Um. I'm kinda rich. So, I told him I'd pay for all his repairs *and* give him an extra $20,000 for his trouble."

"Wow! I guess that *would* take the sting out of it." He stared into space a moment, "I suppose you didn't actually need my help with that jerk at Tres Locos?"

She gave him a brilliant smile, then leaned over to give him a hug. Quietly into his ear she murmured, "I'll take all the help I can get from my friends. That kind of help's as precious as gold!"

Chapter Six

Axen knocked on Colonel Ennis' door. "Can you use a new El Tee on your flight crews yet?"

Ennis grinned, "You finally going to turn Donsaii loose and let her do something useful?"

Axen shrugged, "Yeah, she's *completely* wasting her time in class now, just as well put her to work."

Ennis said, "I'll have Smith assign her a slot."

***

Ell finished hooking up the new power supply in her setup. She opened the valve and put some pressure in the chamber without shooting for an exact setting like she'd done last time. She energized the chamber and asked Allan to turn off the lights. She knelt and peered under the table. The sparks were back! Only a few, just above the carpet though. Her eyebrows drew together, then rose and she quickly turned down the power delivered by the new supply. Sure enough a line of sparks now extended from the bottom of the table down to the carpet. Some of them *must* have been appearing in the apartment below for a minute or so there! She hoped no one downstairs had noticed!

She turned the power down further until there weren't any sparks near the carpet so she could be relatively certain none of them were still appearing in the room below. Then she adjusted the pressure in the chamber and wrote it down after closing the valve tightly. While she'd been waiting for the new power supply she'd set a pressure and checked it three days running to establish that the chamber didn't leak and that the gauge was accurate enough to show even small changes.

She couldn't wait to see what it read tomorrow!

***

Tech Sgt. Apert leaned back in his chair and put his hands behind his head as the RQ-7 he controlled began a long straight run to the PRC coast. It was under AI control, so it didn't need any input from him. He turned to Jones, flying the other bird in his flight, "So Sarge, what have you heard about our new El Tee?"

"Hmmpf. So young the paint's still drying. Graduated UAV school early. Real early, so she's probably smart and knows all the technical stuff, but probably can't fly worth a shit." He turned and looked at Apert with a lifted eyebrow, "She's that girl who won all the Olympic gold medals in gymnastics, so when she goes to jump on your ass she'll be able to get a lot of height on her jump."

"Really? *She's* already graduated?"

"Did that early too, I hear."

"Well, it doesn't matter whether she can fly does it? That's what she's got us and the AI for. Hmm, if I remember right from watching her in the Olympics, she'll be easy on the eyes."

"Apert, is that *all* you think about?"

Apert shrugged, then jumped as a young sounding female voice came over his shoulder. "Sergeant, how long have you been getting pinged by that PRC radar?"

Apert cast a panicked glance over his shoulder to see a Lieutenant's bars on the woman's shoulder, then back at his station seeing the blinking red light for which he'd turned off the audible alarm. "Um, I'm not sure..." *Damn it, PRC radar'd never touched them this far off the coast before!*

"Turn right thirty degrees to minimize your profile, then take your altitude up. That radar should be ship based and easy to elude. I doubt they've actually picked you up yet."

"Yes Ma'am," he said, complying with the order.

"Next, I suggest you turn your radar detector's audible alarm back on."

"Yes Ma'am. It's just that, near Okinawa, it goes off all the time." Assuming she wouldn't know why, he elaborated, "From our own radar."

"I believe checking out those alarms might be good practice for you."

"Yes Ma'am," he said, hoping he didn't sound as surly as he felt.

She stood behind them. The two enlisted stared straight ahead at their machines, wondering how a brand new butterbar lieutenant had gotten the drop on them. They were supposed to be teaching *her* the job, not the other way around. Eventually, the radar ping detector sputtered out and became silent. She said, "Everything seem copasetic at present?"

"Yes Ma'am."

"Good, let me take a moment to introduce myself." They turned around and saw a young girl who looked like a recruiting poster for a fresh out of high school enlisted, not someone who should have those lieutenant's bars on her BDUs. "I am, as you have presumably guessed, your new El Tee, and I *am* 'so new my paint's still wet.'"

Jones heart sank at this evidence she'd heard everything he'd had to say about her. He came to his feet and to attention. "Sorry Ma'am. Won't happen again."

She tilted her head minutely, while looking steadily at him, though his eyes were focused on the wall behind her. "Your assessment, Sergeant Jones, was remarkably correct, though perhaps somewhat lacking in the respect that should be shown an officer." She turned to Apert, "Your appraisal, however, Sergeant Apert, was incorrect. It *does* matter if I can fly. If I'm to supervise you, I must know your job as well as my own. Sergeant Jones was also correct," she grinned, "in that I *can* get a lot of height on my jump, so I'd suggest that you be more respectful when speaking of your officers in the future?"

Apert also came to his feet and to attention. "Yes Ma'am. Won't happen again Ma'am."

"Okay, eventually we need to talk about how we're going to run this team, but for now I want to watch this flight and ask you questions, both to be sure you know your jobs and so I understand the job and my role in it better."

~~~

Apert and Jones had been confident that they knew their jobs before that flight. Donsaii, however, peppered them constantly with questions, undermining their assumptions about the flight, their UAVs, their skills and the very nature of their job. Instead of just flying to the waypoints set by command, to photograph the items specified, she constantly watched the terrain, asking them what the various structures were and having them zoom in on the structures to confirm or determine their nature. They'd never run a flight this intense before and weren't sure whether to hate it or take pride in it. When their replacement shift arrived, Donsaii looked Apert and Jones up and down, then said, "Looks like this team could use a little PT. I think we should take a run every day at end of shift. Today I'd like you to run me over and introduce me to the UAV maintenance crew."

Apert restrained himself from rolling his eyes but shortly found himself huffing along with Jones and Donsaii as they made their way over to the hangars. It was only about a mile and a quarter, but Donsaii looked like she was completely exhausted by the time they got there. This surprised him since she was supposed to be such a star athlete. After a period with her bent over, holding her knees while Apert wondered if she was gonna puke, she took a deep breath, stood up, smiled and said. "Let's go meet the maintenance guys."

Apert thought that, hard as that little run had been on her, she probably wouldn't take them out for any more exercise in the future. He turned out to be wrong on that count as well.

Jones knew Chief Master Sgt. Milton and introduced Ell to him. By the time they found him she was beaming and full of energy again. It was as if she hadn't just looked like death warmed over when she finished the run. "Chief! Thanks for meeting with us. As you can tell, I'm so brand spanking new my 'paint's not even dry,'" she smirked at Jones, "and I'd really like to understand the machines we fly from inside those boxes across the field. Can someone show us around the guts some?"

Milton's eyes narrowed. "Didn't they bring you over here to look at the birds during your training Ma'am?"

"Yes they did," Ell said cheerfully, "but they really only showed us the outsides. I'm hoping you've got one opened up so we can see what's inside? Or maybe we could come back tomorrow?"

Milton'd never had this happen. On the other hand, in maintenance they always bitched that the geeks flying their machines didn't understand or even care what they were flying. He quirked a lip, "No problem Ma'am, we have an RQ-7 opened up over here." He began to walk that way and started the superficial spiel that he usually gave on tours. When they got to the actual machine though, she interrupted him with a series of questions. Tough questions which were far more perceptive than any he'd ever had before. After going over the airframe, to Milton's astonishment she was soon head down and ass up, deep into the command and control section of the bird. When she'd asked him her fifth question about the comm section that he didn't know the answer to, he began to get frustrated.

In a chipper voice from down inside the canopy, Donsaii's voice said, "I can tell you're getting aggravated with all my questions, Chief. Can you just have one of the guys who works on the comm section drop by to fill me in? That way you and my men, Apert and Jones, can get on about your own business."

Milton assigned one of the comm guys to her and walked away, shaking his head. *She may be gorgeous but*, he thought, *but just like all the rest of the El Tees in the world, this one's a pain in the ass.*

Laurence E Dahners

***

Ell came in the door and swept past Amy sitting at the dinner table waiting for their daily report. She stepped into her "office" and looked. Her heart leapt as she looked at the pressure gauge for her chamber. It was definitely lower! Her port *must* be allowing some gas to escape. Presumably the egress of the gas was heralded by the energy leak that created the sparks she could still faintly see beneath the table. The continued presence of the sparks suggested that she finally had a power supply that'd hold up to the demand.

Amy had to call her three times to get Ell to come to dinner, and even after she was there, her eyes kept defocusing while she ate.

Amy finally gave up trying to talk to Ell about the day's issues, none of which were all that important anyway. Ell sat at the dinner table for almost an hour, then had Allan order parts for an improved power supply she hoped would deliver a highly filtered and stabilized, fluctuation free current with which to energize her port and thereby narrow the range of distances over which the ports opened. It hardly seemed useful to send something through a port and have it return to this universe much nearer or farther than intended!

She fell back to thinking again. What if I define both the entry and exit points for entry into the fifth dimension with quantum entangled pairs? One member of the pair at the entry and the other member at the exit? The paired entanglements would then exactly define the two points in this universe that the ports would join. Actually, she realized, the electronics would be far simpler. However, it'd take a lot of quantum pairs, distributed around the entrance and exit of the port. She wanted a bigger port than the one she'd made so far, so flow through the port'd be faster. Fast enough that she wouldn't have to run the port all day just to detect a tiny drop in pressure.

She ran the math. It should require a lot less power to make two defined ports connect than to send material through a port when she'd only defined one end of the connection.

Her shoulders sagged, it'd take a long time to create enough quantum entangled pairs and micro-manipulate them into position to make a significantly bigger port.

***

Millie looked over her class and said, "Today we spar. I not teach you something new. Instead, we see how you do with what you have learned so far."

Gary looked at "Raquel" out the corner of his eye. After the attack in the pizza parlor he'd realized that she must normally hold back from what she could actually do when she was in their classes. But, he'd actually been holding back some too, as a guy, not wanting to hurt the girl he had a crush on. He wondered how he might do against her in a sparring match where the moves weren't scripted by Millie. Besides he couldn't just let a girl beat up on him in a sparring match in front of the whole class, could he?

Millie laid out rules for the sparring that were intended to keep anyone from getting seriously hurt. She held up a finger, "A real fight over quick. Serious throw or strike end it quickly—so today we all take turns in the center of the ring. Each match will only last as long as it takes one of you to score what I think is solid strike or throw, then the next pair will be up." She pointed, Cheryl, you and…" Millie's eyes swept along, "Robert. You two will go first."

Cheryl's eye's opened wide, "But, I've never worked with him… he's too big!"

Millie put her hands on her hips, "So if you attack' by a big man, that what you going say? 'Excuse me, but you *too* big?'"

A nervous laugh rippled around, then Millie said, "I little, *and* old. Robert, you come attack *me*!"

Moments later Robert was uncomfortably circling around the tiny Millie. She promptly began taunting him, "Come on, you afraid of little ol' me? You waiting for me get even older?"

Eventually Robert stepped forward, reaching out for Millie. She grabbed his wrist and spun in under him. He flew over her to land heavily on his back, slapping down as taught. Despite making a pretty good landing, when he got back up he looked like he was having a little trouble drawing a deep breath.

Millie said, "Now. You thinking that this only happened because I have a black belt? Let us have someone else try," her eyes lit on Ell, "Raquel, we have you and Alexander spar next."

Gary's eyes widened. Alexander had to weigh well over two hundred pounds! How in the world did Millie expect Raquel/Ell to deal with him? Alexander looked pretty uncomfortable with it too. He stepped out on the mat across from Ell who stood with her head tilted slightly, considering him as if he were an interesting specimen. Nothing happened until Millie sighed, "Raquel, you must attack Alexander. He timid because he fears he migh' hurt..." Millie's voice halted as Ell spun in under Alexander's arm and sent him flying through the air over her back. He landed badly, flat on his back with a loud whoosh of air. He lay there gasping, with his wind obviously knocked out of him.

Ell calmly stepped over him and knelt at his head. Saying, "Sorry Al." she pulled up on his shoulders, then let go. A moment later she lifted his shoulders again.

Millie raised one eyebrow quizzically. "Raquel, what you do there?"

Ell looked up, "He got the wind knocked out of him. When that happens, you can't pull in a breath. Pulling up on his shoulders fills his lungs for him. It should make him feel better." She looked down at Alexander, "Is it helping you Al?"

Al nodded. After a few more breaths he stood back up, glancing repeatedly at Ell with a mixture of awe and embarrassment.

Millie exclaimed, "I not know I could help person with no wind!" She shrugged, "I try it next time that happen." She turned back to her class, "Cheryl, you ready to try now?"

The class went on, each of them getting turns in the ring. When it was over Gary found Ell next to him. She quirked an eyebrow, "Feel like some pizza?"

"Sure!" Actually Gary had spent much of the past week looking forward to the possibility of pizza with Ell. "But, I think you should let me buy. I'm feeling like a kept man with you always buying my pizza for me."

"You can buy if you want, but trust me, I've got more money than I can spend. You shouldn't waste yours. Actually, you can buy your way into my heart and pizza fund with some nanotech.' She raised her eyebrows, "I'd really like some nanotori. You know, the nanotubes bent in a circle to make a hula hoop type structure?"

"Sure I know what a nanotorus is. Nanotubes are my life. But," he frowned, "you can buy nanotori commercially, why do you want some from me?"

"Well, actually because I want big ones where the torus has at least a 2mm inner diameter, and I need them in pairs that are *exactly* the same diameter."

Gary frowned. "Oh, now *that's* something difficult all right. I can make you big tori by the thousands, but you'd have to sort through them to find pairs that are the same diameter. Would that do?"

She smiled at him, "That'd be very cool. I'll buy your pizza then?"

He grinned back, "Deal."

***

Though Ell had already graduated, when the graduation was held for the rest of her UAV training class she was invited back for the ceremony and to pick up her diploma and ribbon. After the ceremony the class decided to go out for a celebration. They gathered with exuberance at "The Flight Risk," a civilian bar near the base where mixing of enlisted and officers wouldn't be frowned upon.

Even though she'd be with a military group, Ell let Steve know she was leaving base, and she saw him sitting at the bar when she entered. Barrett and Randy had a table near the door.

Ell'd barely told Allan to arrange to pick up everyone's tab when Axen said, "All right now, as congratulations I'll buy you monkeys your first beer!"

As the group jostled around the bar putting in drink

orders, Axen shouted to the group, "Hey, some anonymous patron bought *all* the drinks for you fools, even the first one I was gonna get! Drink up! But, remember *some* of you have duty tomorrow."

The exuberance increased with the announcement, along with wonderment that *anyone* would give them an open tab. There was speculation that somebody in the group had wealthy parents or that some wealthy veteran in the bar had sponsored them. Fortunately, no one considered Ell since she'd so carefully suppressed any news of her newfound wealth.

Axen grinned at Ell, "I hear you've completely intimidated your crew already?"

"Oh no Sir. I *am* making them run with me after every shift, but I don't have enough endurance to actually intimidate them."

He smiled, "*I* heard that your introduction to them involved catching a couple of experienced UAV pilots with their audible radar detect alarm turned off?"

"Well yes sir." Ell was surprised. She hadn't told anyone, so the guys must have commiserated with friends and let the story out themselves.

"*And* being painted by PRC radar."

"Uh, yes sir."

"Well they think you're Hell on wheels, congratulations."

Sasson, dropped by and winked at Ell, "Hey, Donsaii, just wanted you to know I've forgiven you for wrecking my takeoff on your first day."

Axen said, "You know Sasson, if you hadn't pissed her off when you first met her I think she might have been content to let you graduate first in the class."

Sasson grinned, "Sir, I now realize that, in your wisdom, you put her in the class with me *just* to prove to me that I wasn't as shit hot as I thought I was."

Ell looked back and forth between the two of them with an amused expression. "All about you, eh, Sasson?"

Sasson said, "Of course. Anyway, I'm here to challenge you to a game of pool in hopes of redeeming my lost honor?"

Axen said, "I'll get in on that action. I want to be able to tell my grandkids I beat an Olympic athlete." He looked around the crowd, "We just need a fourth."

Ell glanced around and saw Amy come in the door. Amy came directly over to Ell. "Hey, congratulations!"

Ell introduced Amy to Sasson and Axen as her friend. "You want to play pool with us? I need a partner."

"Sure."

Sasson said, "All right, we've got a girl for each team!"

Ell grinned at him, "'Fraid you'll lose to a couple of girls?"

"Oh my goodness, Major, looks like we're going to have to put these ladies in their places."

While the guys were getting a pool table, Ell turned to Amy and asked quietly, "Is there a problem that brought you here?"

Amy grinned, "Nope. I could say I just didn't want to miss our regular evening debrief, but actually I felt like an evening out, and your grad celebration seemed made to order." She looked around the room and raised her eyebrows, "And there're some hunky guys here, just like I hoped."

"Great! But remember, with this group, you're my friend, not an employee. Also, remember that as Ell Donsaii I don't even know Steve or the guys." Ell really liked Amy. She was pleasant, smart and fun to talk to.

She genuinely liked what she was doing to make Ell's life easier and she'd worked hard to understand the lab equipment Ell had in the "office." she often ran Ell's physics experiments for her while Ell was at work on base. Their relationship had become more like a couple of partners on a project than employer-employee. Ell hoped she could teach Amy how to use the micro manipulator to position entangled molecules for the entangled pair portals she'd started work on.

Claiming "rank hath its privileges" Axen broke, but didn't get anything in.

Ell was surprised when Amy put in three balls in a row. She whispered, "Hey! You didn't tell me you could play."

Amy gave Ell a gentle nudge with her elbow, "A girl's gotta have *some* secrets."

Sasson turned out to be *very* good, smoothly putting in five balls before getting stymied.

Ell wondered what to do. She didn't want to use her physical skills at or even near their limit, thus appearing freakish. She settled for putting in a couple of balls and purposely left Axen a good leave. Axen proceeded to put in the guys' last two balls and then the eight to win the game. Ell realized the two officers were both pretty good at pool. Sasson good naturedly crowed about the win. "You ladies want to split up onto different teams now?"

"Hah! You think we'd split up just because you fellas got lucky in *one* game?"

Part way through racking the balls, Ell saw Amy tense up. She looked where Amy's gaze was focused and saw a big man with slicked back hair. He was wearing a suit and standing just inside the door. Not typical attire for bars near the base. The man was staring at Amy. Ell lifted the rack off the balls and quietly asked, "Is that Felton Bonapute?"

Stiffly Amy said, "Yeah, I wonder how the SOB knew I'd be here. This isn't a place he'd *ever* show up by accident..." She shrugged, "I'll go talk to him."

"No! You do *not* want to meet him over near the door. Make him come into friendly territory. As to how he knew you'd be here, he probably has a tracker on your car."

Ell heard Steve's voice in her earphone. "That's Felton Bonapute. Do you want us to take care of him?"

Ell quietly said, "No, I hired you guys to *defend* me. If I need to go on the offensive, I should do that without dragging you into it. Please stand by in case I *do* need defending." Then Ell asked Allan, what he'd learned about Felton Bonapute so far.

Allan responded in her earphone, "He lives a life hundreds of thousands of dollars more expensive than his salary from Casino Real would finance. He's been arrested twice on suspicion of trafficking in narcotics and three times for complaints of violence against women. None of those arrests have led to convictions, all of them being overturned on technicalities. One of those women was later murdered. I've run an evaluation of the status of his previous employees and determined that three other women who've resigned from employment under his supervision at Casino Real have also been murdered. No one else seems to have noticed this connection, but I would advise against going anywhere with him. On his income tax he's underreported his income, declared dependents he doesn't have and taken deductions for charities that he doesn't actually support. He has..."

Ell said, "Thanks, that's enough."

Sasson broke the rack and put in a stripe. Bonapute started shouldering through the crowd in their direction. Ell brightly said, "You're up next Amy."

Amy shook herself and started nervously chalking her cue.

Sasson put in a ball. Ell could feel Bonapute coming up behind them. Glancing at the mirror over the bar she checked his position.

Sasson put in another ball. Dang! Ell had been hoping that Amy would be shooting pool by the time Bonapute got to the table. Ell shifted to put herself between Bonapute and Amy.

Sasson put in another ball. Bonapute shifted to the side so Ell wouldn't be between himself and Amy. "Hello, Ms. Reston. I believe we have some unfinished business." His tone dripped venom.

Ell turned to him, "Mr. Bonapute I presume?"

Bonapute turned angrily to eye Ell, "Yeah!" he hissed, "Who the Hell are you?"

"I'm a friend of Amy's. Since Amy told me what a lowlife scumbag you were and how you treated her when she worked for you, I've done some research. I note that three women have been murdered after leaving your employ in the past several years. The police don't seem to have noticed you as the common denominator. Care to comment before I turn that information over to the authorities?"

Bonapute's eyes widened momentarily, then narrowed. "Sounds like you're as big a problem as my friend Amy here, aren't you?"

Axen looked back and forth at the two of them, "What's the problem here Donsaii?" Sasson straightened from the shot he'd been lining up.

Without looking away from Bonapute's eyes, Ell said

in a clearly carrying voice, "Mr. Bonapute here, is a drug dealer who's escaped prosecution on legal technicalities, *doesn't* pay his taxes, beats women and has likely murdered three of his former employees. He's come here because he's got a bone to pick with my friend Amy, *another* former employee of his."

Axen and Sasson stepped closer and several of the enlisted at the next pool table also stood and moved their way.

Bonapute hissed, "Who the Hell do you think you are?"

Ell saw Steve step up to a neighboring table and set a bag on top of it, then reach inside. Realizing he must have his hand on a weapon, she gave him a brief head shake and answered Bonapute, looking hard into his eye, "As I said, 'I'm a friend of Amy's.' Now, I'm Amy's friend who's called the police."

Bonapute screamed, "You're gonna regret this!" and stepped back, but his way was blocked by a couple of large staff sergeants. He reached into his jacket.

Ell cursed at herself. *Of course* a guy like Bonapute would be carrying a weapon! Why hadn't she seen that taunting this jerk could create a situation that might get out of hand? Cringing inside at the danger to her and everyone around her, Ell let the zone drop over her. The world slowed, her heartbeat throbbed in slow thunder and she stepped closer to Bonapute.

Bonapute's hand cleared back out of the jacket with a pistol.

Ell began to swing her pool cue up from where it rested on the floor.

Bonapute swung the muzzle toward Ell.

Ell willed her pool cue to move faster. In the zone, everything seemed to move like it was being dragged through sand! *Nothing* she could do could make the cue move fast enough, but she saw his wrist bobble the gun to her left and she adjusted the trajectory of the cue. The barrel of the gun turned to a black gaping maw as it pointed directly toward Ell and she saw his finger begin to contract around the trigger. She dropped her head out of the line of fire as the gun roared. The bullet flew toward her as she moved her head to the right. It passed by, tugging on her hair.

The smoking black hole of the muzzle disappeared as it rose from the kick, and she found herself looking at the bottom side of the barrel. *Finally,* her pool cue struck Bonapute's wrist, driving hand and gun upward. Then the gun twisted as the cue struck it too, ripping the weapon from Bonapute's fingers, but turning the barrel sideways.

As the gun pulled out of Bonapute's hand, it went off again! Ice slid down Ell's spine as she watched the bullet track toward Sasson. Her gut unclenched as she saw it pass through his shirt to imbed itself into the wall behind him.

The gun, free of Bonapute's broken hand, flew up to strike the ceiling. It began to spin and fluttered out toward the crowd.

Ell's stomach clenched again. Panicked that the un-safed weapon might go off again if the trigger caught on something when it landed, Ell leapt up and out after the turning pistol, kicking off the pool table next to her and stretching out into the air after the gun.

At first she wasn't sure she'd given herself enough height with her leap, then when it was evident that she'd be able to reach the weapon, she worried that the gun might go off if she grabbed it badly.

She slowed her stretch for it, letting the handle go

by with trepidation that she might not be able to reach the barrel when it came around. After the handle passed she stretched a smidgen more to grasp the barrel of the weapon as it came around. She touched down one hand on the rail of the next pool table, flipping herself end for end and dropping to land feet first on the other side of the table.

Not wanting a keyed up crowd seeing her with a weapon in her hand, Ell safed it and set it down in the middle of the pool table before most people in the room had any idea what'd happened, though most had heard the argument and everyone heard the gunshots.

She turned to look toward the bar at the area behind where she'd been standing when Bonapute shot at her. At first all she saw were people down on the floor like you'd expect with gunfire. Her heart hammered with fear that one of them had been struck by the bullet that parted her hair. Then, with a huge sigh of relief, she recognized that the broken mirror behind the bar was where the bullet actually struck.

Shouts broke out around the room. Bonapute initially dropped to his knees, cradling his broken hand, then raised to a crouch, still holding the hand and starting to slink toward the door. Ell's alto command voice cut clearly through the chatter, "Sergeants!" The two large NCOs who'd stopped Bonapute before looked sharply her way. "Stop that man!" She pointed.

A moment later Bonapute was held in an unyielding grip. Reaction avalanched over Ell from the near disaster and she began to shake.

***

Colonel Ennis looked bemusedly at Ell. She again stood at parade rest in his office.

Staring at the wall over his head.

Axen had not only described the events at the graduation party, but had sent Ennis the video file from his AI. The colonel had watched the sequence repeatedly. He suspected that Donsaii had deliberately goaded Bonapute into rash action, but Ennis himself would want Bonapute to act rashly and be delivered to jail if the man was guilty as accused. Ennis ruefully thought he would have goaded Bonapute himself—if he could move the way Donsaii could. The speed and the amazing athleticism exhibited by the swing of that pool cue and the midair catch of the flying gun was simply astonishing. After a few moments he said, "Ahh, crap! Sit down Donsaii."

He waited until she'd taken a seat, though she still sat at attention like a brand new Academy Cadet. "Personally, I think you did the right thing. Felton Bonapute needed to be off the streets and you made it happen. I'm not sure about your judgment, goading a suspected killer to action in a room full of innocents, but if you hadn't goaded him, he doubtlessly would have gone on hurting people in back alleys.

"However, no matter what I think, the rules say that incidents like these must be investigated and that until the investigation is completed you are to be kept away from all combat roles. In other words, if you're unstable or spoilin' for a fight, we ain't turning you loose with a major combat system. So the question is, what can I do with you?"

"Sir, if you don't mind, I'd like to get some experience over in maintenance?"

Ennis' eyes widened, then he threw his head back

and laughed unreservedly. "Never..." he wiped an eye, "never thought I'd get a *request* to be assigned to maintenance. You are no end of surprises Donsaii! You've got your wish. Maintenance it is."

***

Chief Master Sergeant Milton cast a gimlet eye at Captain Danson as he approached with a Lieutenant. The selfsame fine looking El Tee that'd been over here a few weeks ago with more questions than Nevada had cacti. Danson said brightly, "Sarge, this is Lieutenant Donsaii, one of the flight leaders from across the way."

Milton's eyes widened as he recognized the name. This was Donsaii? To hear people tell it she was ten feet tall, breathed flame and leapt over tall buildings. His mental image just didn't jibe with this slender reddish blond girl who looked like a model. He'd heard a little about the incident over at The Flight Risk and been offered some video from peoples' AIs though he'd turned them down.

Captain Danson continued, "She's been taken off flight duty for a few weeks because of some technicality. She actually asked to come over here and learn more about maintenance." From Danson's bright tone, he thought this was *great*. Danson often expounded the belief that the UAV pilots should be *required* to spend some time working in maintenance so they'd have more respect for the birds they were flying.

"We've been introduced, sir." Milton said, dryly. "What did you have in mind for the El Tee?"

"Well she's particularly interested in the command

and control comm systems so I thought you could have her supervise that section, though she'll probably only have time to *begin* understanding the system before she goes back to flying."

"Yes Sir." Milton said, thinking he should request that video from the Flight Risk after all.

~~~

After the Captain left, Milton took Ell over to the small section that worked on the communication elements of the birds and introduced her to Master Sergeant Nuñez. As he walked away he heard the Lieutenant requesting a download of the technical manuals for the RQ-7 and the old MQ-9 Reapers. She sounded like she intended to read them! No one *read* the manuals; they only used them for reference when they couldn't solve a problem!

Milton returned to his office and read the public file on Lt. Donsaii.

This is the girl that won the gymnastic Olympics with perfect tens a few years ago!

My God, the woman has a Medal of Honor!

How could a kid that young have a Medal?

He read through the public documentation on the award. Holy crap! She might not have earned it in a war zone overseas, but stepping back into the jaws of death to take on terrorists that were Hell bent on killing everyone in their grasp deserved a Medal of Honor—no matter how you looked at it.

***

The next morning the video from the Flight Risk

Laurence E Dahners

arrived and Milton watched it a couple of times. He was leaning back in his chair, staring at the ceiling, trying to make sense of what he'd just seen when Nuñez came in.

Nuñez looked pissed, "Chief, the new El Tee you dumped on us..." He shook his head disgustedly, "She's got her head *way* up her ass!"

"What's the problem Nuñez?"

"She spent one evening reading manuals and she's in there telling everyone in my section how to do their jobs!"

"You know Nuñez, I thought officers were *supposed* to boss NCOs around?"

Nuñez rolled his eyes. "*Not* wet behind the ears lieutenants."

"What's she wanting you to do different? Captain's gonna want a specific basis for a complaint if we go up the chain."

"Well first off she starts raisin' Hell 'cause the guys aren't wearing gloves working on the circuit boards. I know the manual says you're *supposed* to wear them, but they make it hard to feel what you're doing and the guys make more mistakes. The gloves really slow us down and nobody's gotten hurt working bare handed. And..."

Milton put his index finger up calling for a pause, "Nuñez, haven't we been having a high early failure rate on our circuit boards?"

Nuñez blinked.

"Did you know your Lieutenant won a Congressional Medal of Honor?"

Nuñez' eyes blinked again at the non-sequitur, then widened.

"It's been my impression they don't usually give the

Medal to people who have their heads very deeply implanted in their asses? I'll bet if you look into it carefully, maybe read the manual, you'll find that there's some problem—for instance that oils or acids from our hands cause early degradation of some of the circuit board components. I'm gonna further suggest that you do just what the El Tee says to do, unless you've got a good reason not to."

Nuñez looked a little glazed. He turned and started out of the office.

Milton called after him, "Before you get in any real fights with her, you also might want to look up and see just *how* she won that Medal."

***

Amy grinned, "Felton Bonapute was denied bail. Seems that they've found some DNA evidence on one of the murder scenes that implicates him."

Ell swallowed and said, "Great, we don't want him getting out again." She held her hand up for a high five.

Amy grinned, "I think I might have the hang of how to move your entangled molecules? You want to show me how you want me to position them? I should be able to do some tomorrow."

"Yes! Come on in and let me take you through it. I'd love it if I didn't have to do all of them myself!"

~~~

Ell spent about 20 minutes showing Amy exactly how she wanted the entangled molecules positioned. After Amy successfully positioned one she pushed back from the table, "Whew! I can see why you don't want to do them all yourself!"

"It *is* a huge pain, but you'll get better at it, they won't all take this long."

Amy said, "Now, about dinner."

"Oh, yeah. I'd forgotten. I *am* hungry; what do we have tonight?"

"Sorry, I didn't get time to make dinner, and it's Friday night, so I made a reservation at this new little restaurant about three blocks from here."

Ell frowned, "I really don't want to take the time. Just order something in so I can keep working on this," she waved at the micromanipulator, "a little bit more."

Amy put her hands on her hips. "*Absolutely* not! You put me in charge of ensuring you had some kind of social life remember?" She glared impressively, "*That* means going out occasionally, at least on the weekends, even if it's just for dinner."

Ell raised an eyebrow and tried to frown again, "I put you in charge of my social life?" A little grin broke through, "I don't remember tasking you with that."

Amy looked up as if studying her HUD, "It's right there, a sub-clause to the overall directive to do whatever it takes to make you happy. I take you to Tres Locos. I take you to Martial Arts. I make sure you meet young men—*now* I'm taking you to dinner."

Ell gave her a resigned smirk, "Okay, okay," she waved her hands in submission, "We'll go out. I'll *have* a social life. It'll be good for me, right? Just let me put Raquel on a little better."

~~~

Ell applied the prosthesis to her nose, added to her makeup and got her wig back on, then met Amy back out in the front room. They walked the three blocks to the newly opened "Sal's." It appeared to be an upper scale Italian eatery. Amy stepped up to the hostess station, "Reston reservation?"

The hostess glanced at her slate and said, "Yes, Ms. Reston, the rest of your party's already here."

As the hostess led them toward the back Ell raised an eyebrow at Amy, "Rest of your party?"

"*Social* life, remember?"

As they walked deeper into the restaurant, Ell saw Barrett and Roger from her security team sitting at one of the tables, then she saw Gary sitting at a table across from two women and a man? Gary looked up at her and smiled, then Ell's mother and Gram turned in their seats to look at her!

Ell gave a little shriek and ran to her mother, giving her a big hug. As they did so her mother whispered in her ear, "Happy birthday Kiddo."

Ell drew back and stared at her Mom. "Arggh, is it October 23rd? I hadn't been paying attention!" She shook her head, "Dang, I'm getting old." She grinned, "Nineteen! Next thing you know, I won't even be a teenager anymore." She turned to her Gram and gave her a hug too. "Looking good Gram!"

Gram winked at her, "Yeah, well someone done went and took all the stress out of my life. I've been taking better care of myself." She whispered to Ell. "I just need to find myself a man like the one your mother's got and I'll be all set."

Ell turned to look at the man at the table. It was Miles Duncan, the policeman who'd helped the night Ell was kidnapped. He'd progressed further and further into boyfriend status with Ell's mom. They shook hands. He leaned close and said, "Not that I'd wish a kidnapping on you, but meeting your mother the night you were kidnapped was the best thing that's ever happened to me, El... Raquel."

Ell grinned at him and said quietly, "Thanks for remembering to use that name."

Gary had waited patiently through the family reunion, now she turned to him, "Gar'! Thanks for coming out!" She gave him a hug too, tight and fierce.

~~~

Gary thought, *Wow, she feels...so great*!

They sat and ate an enthusiastic dinner, talking about old times and new adventures. From meeting Amy, to flying UAVs, to Felton Bonapute. When they got around to the Chinese, Gary described that encounter in a low but intense voice. They even managed to get through the meal while only calling "Raquel" Ell one time, when Gram slipped in her enthusiasm. Though everyone else was full, Ell ordered tiramisu and the restaurant brought it out with a candle and a cheery rendition of "Happy Birthday."

Ell's mother reached under the table, "It's hard to get a present for a girl who can buy anything she wants, but Amy tells me you've been enjoying dancing at a Western type bar so I figured I could at least dress you in style."

Ell opened the gift bag enthusiastically and pulled out a red silk western shirt with piping, embroidery and mother of pearl snaps. "This'll be fun!"

Gram got out a small box and passed it over. When Ell had it opened it proved to contain her Grandmother's prized opal necklace. Her Gramps had given it to Gram and, as a child, Ell had often mooned over it when looking through her Gram's jewelry. Ell's eyes quickly misted over and by the time Gram had fastened it around Ell's neck she had to dab her eyes and blow her nose.

Amy said, "Now *that's* a hard act to follow!" She held out an envelope. When Ell opened it she found a set of tickets to take the family to Cirque del Soleil the next night.

Suddenly Ell was embarrassed to realize that Gary'd feel *he* owed her a present too. Her impulse was to try to get everyone up and moving, thus showing she didn't expect a gift from him, but he pulled out a small glass bottle and handed it to her saying, "My gift is the ashes of my heart."

Ell held it up and saw that it had a faint dusting of black ashy material in it. She turned to him excitedly, "Tori?!"

He nodded, "They aren't all exactly the same size, but I worked out a way to make them all pretty close to the same size, so a lot of them *should* be the same size."

Ell gave him another hug, "Thanks Gar'!"

Curious E,ll's mother said, "What is it?"

"Carbon nanotube tori, or toruses. I've been wanting some for my research and so I tracked Gary down because he makes nanotubes." She said grinning at Gary, "He *thinks* we accidentally ran into each other at 4MA, but actually I'd relentlessly pursued him, hoping he'd agree to make me some tori. Now he's probably wondering if it's really even my birthday."

Gary raised an eyebrow, "Hah, it was well worth it, just for that one measly kiss you gave me at Tres Locos."

Chapter Seven

Felton Bonapute's eye fixed the man on the other side of the glass barrier. "Not just her, but that red headed Air Force bitch that broke my wrist too. You'll get the rest of your money when I hear what I want to hear about them." He held up his good hand with a finger extended like it was a gun, then pulled an imaginary trigger.

He hung up the phone.

***

Nuñez rapped on Milton's doorframe. "Come in." Milton said, leaning back in his chair, taking off his glasses and rubbing his eyes.

"Looks like we need to issue you some refurbished Mark 1 eyeballs, Chief."

"Yeah, yeah, you're gonna be old someday too, Nuñez. Or," he growled with a fake glare, "maybe not!" Then he grinned, "What's your shit hot El Tee doing this week?"

Nuñez rolled his eyes, "The boys are wearing gloves. I checked, you were right about the oils and acid pH being bad for several of the components. I also looked her up; she's just as impressive as you said."

Milton said, "Here watch this." He threw a video

record from The Flight Risk up on his big screen and they watched it together.

"Holy crap boss man! What just happened there?"

"Here it is in slo-mo." The video ran again.

The two men looked at each other. Nuñez said, "Remind me again about how much I *don't* want to piss her off?"

Milton rubbed his head, "You're tellin' me, that dude's wrist ain't never gonna be right." He leaned back in his chair again. "So, why're you invading my sanctum today?

"Well it's the El Tee again."

Milton rolled his eyes. "I sure hope it's not more places where she's caught your boys not following the book?"

"Naw. She knows the manuals better than anyone I've ever met and she keeps teaching people who *think* they know their job how to do said jobs better—which *can* be pretty annoying when you think you already know your job. But I'll admit, she doesn't slavishly follow the book. When it says to do something the long way and we have a shorter, better way, she pats the guys on the shoulder. She's shown us how to do several things better and faster than the manual herself. Nowadays, when she tells us to do something different, I ask why. She's always got a good reason."

"So, what's the problem?"

"Well, she's brought in a chip she says she had fabbed just for the RQ-7 comm system."

"A what?"

"A chip. Plugs into one of the spare BXA ports on the comm board just like it was made to go there."

"What the hell's it do?"

"Improves comm, she says." Nuñez shrugged. "She

says she had it fabbed to mil-spec just for our UAVs."

"Why's she talking to you instead of the Captain?"

"Says she wants to be sure it works right before she shows it to any brass."

Milton rubbed his head. After a bit he said, "And you're thinkin'... what?"

"Damned if I know Chief. I *want* to trust her. But someone wanting to put homemade chips in our birds? Chips that I don't *really* know what they do? What if she's a spy... or something...? Hell I don't know. Just thinkin' about it makes my head hurt."

Milton didn't say anything for a long time. Then he asked, "Did she say how this chip's supposed to work?"

Nuñez chuckled, "Yeah. Some kind of quantum technology she calls 'photon gluon resonance.' Says she has a patent for it, but because she's in the Air Force, the Air Force has a royalty free right to the technology."

"Cripes Nuñez! That sounds great, but I *still* don't know how it works or how we'd use it!"

"She's got a matching chip that she says plugs into the control station. She says, with those chips in place, data transmission won't have any satellite transmission latency and that transmission rates will be so much faster that we can send *all* the imagery at full resolution, not have to select the images we want to send right away and store the rest for transmission when the bird gets back to base."

"*Won't* have satellite transmission latency?" Milton's brow furrowed. "That latency is from how long it takes a light speed signal to get to the satellite, get sent around the world to another satellite and back down to the control station. How in the Hell would a *chip* make light speed transmission faster?"

Nuñez threw his hands up. "You wanna ask her

yourself Chief?"

"No. You install her chips. Use one of the birds that're in for maintenance. Put her other chip on your testing control station. Then check out the maximum data transmission rate and measure the satellite transmission latency and tell me what you find out. Then we'll go talk to Captain Danson about this."

Nuñez shrugged, "Okay." He got up to leave.

"Nuñez?"

"Yeah Chief?"

"Slip an RF detector into your testing setup. Measure any radio transmission from the setup before, then after her chips are in there working. Then we'll have an idea whether she could be diverting any information. I'd trust that woman with my life, but I've heard the best spies *always* seem... too good to be true."

Nuñez' head tilted as he considered, then he said, "Can do," and headed on back down to his shop.

***

Ell finished wolfing down her lasagna while Amy went over some changes in her investment portfolio that Ell's advisor had suggested. She said, "Okay, tell them to go ahead with the investments in mining and industrial manufacturing. Pull out of orbital launch and ask them to *please* stop suggesting communication stocks."

Ell looked down from her HUD at Amy, "Are you ready to look at your micromanipulations?"

Amy shrugged as she made some notes. "Sure." She wondered how Ell made decisions about how to invest millions of dollars in a heartbeat like this? *Was* she making wise decisions? Or was she just making quick decisions so she could get back to her beloved research? "Why do you hate communication stocks so badly?"

Ell looked at her pensively, "You've got a PGR chip on your headband and you know what it does right?"

Amy's eyes widened and she covered her mouth, "Oh! You think comm stocks are gonna tank when your chips hit the market?"

Ell tilted her head and shrugged, "Yep. I feel kinda bad about it, but not bad enough to ride 'em down."

They went back to Ell's office/lab where they carefully examined Amy's positioning of the entangled molecules around the upper member of the pair of connected portals Ell was trying to construct.

~~~

After Amy left to go back to her apartment, Ell began assembling the new components she hoped would filter and smooth the current output of her big power supply. It actually didn't take all that long to place the components in series between the power supply and her port chamber.

She switched it on and had Allan turn off the room light. She slowly leaned back to look for the telltale sparks.

"Damn," Ell muttered, *No sparks!*

She felt the power supply, it was only warm. She leaned down and sniffed. No burning smell. Frustrated, she stared at it a minute, then disconnected it, hooking up her multi-meter to determine whether the power supply was in fact delivering the correct power. It was, but it was only about 20% of the expected current! Her current smoothing circuit must be consuming a lot of the output from the power supply.

A smile crossed her face as she had Allan turn the lights off again and began slowly turning up the control knob on the main power supply, peering under the table. Sure enough the sparks appeared and slowly drifted down, farther and farther from the chamber as she increased the power. They were much more tightly clustered than they'd been before she'd installed her smoothing circuit. "Yes!" she murmured. Then she sighed in frustration. If her "smoothing circuit" consumed this much power, would she need an even bigger power supply?

***

Milton's AI spoke in his earphone. "Master Sergeant Nuñez relays a message that they're about to begin testing transmission rates on the El Tee's new chips if you want to mosey on by."

Milton pulled his head back from where he'd been watching tests on the airframe of one of the UAV's that'd made a rough landing. "Carry on, Sarge."

He wandered outside and looked around for a RQ-7 parked outside where it could get line of sight to a satellite. Sure enough there was one out a couple hangars down. Whistling tunelessly, he started that way.

~~~

When Milton walked up to the little group he saluted Ell. She hid a smile. She'd been able to tell that Nuñez was very nervous about installing her chips and suspected he'd go up the chain somewhere. She appreciated that he'd respected her wish not to go to Captain Danson until she was sure the chips worked.

Nuñez looked up and said brightly, "Chief, Lieutenant Donsaii's given us some improved communication chips for the birds. We're just about to test them out."

Ell kept a poker face at this transparent attempt to make it seem like Nuñez hadn't already filled in the Chief Master Sergeant about the whole thing.

For his part the Chief raised his eyebrows and said, "How're they working?"

Nuñez shrugged, "Well they've reduced the satellite transmission latency to zero." He raised an eyebrow. "Of course if the chips were simply transmitting data from the one here in the bird, to the one in the control console over there, directly, instead of sending it up to the satellite and back, we'd get the same measurement."

The Chief cleared his throat, thinking that had to be what was happening. If the chips were radiating directly to one another, that would hardly be useful when the bird was on the other side of the world. "What about data transmission rates?"

"Pretty amazing Chief. With the equipment we've got, we can only test transmission rates up to a hundred terabytes a second, but it does that flawlessly. The bird doesn't come close to producing that much data so our setup doesn't have any reason to try to test higher rates. But, how it's doing that over a satellite link, or even direct transmission from one chip to another, I have no idea."

Milton frowned, sure he must have misheard. "A hundred Tb per second?"

Nuñez raised an eyebrow and nodded.

Milton turned to Ell. "That's pretty amazing Lieutenant. What's Captain Danson plan to do with this tech?"

Ell grinned crookedly at the two senior NCOs, looking back and forth from one to the other. "Chief, I feel in my bones that the Master Sergeant has already told you I didn't want to tell Captain Danson about it until I was sure it worked."

The chief grunted, "That's as may be Ma'am. But we're not sure we should be installing unapproved electronics on Uncle Sam's birds without higher authorization than yours?"

"Good, and you shouldn't. But we haven't proved much yet. I'd like you to help me do a better test, still without putting one of Uncle Sam's birds in the air. I can hear the reasonable doubt in your voices about the results we're getting with this test. But, if we ship a chip to Okinawa and do a test around the world, then you'd have to believe the latency test right?"

"Um, yes Ma'am." The Chief's brow crinkled. "But how would we measure latency?"

"Oh, there's an algorithm in the console to send round trip pings to a bird and measure latency. The AI needs it to determine how far ahead it has to plan during landings."

"How do we know the ping went there and back?"

Ell laughed, "Good point. The outgoing signal's supposed to be modified by the bird before it's returned, specifically to confirm it went there and back. If I wanted to cheat, I'd have to reprogram the console software so that it modified the signal all by itself. When we get around to doing the test, you and the Captain might just have to trust that I'm not so devious as to trick you that way. It'd be pointless to fake the test anyway because flight control sucks with latency. Any pilot can tell when they're flying a bird with latency. So once we tried to actually *fly* a bird it'd up be obvious whether there was latency or not."

The chief frowned, "But there'd *still* be latency. I doubt even the hottest pilot could tell for sure the difference between some latency and a little less latency."

Ell grinned back and forth at the two NCOs again. "Sergeant Nuñez thought I was crazy when I told him there wouldn't be *any* latency so he didn't relay that part of the story to you, did he?"

"Um, he might have said it, but I might not have believed it. *No one* would really believe that, I don't think."

"Good for you Chief. So let's find out for sure. What I want to do is repeat this test with a bird on the ground in Okinawa so we'll be able to prove for sure whether I'm crazy or not." She shrugged, "In a few months no one'll have trouble believing. I have a paper coming out in Nature documenting the phenomenon. Also a company based on my patent for this technology will start selling product shortly after that. Right now the company's still keeping it under wraps so they're having me hold publication."

~~~

Milton and Nuñez looked at each other a moment. It was obvious to Ell that they were wondering just how far off her hinges she'd fallen. Finally Nuñez spoke, "I say let's give this crazy notion the benefit of the doubt and send a chip over. I've got a buddy in Okinawa UAV maintenance; I can get him to plug it in. If it works, we can tell the Captain and congratulate each other on our wisdom. If it doesn't, we can have the Captain call the guys with the straight-jackets."

Milton raised his eyes to the heavens for a moment, then nodded.

Ell grinned and clapped her hands together, "Thanks guys. If it works, you owe me a beer and I'll owe you a car." She handed Nuñez a box, "Just in case it works," she winked, "here's enough chips for all the UAVs in Okinawa so we don't have to send another shipment." She grinned at him and walked back into the hangar.

The two noncommissioned officers looked at each other a moment. Finally Nuñez said, "She's either crazy or amazing. So far the evidence points at amazing. Did you understand that wager about a 'beer and a car?'"

"Nope, but Martha ain't gonna let me buy the young lady a car, so I hope it only put me on the hook for a beer."

***

Amy raised her eyebrows as she watched Ell consume her hamburger. She said, "I don't think I'm *ever* gonna be able to come to grips with the way you eat so much without getting fat! I'd be a blimp!"

After dinner Ell showed Amy the sparks she'd been producing with the current setup. Then Amy had her examine the ring of entangled molecules that she'd finished aligning that afternoon. Despite the many days and evenings Ell and Amy spent aligning the molecules in the two rings, the circles they had created were still microscopic. Ell sighed, but you had to start somewhere and they were bigger than the single ring that was producing the sparks. She'd hoped that a single ring could send something through the 5th dimension to reappear somewhere and so far it seemed that she could do it, but the material sent through—just gas so far—seemed to be reappearing in this universe over a pretty broad range of locations. This dashed her hope that she could send something, herself perhaps, somewhere in an instant. If she were to try to transmit herself up to a satellite in orbit, some 300 kilometers up, with a 10 percent or 30 kilometer margin of error, she'd most likely wind up a long way away from the station and therefore in some pretty serious trouble. However, if there was a receiving ring at the space station and she could step instantly from one to the other, that'd be pretty cool. Who knew what she'd learn from activating this newly built pair of rings? Tonight she'd work on assembling the equipment to energize the receiving ring.

***

Ell knocked on the doorframe of Chief Milton's office. He stood, saying, "Yes Ma'am?"

"Hey, Chief, I just dropped by to tell you I've been reassigned back to flight operations tomorrow. I'd like to thank you for having your guys teach me about the insides of the birds."

Milton grinned, "El Tee, anytime you want to come back and *pretend* to learn from my team, while you actually whip 'em into shape for me, you'll be very welcome to do so."

Ell gave him her trademark crooked smile and said, "Thanks! You might suspect that I have an ulterior motive in dropping by?"

Milton sighed and rolled his eyes. "Yes Ma'am. Nuñez already told me your chips were in Okinawa and that I could expect you to be dragging me down to watch the testing sometime soon."

"Aw, Chief, you sound like someone who *doesn't* want to go see what happens!"

Milton's eyes crinkled as he got up and came around his desk, "True, but someone's got to keep an eye on the leprechaun. It seems I've been given that dread responsibility."

They walked over to the maintenance section's test console where Nuñez waved Ell into the remote pilot's seat. She sat and keyed open the microphone, saying, "Sergeant Davis? Do you read me?"

After a momentary pause, Davis' voice came back from Okinawa, "Yes Ma'am, we read you five by five."

"And the bird you have there, RQ-7, five eight niner, is engines and weapons disabled, but otherwise pre-flighted and checked out ready?"

Pause, "Yes Ma'am."

"Okay, I'm going to test the control surfaces—ailerons right, left—flaps down, up—rudder right, left—elevator down, up."

Pause, "All checks, Ma'am."

"Fuel reads full…" Ell went on to confirm all gauges and electronic controls per a standard preflight.

After another brief satellite transmission pause, the sergeant said, "All confirmed, Ma'am."

"Okay, Sergeant, now I'm asking you to jack that new chip into the tertiary radio jack on the comm board."

"Done, Ma'am." the sergeant said but his voice was distorted with a "chorus" effect as if he and a friend were saying the same words.

Nuñez frowned, "What happened to that 'five by' signal we were getting?"

Ell grinned up at him, "We're getting two signals now. One of them is immediate and the other is delayed a few hundred milliseconds by satellite transmission." She turned back to the microphone, "Sergeant, please un-jack the primary radio from the comm board."

"Are you sure Ma'am?" The transmission remained fuzzy but he was obviously wondering how they'd communicate with the comm board unhooked from the radio system.

"Yes, go ahead. If you can't contact us after it's un-jacked, just plug it back in."

His answer, "Done, Ma'am," came back clearly and immediately, without the momentary pause that'd been present before. Nuñez and Milton looked at one another with eyebrows raised.

Meanwhile Ell began repeating the preflight checks she'd just performed, again getting positive responses. Finally, Ell pinged the bird to determine transmission delay. The digital readout said "0 milliseconds." She turned and smiled up at the two sergeants, then said to the microphone, "Sergeant, I'm going to turn the bird's camera onto something interesting. Make sure everyone's clear of the mechanism?"

"Clear, Ma'am."

The screens on the console had been showing the pavement below the RQ-7. Now the views swung up to show the airfield at Okinawa in color, UV and IR. Ell rolled her chair back from the console and looked up, "Chief, would you like to wiggle the joystick for the camera control to get a feel for the latency?"

Bemusedly, Chief Milton leaned over and moved the joystick, noting that the image of Okinawa moved instantly as he moved it, rather than with the momentary delay he'd experienced with distant craft in the past. He motioned, and Nuñez wiggled the stick. He and Nuñez looked at one another again. Finally Ell reached out and rolled a scroll wheel, zooming the color image in on a man across the runway until his face filled the screen. "Please note, I've just used the console's digital zoom to confirm that we are looking at a full digital download of the camera's 200-megapixel video images rather than the compressed, low res four-megapixel images that we'd get from the standard comm link." She bounced enthusiastically up out of her chair, "Think we're ready to talk to Captain Danson?"

The two NCOs looked at the grinning lieutenant, then at each other, then shrugged as one. "Might as well," Milton rumbled.

***

Stimson looked up at a knock on his doorframe. Varnet stood there, as rumpled as always. He said, "Our geosynchronous Asian observation satellite just went down."

Stimson grimaced, "What happened to it?"

Varnet rolled his eyes, "Space debris or meteorite is the assumption. I think the 'debris' consisted of steel shot placed on an intersecting path by our friends the Chinese."

"Do you have any evidence?"

"Just a gut feel. They needed to test their weapon on our equipment close to the time of their attack on

Taiwan so they could be sure it worked, but we wouldn't have time to analyze what happened, much less develop a response."

"Great!" Stimson moaned. "Have you figured out what we can do about it?"

"I still think we should find out how this new communications technology company PGR Comm is coming along. The one that's based on the Donsaii theory."

"Come on, Varnet! We need something now! Not your pie in the sky, futuristic, wishful thinking! I'm going to set a meeting with the Secretary tomorrow or the next day. I want you to have something concrete by the time we talk to him."

***

Ell finished assembling the energizing circuit for the second chamber. It had what she thought of as the "receiving ring" inside it, even though either ring should be able to both send and receive. The pressure gauge attached to it read one atmosphere. She went over to the other chamber on her main lab table. The gauge on that chamber also measured one atmosphere, but she opened the valve and pressurized it to five atmospheres, sealed the valve and watched the gauge a moment to make sure it was holding stable. She flipped the switches to energize the ring in the chamber and walked back across the room to power up the second chamber too. As she watched the pressure rose a little! *Could the flow through the new, bigger ring be that fast?* Then she remembered that the pressure always rose a little, because energizing the ring heated the chamber some. Although... her calculations suggested that the amount of energy required to successfully energize a port from one ring pair to another was much smaller than the energy required to open a port without a ring at the other end. Since she wasn't running as much current, the chamber might not be heating as much? She'd just have to wait and see after she'd de-energized them and they'd cooled down tomorrow.

***

The diver snapped the ring shut around the cable and ascended to the surface, trailing an antenna wire. Before heaving himself into the boat he nodded sharply once at his officer. As the boat silently headed back to its tender an encoded signal went out indicating that the last of Okinawa's and Taiwan's submarine fiberoptic cables had a detonator attached to it.

***

Amy and "Raquel" walked into Tres Locos again. Ell hadn't gotten off base until nearly 8PM. She and some of the guys from her maintenance crew had run a mile and then Ell had showered, put on her new Western blouse and jeans and driven over to meet Amy at the bar. She'd put on "Raquel" on the way. With their later arrival this time, the place was crowded. Ell's growling stomach had her hustling over to the taqueria on the west wall for a Grande burrito.

Amy watched Ell wolf down the burrito. "My God,

the way you eat!" A worried glint came in her eye, "Are you purging when I'm not looking?"

Ell wiped her lips in embarrassment, "Sorry, no, I must just have a fast metabolism." She took a swallow of her Coke. "It'll probably slow down when I'm older and I'll have to watch my weight like everyone else."

Amy laughed, "At least you didn't say, 'when I'm as old as you.'"

Ell grinned, "*You're* not old! I'm gonna get some nachos, do you want anything?"

"A Grande burrito *and* nachos?! My God girl! You just trying to put me in my place?!"

Ell shrugged and grinned. "If I'm gonna dance, I'm gonna need some energy," she said as she headed back to the taqueria.

Amy'd found a table near the dance floor, although all the ones right next to the floor were taken. Ell plopped down with her Coke and nachos and began wolfing most of the nachos as well, though Amy had a few. While she ate, Ell watched the dancers. There were many more out on the floor this time of night, some swing dancing around the edges with freestylers and line dancers out in the middle. This night some of the freestylers had amazing routines going—she watched as a guy dropped to the floor and began whirling around break-dance style, then leapt back up, did a back flip and dropped into the splits. She wanted to watch him more, but her line of sight was blocked by swing dancers much of the time. Ell leaned over to Amy and said, "Sorry to say, but I like this band a lot better than the band you like. The one that was playing last time?"

Amy punched her gently on the shoulder, "This *is* my favorite band you doofus. Last time you made us leave while the warm up band was still playing!"

Ell put her hand over her mouth and raised her shoulders, "Oops!"

"Yeah, you're such a party pooper."

"Well, do you think anyone will ask us to dance?"

"Let's get out there so they'll know we'd like to." Amy got up and grabbed Ell's hand.

They walked out into the middle and Ell thought Amy was going to join the line dancers again but she stopped where the freestyle dancers were and just started moving to the rhythm. Ell found herself near the guy who'd been breakdancing earlier and watched him with great interest, fascinated by the spinning he did on the ground and the way he kept time to the beat even while doing semi-gymnastic maneuvers like flips.

~~~

Dan noticed the tall slender brunette watching him. She was pretty, though she was only shuffling her feet to the rhythm. Well he didn't actually care if *she* could dance; his chances were better, the more impressed she was with what *he* could do. He winked at her. To his amusement she blushed! She looked away, then shrugged and turned back to watch him. He upped his game a little with a back-flip, front-flip combo then moved over in front of her. He started imitating the simple shuffle she was doing, even the little hip shake she put in on the four beat, though he emphasized his hip move to keep it from looking effeminate.

She emphasized hers too.

Dan threw in an arm pump on the two beat.

She imitated it.

He circled his finger, then spun around starting on the one.

When he faced her direction again, she was completing a turn too! Usually he had to do this several times before a girl got the idea of following him, some never did. She had a huge grin on her face, as if she loved the game he was playing. He made a three quarter turn and she did too so that they finished side by side and quite close. He gently bumped his hip against hers a couple of times then twirled away. To his amazement she twirled a reciprocal to his—it was like she either knew what he was about to do, or was able to duplicate his movements so quickly it looked like they were doing them together! He raised his eyebrows in an exaggerated expression of surprise then winked at her again.

~~~

Ell'd been embarrassed when the dancer first winked at her, showing he was aware of how intently she'd been watching him. At first she turned away as if to pretend she hadn't been watching, then decided to just go with it. When he started leading her in little moves, she was even more surprised, but really enjoyed matching what he did. After the twirl she saw him crouch forward in obvious preparation to throwing himself up into a backflip so she did too. As soon as he committed to the backflip so she felt sure he was doing one, she flipped with him.

~~~

In astonishment, Dan saw the brunette landing from a backflip in synch with him! He did an immediate front flip but, holy crap, she matched him on that too! He'd helped girls do backflips before, but he'd had to work with them to teach them how. He'd never danced with a girl who could actually *do* one without his help! He'd been *so* sure this girl couldn't dance. Now he was *determined* to prove he could do things she couldn't. He dropped to the floor to do a "windmill" and this time he felt some relief that she kept dancing upright and simply watched in apparent fascination while he spun. But, when he leapt back to his feet, she dropped to the floor where he'd been and windmilled in the same fashion he had!

Exactly the same fashion.

She leaped back to her feet with an exhilarated smile plastered on her face. She looked like she was just having the time of her life, rather than trying to embarrass him by showing how easily she replicated his moves. The crowd noticed them and began forming a ring around them, clapping and watching. Dan saw the girl dart her eyes around the crowd. She seemed a little distressed. He briefly wondered why. Excited about the attention Dan started doing even more complex elements. To his great sadness, the brunette resumed her simple shuffle, slowly backing away into the crowd around him and clapping along with the rest. It was as if she thought *he* was what'd attracted the crowd's attention, when he knew damned well it was the simple perfection with which she'd performed such astoundingly athletic moves. Wearing boots no less!

~~~

Ell really enjoyed dancing with the guy. When a crowd gathered around, she realized she was once again exceeding what other women could usually do. She was attracting attention she didn't want. Slowly she drew back into the crowd and out of the sudden spotlight.

~~~

Dan, alarmed at the loss of his new dance partner yelled, "Hey girl! Show us what you can do." She shook her head at him and turned to walk off the dance floor. He followed her to a table a little ways from the floor. She was gulping down a drink. "Hey, what happened? You were *great* out there, why'd you quit?"

She wiped her lip and grinned, "Shy."

"Shy?! You've *got* to be kidding! You dance better than any girl I've ever seen and you're gonna try to tell me you're shy?"

She shrugged, "Yup." She took another sip of her drink.

"Dan," he said, putting his hand out for a shake.

She took it and gave it a firm shake, "Raquel."

"Only one word at a time?" He quirked an eyebrow.

She grinned and shook her head.

"None sometimes?"

She nodded, still grinning.

He held out his left hand, "Swing dance?"

She tilted her head and narrowed her eyes, "Fancy?"

"Not if you don't want to."

"Okay." She let him lead her back out to the floor where she proved to be an impeccable follower at swing also. When he tried to initiate a lindy flip or a jump she just ignored him, but even doing standard turns, cuddles and pretzels, her elegant coordination and grace attracted eyes from all over the dance floor. When the song finished, she thanked him and went back to her table despite his request for another dance.

Back at the table Ell frowned at Amy, "Everyone keeps staring at me. Is my wig crooked?"

Amy laughed, "No, it's just that you're so elegant, even doing a simple dance. The eye just sticks to you."

Ell stared at Amy in disbelief. "I'm going to the bathroom to check."

Amy followed her and watched her check her image from all sides. "There isn't anything wrong with your wig. You're pretty and soooo *damned* graceful, believe me, graceful is always gonna attract the crowd's eyes."

Ell rolled her eyes and they went back out into the bar.

They danced on and off for another hour before heading home. As they walked out of the bar Ell noticed a man in a ball cap lean up away from the wall and trail after them. She glanced up at her HUD, "Allan, who's the man behind us?"

In her earphone Allan said, "Unable to identify. He kept his face in the shadow of his cap and has hair across his eyes. Infrared imagery's not identifying him either because of infrared defects. These may be due to silicone facial prosthetics. I suspect he's actively trying to avoid being identified. Caution advised."

Ell suddenly turned to face the man, "What do you want?"

Amy took a few more steps before she realized something was happening, then she stopped, turning as well.

The man made a dismissive wave at Ell, "Just wanna talk to your friend there."

Ell looked hard at him. He didn't have any evident AI equipment and was wearing some kind of facial disguise with grossly exaggerated features to derail video identification. The fact that he wasn't making an audio-video record himself and was trying to block his own recognition on anyone else's video record represented a strong sign of criminal intent.

She glanced around. They were alone in the parking

lot so Ell didn't have to worry about bystanders like the past few incidents. Her stomach still clenched. She wondered briefly why her life had *so* much drama. Watching his hands carefully, Ell stepped between the man and Amy, again saying, "What do you want?" She put her left hand inside her little purse and freed the strap off her shoulder, falling into her zone.

The man peered past Ell and then started to shoulder past her, saying, "Stay out of this." Then he said, "Amy, where's your redheaded friend?"

Ell blocked him again and said, "*I'm* her redheaded friend. Are you a buddy of Bonapute's?"

The man's eyes flickered wide and he scrabbled behind his back with his right hand.

Ell's hand, protected in the purse, flashed out to smack the man in the crotch, then as he bent forward, she kneed him in the face. Knowing she was in the zone, Ell pulled the blows, but they still hit *hard*. He staggered back into Steve who'd come out of the bar just a little behind Ell and Amy.

The man was dazed and Steve caught him to keep him from falling. Steve lowered him to the ground and slipped plasticuffs onto him. Wide-eyed, Amy said, "What just happened?"

Blood started to pour out of the man's broken nose as Steve patted him down and pulled a gun out of a back holster with two fingers.

Allan said, "I've reported this incident to the police and they estimate arrival in five minutes."

The man said, "Wha', wha' habbened? Why' 'jou hi' me?"

~~~

When the police arrived they removed the crude

silicone facial prosthetics and identified the dazed man as Everett Gilmer, a low level criminal known to associate with Felton Bonapute. He'd been suspected of being a hit man for the mob, but the evidence had always been weak. Though Ell'd been worried about the fact that she struck the man prior to his demonstration of certain criminal intent by pulling out his gun, the police accepted the evidence from Steve's AI's cameras showing Gilmer's right hand reaching behind him for the gun in the holster at the small of his back. Ell sighed in relief.

~~~

When Ell got home she turned off the energizing circuits on her. A quick check showed that the two chambers now read nearly the same pressure of just over three atmospheres.

The pressure had equalized between the two chambers—through the port!

Chapter Eight

General Wang looked around the table at the assembled officers of his command. After a long pause, he said, "The current situation nearly meets the specifications laid out in our ideal scenario. The American Carrier Battle Groups are presently far away and won't be able to return quickly enough to interfere. Are you all clear on your roles in operation Small Dragon?" Nods came from all around the table. "Do any of you have concerns about your ability to carry out your roles?" No one spoke. "Does anyone feel that there's a contingency we've left unaddressed?" Still, no one spoke. He slid his chair back, "Very well, I will see if our political leadership has the courage to proceed."

***

Apert walked up to his station and found the El Tee sitting at it, almost finished with preflighting his bird. It looked like Jones was desperately trying to catch up to her in preflighting the other bird. Apert looked at his watch, he wasn't late! He cleared his throat, "Ma'am, is there a problem?"

Donsaii turned and grinned up at him, "Nope. I just wanted to take a bird up myself. Be sure I haven't gotten rusty after all the time I spent over in maintenance. You watch over my shoulder and make sure I don't screw anything up, okay?"

"Yes, Ma'am. Uh, you have the AI disengaged."

"I know," she waggled her eyebrows at him, "not much of a challenge taking off with the AI doing all the work."

"Um, Ma'am, we're not supposed to seek a challenge with Uncle Sam's expensive planes? Takeoff and landing on manual is pretty sketchy with a trans-Pacific satellite delay."

"Hah! I've fixed the delay, watch this." She rotated the camera around to point at the bird's right wing, then wiggled the joystick side to side.

The aileron moved up and down just like it was supposed to and Apert wondered what he was supposed to be seeing. Then his eyebrows rose. When she moved the joystick, it should have taken a couple hundred milliseconds for the signal to travel around the world to the bird, then the image from the camera should have taken a couple hundred milliseconds to come back around the world to the monitor screen! There should have been at *least* a half second delay before he saw the aileron move. For a moment he thought the bird must actually be on the runway here at Nellis, but then he saw the ocean in the distance!

Jones had been watching the byplay. He turned his camera to his own wing and wiggled the joystick. The normal delay was still present. "How'd you do that Ma'am?" he asked wonderingly.

She grinned crookedly back and forth from one to the other, then said, "While I was in maintenance I had a couple of special chips made up and installed on our RQ-7s. We're taking them out on their first flight. If they fail, we can always fall back on the regular comm on channel 1. We're using channel 3 with the new chips, change yours to channel 3 and you should be latency free too."

~~~

Jones looked down and flipped his own board to channel 3, and wiggled the ailerons again—the response was immediate! For a moment he wondered if she had permission to do this. But then Captain Danson from Maintenance showed up "to watch." A few minutes later Donsaii had them rolling their birds down the runway and Jones abandoned himself to the complex task of performing a manual takeoff.

~~~

An hour and a half later, Danson long gone, they coasted in over the PRC coast near Quanzhou and the El Tee exclaimed behind them, "What the heck's been going on while I've been gone?"

Apert and Jones froze, wondering what they'd done wrong. Apert scanned his board without seeing anything out of the ordinary, then risked a glance back at the El Tee. He saw with some relief that she was focused on the screens, not on what he was doing. He looked back at the screen himself, wondering what she was seeing that he wasn't.

Moments later Donsaii was having them zoom in on the port. Apert thought there were quite a few more ships anchored and docked than usual and wondered if that was what had her excited. In a moment the AI took control of their cameras and began shooting images of the port and surrounding water, so someone up the chain obviously had an interest in what was happening too. The AI soon completed its assigned shots and relinquished control. The El Tee immediately resumed zooming in on the various ships, obtaining detailed video of what they were doing. Then she scanned inland over the Chinese Naval base where there appeared to be enormous numbers of personnel, containers stacked high, endless rows of military vehicles and acres of what looked like tent housing. "My God!" the El Tee breathed, "They're going to invade Taiwan!"

She told her AI to contact Colonel Ennis…

***

Varnet shambled into Stimson's office. Stimson looked up in trepidation; Varnet never came with good news. *We're meeting the Secretary this afternoon!* Irritably he barked, "What?"

"Got some astonishing imagery from Quanzhou's Naval base."

"What's it show?" Stimson was irritated to have to ask the followup question.

"It shows a huge military buildup, same as we've known about for some time now. The astonishing thing's the imagery."

In exasperation Stimson lifted his palms and raised his eyebrows, "What's special about it?!"

"It's an enormous file of two hundred megapixel electro-optical, UV and IR video that's been arriving real-time from a couple of RQ-7s that are overflying Quanzhou at present. The time stamp and the early morning shadows confirm that the images are coming from UAVs that're currently in the air."

"So?"

"So, we get low quality video, or an occasional high res image over the satellite link. This kind of imagery has to wait for the UAV to land and download to undersea fiberoptic cable."

Stimson frowned, "How's it being done?"

Varnet grinned, "You're not gonna like the answer."

Stimson rolled his eyes, "Why? Is the PRC forwarding it to us or something?"

"Nope. I was *so* astonished by the video and images that I contacted the commander of the surveillance flight."

"And?" Stimson said dangerously.

"And the commander of the flight was a certain Lt. Donsaii. That selfsame Donsaii with the patent I've been telling you about."

"What!"

"In one overflight this morning that bright young lady figured out that the PRC is going to invade Taiwan, and she's solved the problem that you set for me... I might add, just like I hoped she could." Varnet cocked an eye.

Stimson rolled his eyes again, "Explain."

"She actually *watched* what her cameras were seeing! You know most of the pilots for the UAVs just make sure the planes make the waypoints we set them, so the AI can take the images we programmed." Varnet waggled his eyebrows. "But she actually took an interest in what was happening at the..."

"Yes, yes. I get how she figured out that Taiwan might be invaded. How has she solved the problem I set you?!"

"Ah," Varnet's eyebrows rose, "she's installed some of her PGR chips in the bird and that's what's transmitting all that data."

"So it's sending a lot of data. That's good, but how does that solve our problem?"

"Those chips don't use satellites." Varnet lifted an eyebrow.

Stimson's scalp tingled.

***

When they'd landed the UAVs from their flight over the PRC coast Ell leaned back and said, "That, men, is a serious mess. I can't believe the Chinese think they can invade Taiwan. It's like they think we won't notice!"

As they stood up from their stations Ell looked at Apert and Jones, "You guys been keeping up our running program while I've been gone?"

They looked at the floor. Jones shook his head minutely.

"Well, well, well! I'm so ashamed of you." She grinned at them, "Let's grab Sykes and Tarrant and go try to get ourselves back in shape."

***

The President looked around the room at his advisers, "Let me make sure I understand what you're telling me. The PRC can shoot down all our satellites..."

The Secretary of Defense interrupted, "Just the ones over, or crossing over Asia."

The President glanced exasperatedly up at the ceiling then said, "'All our satellites over Asia.' And, they're poised to invade Taiwan?"

Heads nodded reluctantly. Those that didn't kept

their attention focused down on the table or slate in front of them. Few met his eyes.

The President continued, "And you believe that sometime in the next few days they'll do so?"

Heads nodded again and SecDef said, "Yes sir."

"Why?"

"The PRC has claimed Taiwan since..."

"No, no, I know why they want to invade, but why shoot down our satellites first?"

"Ah. Yes sir. Satellite observation's a tremendous force multiplier. If we know exactly what the opposition's doing we can respond with precision and foreknowledge. Our current military doctrine depends on satellites so extensively that you could liken doing battle without them to boxing while wearing a blindfold. Of course, Taiwan's satellites would also be taken out and so both parties on our side would then be fighting blind."

"What about our vaunted reconnaissance aircraft?"

"They would still function and could give us much of the same data, but they depend on satellites to transmit their data back to us when the planes are out of line of sight. Therefore the information they delivered would be significantly delayed. The Chinese would know what we were doing but we wouldn't know what they were doing until it was too late."

"Can't we take out their satellites to put them on an even footing?"

"We can take out some, but they've put up huge numbers in the past few years. We're not sure which are observation sats and which are the sats that took hours out. And we really don't have very many of our own killer satellites up at present."

"What *are* we doing?"

"We've notified Taiwan and they're on high alert. I've sent three carriers toward the area, but right now they're all far away. The carriers will not only project force to the area, but they can also put up ELINT aircraft that increase our line of sight communications distance. Unfortunately, those craft radiate electronically so they can be readily targeted and taken out by the opposition. The Air Force is moving craft to Okinawa and already has a large UAV surveillance wing there. We have submarines moving to the area, but they're relatively slow and communication with submarines is difficult because they can't receive radio while they're underwater. Unfortunately many of our GPS guided weapons depend on control through satellite communications as well."

"Is there any chance of this going nuclear?"

"We don't think so. The PRC wants Taiwan, not a smoking crater."

"Are we doing anything to improve our situation regarding communication and observation? Launching more satellites?"

"We can launch a few, but they've been planning this for a long time, they'd probably just shoot them down. Um, you remember Ell Donsaii?"

The President blinked at the apparent non-sequitur, then it clicked for him, "The young Air Force gymnast I gave the Medal of Honor to? What on Earth does she have to do with this?"

"She's a Lieutenant now, flying UAVs out of Okinawa from Nellis. Do you remember that she'd also written a hotshot quantum physics paper?"

The President frowned at the second non-sequitur, "Yes."

"Well based on her theory, she's patented some

communications technology that's letting us download imagery from our UAVs without using the satellites."

"Really? Do we get the same quality images?"

"Really. Apparently we get much better images, much faster. Though of course, they're from aerial assets, not from satellites."

"And these chips are already in place?"

A barked laugh, "Apparently, the Lieutenant believes in that old adage, 'Better to ask forgiveness than permission.' She's installed her chips in several UAVs without asking if she was allowed to do it. I don't have to tell you how long it would have taken to get permission?"

The President rolled his eyes, "Give the girl a cigar!"

"I've sent a team out to evaluate this technology in person, but the stuff she's installed is working great! I'd like Presidential permission to fast track getting her stuff out to all our craft so we won't be dependent on satellite comm tech? I want to send it even before I'm sure it works reliably… because we're under a *lot* of time pressure."

"You've got it." The President turned to an aide, "Assuming it actually works, start figuring out what kind of commendation we're going to need to hang on the girl for this one?"

President Teller turned back to the table, "Okay, assuming we can surprise the PRC with our ability to watch them despite their shooting down our satellites, it seems to me that our dependency on satellites for command, control and communications is still a problem?

"Yes sir. I'm presently hoping that Lt. Donsaii's chips will help there too. The ones that are in Okinawa at present, we *think* only plug into the comm boards for our recon aircraft. However, I think her company may be planning to announce chips that can be used for other forms of communications too. Maybe they've already manufactured some general use comm chips we can send to Okinawa, Taiwan and the fleet?"

"Let's talk to her." The President glanced upward as he spoke to his AI, "Get Lt. Ell Donsaii on the line please."

***

Sykes and Tarrant were surprised when the El Tee, who'd been sitting quietly behind them, watching their screens as they overflew Quanzhou, suddenly said, "Okay," stood, then said "Yes, sir." They looked around, but no one else was in their flight control center. She actually appeared to be standing at attention to talk to someone over her AI, which was bizarre

They turned back to their consoles as she said, "Yes sir, the patent's only applied for, but a company called PGR Comm has been founded to develop the technology."

"Uh, yes sir, I did install PGR chips into some of our reconnaissance UAVs in Okinawa."

She winced, "No sir, I didn't have permission."

"Oh! Yes sir!" She sounded upbeat. "We'd be happy to install more. I've already sent more chips to Okinawa. They can quickly be installed on the UAVs there... Sir, I'm hoping you're aware of the military buildup in Quanzhou? I'm very concerned that the PRC is preparing to invade Taiwan."

"Yes sir, of course sir."

"I'm not sure sir; let me ask my AI to find out. Allan,

please determine how many USB type PGR chips have been manufactured so far?"

"Yes sir, I'm sure the company would be willing to put all current inventories at the country's disposal."

"Yes sir, I'll ask them to deliver to a location of the Secretary's choosing."

The El Tee moved to the back of the room speaking to her AI rapid fire as if arranging something. When she came back up she addressed the non-coms, "See anything interesting?"

Sykes looked up at her, "It looks to me like they're moving supplies out into these bulk carriers. Who were you talking to?"

"Um… the President. Have you seen them loading any identifiable weapons systems?"

"They were putting a tank on one as we overflew. President of what?"

"Of the United States. Could you identify the model of the tank? Was it their new Lǎo hǔ?"

"The President?! Holy cripes Ma'am! What did he call you for?"

The El Tee grinned down at him. "He'd heard I'd been assigned some especially inquisitive NCOs and wanted to know what I was going to do about it."

Sykes and Tarrant stared up at Ell wide-eyed. Sykes swallowed, "No, really Ma'am. What did he call you about?"

"Actually he heard a Sergeant Sykes liked my zero latency chips. He said, 'If they're good enough for Sykes, they're good enough to be installed everywhere.'"

"The *President* called to talk about your chips?" Sykes almost whispered in an awed tone.

"Seriously guys, I'm sorry you heard parts of that

conversation. It bears on this China kerfuffle and you should consider it Top Secret, okay? Don't tell anyone outside this room anything about it until it's common knowledge."

Still wide-eyed they chorused, "Yes Ma'am."

~~~

Ten minutes later Lieutenant Sasson stepped into the room and said, "Donsaii, I've been sent to relieve you on this UAV flight. You're to get your ready travel kit and report to travel operations for a flight to somewhere. Apparently, you're supposed to brief somebody on something?" He raised his eyebrows indicating the question.

Ell tilted her head, "No one told me, but I suspect I know what it's about," she looked meaningfully at Sykes and Tarrant. "I think it's on a need to know basis at present. I'll turn these miscreants over to you. So far the flight's routine except it appears that the PRC is loading land assault weapon systems onto those bulk carriers off Quanzhou."

~~~

Ell contacted travel ops about when she was expected to report for her flight.

They told her "ASAP".

She had Mary from the ready team meet her just off base with her travel kit, a box of PGR USB chips she had in her apartment and her flight suit. "I'm not sure where they're sending me or how long I'll be staying, but I may need the team to follow me there. I'll let you guys know as soon as I figure it out."

Mary had to resist the impulse—instilled by her years in the service—to salute the young officer.

~~~

Ell walked into travel ops with her ready bag in hand and a Captain accosted her, "Are you Donsaii?"

"Yes sir."

"What took so damned long?! Let's go!" he started off at a fast trot, out of the building and toward the flight line.

Ell looked around for a transport or cargo plane, however, the Captain took her directly to a two-seater F-35 variant that had a ladder rolled up to it. They handed her a helmet which, to her surprise, fit very well. They must have looked up her database. She was hustled up the ladder and into the rear seat. The ground crewman leaned in to buckle her belts, jack the helmet into the plane's systems and point out the barf bag. To her astonishment, within ten minutes the plane was rolling down the runway and up into the air like a rocket. Once they were in level flight, there was a click on the intercom and a familiar sounding voice said, "Donsaii?"

"Yes Ma'am?"

"Lieutenant Andrews here. When I was yelling at you in basic training back at the Academy I never dreamed I'd be ferrying your ass across the country like some kind of hot shot. Congratulations!"

"Um, thank you Ma'am."

"Hah! I should thank you. I was proud to have known you when I heard you won the Medal and I have a feeling I'll be prouder yet if I ever figure out what *this* is all about. Who are they shipping you over to talk to?

"Um, I'm afraid I haven't been told. I don't even know where we're flying to?"

"Well, well! The right hand doesn't know what the left hand is doing? I'm *so* surprised. I do believe, however that you have 'need to know' where you're going, so I'll reveal to you that we're using accessory tanks to fly supersonic to Andrews AFB in DC where I'm to taxi you directly to a helicopter, so someone *very important* wants you somewhere in the DC area in a *big* hurry."

~~~

Ell identified the Pentagon in the dimming light outside the windows of the helicopter as it swung in to land.

As it settled onto the pad she saw a first lieutenant, holding his hat and making waving motions as if he wanted her to hurry. In a couple of minutes he had her and her bag loaded onto a golf cart. He headed into the building.

She asked, "Do you know who I'm here to meet or what this is about?"

"Nope." He grinned at her, "that's *way* above my pay grade."

"Can we stop off at a bathroom?"

He raised his eyebrows, still grinning, "Are you tryin' to get me court martialed? What'd I ever do to you?"

The golf cart pulled up at a conference room where a Major said, "Is this her?" He looked at Ell's nametag and said, "Good! Have her wait inside." The Major looked up as he spoke to his AI.

The Lieutenant opened the door to the empty conference room. Ell looked at him in desperation. He shifted his eyes to the bathroom signage across the hall. Ell took the situation in hand and stepped across the hall.

When Ell came out she heard the Major in the conference room, saying, "Where the hell'd she go?!"

She stepped quickly across the hall and into the conference room, "Sir, I'm here."

The Major had just begun to glare when the door opened and a blue dress uniform with four stars entered. Ell recognized General Ellis, the Chief of Staff of the Air Force. She remained at attention. As she was indoors she resisted the impulse to salute. Ellis turned to the Major and said, "This her?"

"Yes sir."

The door opened and an Army general in green and a Naval admiral in black entered. Ell suddenly realized she was at a meeting of the Joint Chiefs of Staff! She wondered if she should have tried to change into her dress uniform while she was in the bathroom.

The door opened again and more high level officers poured in, the brass were all shaking each other's hands and sitting down. One of the admirals, whose nametag read "Immenstall," said, "Okay, who's running this briefing? Let's get a move on, it's late."

To Ell's dismay, the Major pointed at her, "Lieutenant Donsaii, sir."

Wide-eyed, Ell didn't even get a chance to clear her throat. An Admiral, sitting behind the nameplate for USPACOM, or Pacific Command, barked, "A 2nd lieutenant? In a flight suit? We've got a PRC crisis in PACOM and someone sends a lieutenant to brief us on communications?! I don't have time for this! I need to get back to my Command!" He started to stand.

The door opened and a man in a suit entered. "Sit down Joe. *You* need to hear from Lieutenant Donsaii more than any of the rest of us." Ell still standing at attention on the side of the room, recognized the Secretary of Defense! Secretary Amundsen walked to the front of the room and surveyed its occupants. They'd all risen to their feet, including Admiral Joseph Larsson of PACOM who'd just been told to sit. "Gentlemen, you are all aware that the PRC's been increasing force levels in Fujian province near Taiwan for weeks now. You may have heard that they've begun placing weapon systems onto shipping as of this morning. What you may not be informed about, is the recent assessment that the loss of our Asian geosynchronous observation satellite likely was not due to micrometeorites, but due to enemy action. It is the assessment of the CIA and NSA that the Chinese have recently put up enough killer satellites to take out *all* our observational and comm satellites that pass over the western Pacific and eastern Asia." A chorus of indrawn breaths greeted this announcement. "Our current intelligence estimate is that they will likely take down all those satellites within the week and invade Taiwan immediately after that. They'll be able to keep taking out the rest of our satellites as they rotate over that part of the world." Everyone in the room blanched. He turned to Larsson, "Joe, I assume that I don't have to tell you what a mess that'll make of your current crisis response plans?"

Larsson swallowed, "My God! How did this happen without anyone putting me in the loop?! I've got to get back to my command and try to develop a response! Now!"

The Secretary smiled grimly, "Yes, but, I'll guarantee that you won't want to leave until after you've heard what the Lieutenant has prepared for us." He turned and waved Ell toward him, "Lieutenant, show us what you've got."

Ell had stepped forward when he waved her up.

Now she grimaced and said, "Sir, I'm afraid I was ordered to get on a plane and then flown here without knowing my destination or my assignment. I do not have anything prepared and, though I can guess, I am not certain of the expected contents of any briefing I'm to deliver?" Ell could *feel* Larsson rolling his eyes, but she kept her attention focused on Secretary Amundsen.

The Secretary grimaced, then turned to the brass and said, "I believe your term for this state of affairs is SNAFU?" He turned back to Ell, "We flew you here to explain your new communication chips to us and help us quickly understand how they might be integrated into solving this crisis? Just give us a brief synopsis of what we should know about them and then you can answer questions.

Before Ell could say anything Larsson barked, "Lieutenant? Who the Hell's your senior officer—the officer who *should* be briefing us on this?"

The Secretary's eyes glinted and then tracked back to Larsson. "Admiral, do I have to give you a *direct order* to shut up and listen?" He paused, then indicated Ell with a wave, "This is Lieutenant Ell Donsaii, whom you might remember was the winner of four Olympic gold medals in gymnastics two summers ago? You may also recall she received the Medal of Honor for her role in stopping the terrorists at that Olympics? I believe that she deserves more respect than your usual second lieutenant and a great deal more than you've been giving her?" Eyes had widened among the officers in the audience. "Finally, Joe, she's presenting, rather than any 'senior officer,' because *she* invented the technology in question." He turned to Ell, "Lieutenant, please do your best to fill us in on the nature and capability of your chips and accept our apologies for the failure of communication that left you unable to prepare."

Ell had been breathing slowly and deeply to keep herself out of the zone. She felt fairly calm, but stepped slowly to her bag and pulled out a pair of PGR chips. "A little more than a year ago, while a Cadet at the Air Force Academy, I published a paper on a new math I'd developed which seems to fit well with observed quantum effects such as entanglement in which particles seem to be joined somehow, even though they are separated by distance. It was my postulate that the particles were joined by a connection through a "fifth dimension" which we are unable to perceive. Therefore communications from one entangled molecule in our universe, to the molecule it is entangled with—by passing through that fifth dimension—appear to be instantaneous to us because the distance in *that* dimension is microscopic. After graduating last summer, I was temporarily detached from active duty to pursue graduate studies in experimental physics. During that time I endeavored to develop a means to use the predictions made in my paper to produce useful communication devices." She stepped forward and handed the pair of chips to the Chairman of the Joint Chiefs of Staff. "This pair of entangled chips can transfer data from one chip to the other at the same rate as can be achieved over the very best fiber optic connections. At present about 20,000 pairs of chips are available and can be distributed to US forces, but they all use USB 5.0 jacks and so fitting them to devices that do not have USB sockets may be problematic. I also made up a hundred pairs of mil-spec chips that fit the BXA ports on the comm boards in our UAVs. Although I don't know how common BXA ports are on the rest of our military comm boards, during my flight here, suspecting this need I asked the manufacturer to rush production on 10,000 more pairs with BXA jacks. The company's current manufacturing operation is small, but they should be able to turn out about a thousand a day. Making chips with other jacks will take longer, due to the need to design those interfaces before we can begin production. Therefore, I hope that BXA jacks are as common on military comm boards as I've been led to believe."

This time it was the Chairman who interrupted with a frown, "Who approved an order of 10,000 chips? And how did you order them during your flight?! You aren't supposed to use military aircraft comm systems to access the net!"

Ell took another deep breath to calm herself. "No sir. My AI's hooked to the net via PGR chips so it wasn't necessary to use the aircraft comm. I authorized the expenditure as..."

The Chairman interrupted again, "You authorized! A lieutenant doesn't have authority for such expenditures!"

Quietly Ell said, "I spent my own money." She took another calming breath.

He frowned, "How much are these chips?"

"In a low production run like this the mil spec versions are about $100 a pair."

"That'd be... a million dollars for 10,000 of them, where did *you* get that kind of money?!"

Quietly, "Sir, the royalties on this invention are quite generous."

The room was silent.

The Secretary of Defense raised his eyebrows, "Might she get on with the presentation now?"

Admiral Larsson had his hand up, but without being recognized, interrupted to say, "What the hell do these chips have to do with the fact that I won't have *any* satellite observation?!"

The secretary frowned and put a finger to his lips, then waved to Ell to proceed.

She said, "You are correct Admiral, that they don't solve the loss of satellite observation. However, the loss of our satellites will also hamstring our battlefield communications, and unfortunately, even our aerial observation platforms currently use satellites to transmit their imagery back to us. We already have PGR chips in a few RQ-7 UAVs, but could very quickly install them in *all* UAVs in order to provide uninterrupted, realtime, battlefield observation. PGR chips would also allow our aircraft to stay in communication with command far beyond line of sight and our aircraft carriers to serve as battle direction centers. This is because they'd provide the ability to obtain data from our aircraft and send directions to them without using satellite linkages. Perhaps most importantly, if the PRC were to cut our undersea fiberoptic lines to Okinawa and to the ROC on Taiwan, PGR chips could substitute for those cables as well."

"What! What's their range?!"

"Unlimited."

"What do you mean 'unlimited?' I want a *range*."

"Theoretically, an unlimited number of light years. Practically, I have tested a chip pair which successfully communicated from North Carolina to Australia."

"With what kind of repeater stations?"

"None."

"How much power does that take!?"

"Five volts."

After a disbelieving silence, "How hard is it to jam or intercept their messages?"

"Jamming or intercepting them is not possible."

"Oh, come on. Everything can be jammed or intercepted *somehow*!"

"These can't be. The message passing from one quantum entangled molecule to the other member of a pair is uninterruptible, uninterceptable and undetectable. This has been tested by numerous individuals and is predicted by the math and theory that made it possible." Ell felt bemused to not only be standing up to, but lecturing the Joint Chiefs of Staff.

The officers were sitting back in their chairs and looking at one another as if wondering if any of the others were being taken in by this unbelievable line of crap. Ell continued. "The chips will not replace satellites, but *will* replace satellite communications. It is important to recognize also that they *improve* on satellite communications in two fashions. First, satellite comm is limited in bandwidth because it is essentially radio, whereas the chips transfer data at much higher data rates that are on par with optical transmission bandwidths. Therefore, for example, the UAVs that I fly out of Nellis normally transfer real-time data via satellite at low rates. These rates allow steady transfer of low resolution video with occasional high megapixel images. The high quality video and the rest of the images must await downloading of the UAV's memory after the UAV returns and lands in Okinawa. Then that detailed imagery is transmitted by undersea fiberoptic cable. However, PGR chips allow continuous transmission of 200 megapixel video directly back to Nellis. Also, the data transmission is instantaneous, thus allowing much improved realtime control of remote aircraft such as UAVs, due to the lack of satellite transmission latency."

Ell saw patent disbelief on the faces in the room, but didn't really know how to convince them without a demonstration of some type. A demonstration she was not set up for. After a brief pause, Admiral Larsson said slowly, "Just how old are you Lieutenant?"

"I'm nineteen sir."

She turned to the Secretary who'd seen their doubt as well. He grinned at her a moment then turned to the assembled officers with a grin that had turned shark-like. "*Believe* it. How old she is doesn't matter. I've seen the data coming from her UAV and it's delivered realtime at rates over a terabyte per second. A couple of reports from her superior officers confirm that it's either instantaneous, or close enough to it that they can't measure the delay. The PRC's going to be stunned at our ability to circumvent their strategy, but only if we get on it right away.

"Now, we need to figure out how to implement delivery of our limited number of chips, over great distances, to many different force elements in the face of this crisis. I expect that we need to send a few chips with Admiral Larsson back to PACOM in Hawaii. Some need to go to each aircraft carrier so they can be distributed to their aircraft, ship to ship comm within battle groups can continue by radio for the time being. Some chips need to be sent to Okinawa to outfit *all* our UAVs. And some need to be sent to Taiwan. Let's work out a plan to divvy them up and then get about our regular business. Lieutenant, how many chips do we have to work with exactly?"

Despite the dubious expressions on the faces of many officers they fell to arguing, each demanding a large share of the available chips for their particular commands. Ell interrupted once to suggest that each designated asset get one of a pair of the USB chips and the other member of each pair of chips be placed in a safe location with one of the servers that PGR Comm was developing to handle signal routing from chip to chip. This would be much more flexible than point to point connections. At least until a lot more chips were available. Thus communication could go to the central server and be routed back out to whichever chip the communications needed to be sent to, like with a telephone exchange, allowing rerouting as necessary. She also suggested that a chip be delivered to each of the submarines in the area to allow them to have high speed realtime communications while submerged for the first time in the history of submarine warfare. The Naval officers present raised their eyebrows at this striking notion.

Over the next several hours supersonic aircraft were dispatched to PACOM in Hawaii, to each of the aircraft carriers, to Okinawa and to Taiwan. Midair refueling was arranged for the aircraft and an initial plan to send all the chips most of the way on one plane was nixed on the basis of not "putting all our eggs in one basket." From the aircraft carriers, chips would be dropped to submarines and other naval elements by the carriers' aerial assets.

At 10PM the Secretary had PGR Comm rousted out to deliver the new PGR chip servers as well as personnel expert in their use via several different military planes to a secure underground location. Per President Teller's request, PGR Comm had already delivered all of their available USB chips to the Pentagon that afternoon.

Secretary Amundsen sent Ell to the secure location

as well, "To make sure it all works!" As he left he said, "Having seen the trouble the Chiefs gave you, I realize a Lieutenant might need some punch to get your job done. In case you meet resistance to setting things up as needed and need command authority from me your AI hereby has permission to contact mine at *any* time. Good luck." He turned and walked away.

Ell desperately hoped the PRC would give them enough time to distribute the chips and get the servers functioning.

Chapter Nine

Ell arrived at the secure location a couple of hours later. It turned out to be one of a number of buried and hardened facilities near D.C., this one belonging to the military. She'd scanned the chips sent to each of the locations in the Pacific and had their paired counterparts with her. A Major Geller from PACOM was with her, but when they arrived they were held at the gate while the Colonel in command of the facility was rousted.

He peered up at his HUD, "I'm to give you access to space to set up a communication facility?"

"Yes sir."

"We don't have rooms with communications hook ups," he said somewhat petulantly.

Ell interjected, "Sir, we just need a secure room with power outlets."

The Colonel turned on her. "Lieutenant, when I want to hear from you, I'll ask you to speak up!" He turned back to the Major, "We only have one room, the command facility, with connection to the secure military fiberoptic network. I'm not sure I should turn that facility over to you. Whoever wrote these orders probably just doesn't know what's actually available here."

The Major said, "I'm told the Lieutenant here is the expert. If she says we only need power outlets, I'd go with a room having lots of power outlets."

The Colonel rolled his eyes, then glanced up and, speaking to his AI, said, "Put me in touch with whoever originated these orders. We need to get this snafu straightened out."

They waited a few tense moments, then the Colonel looked up again, "Yes sir! But the Lieutenant doesn't even know what she needs sir. She's trying to set up communications without access to the fiberoptic..." the Colonel blanched. "Yes sir... Yes sir... Yes sir."

Suddenly, Ell was connected to the conversation also. "Lieutenant Donsaii, are you on the line now?" she heard the Secretary of Defense say.

"Yes sir." She saw that Major Geller must be connected too from the way he looked up and unconsciously straightened his spine.

Secretary Amundsen said, "Lieutenant, I've explained to Colonel Whitt that you are the absolute expert on this issue and that it's a matter of utmost National Security that he cooperate and provide you every assistance you request. Colonel, she has authorization to contact me directly if she meets any more obstruction, but it's *your* job to make sure she doesn't encounter any resistance—from you or anyone else. If she does, it'll mean your career, understand?"

"Yes sir!"

The Secretary said, "I have other matters to attend to," and signed off.

As they rode down an elevator into the depths of the Earth Ell turned to Colonel Whitt and said, "Sir, I've realized that you are correct. We *will* need a connection to the secure military fiberoptic network, I thank you for pointing that out. However, we will be able to just attach one chip to a fiberoptic terminal in your command center though. All the rest of our equipment can be in a separate room."

"There aren't any decent rooms close to the Command Center!"

"Sir, we don't have to be close to it."

"You're *not* going to run fiberoptic line down hundreds of yards of my hallway."

"No sir," Ell thought about explaining it all to him, but thought he'd argue about that also, "We just need to put a chip in the Command Center, everything else can be wherever you want to put us. Also, please let the gate guards know that we expect a delivery and personnel from PGR Comm in the next thirty minutes?"

"We can't allow commercial personnel into *this* base!"

"Sir, I need you to make that happen?" Ell raised her eyebrows.

The Colonel stared at her, thunderstruck, looked for a moment as if he would protest, then said dangerously, "Okay Lieutenant, but I'll be filing a complaint after the fact."

"Yes sir."

~~~

Ell and the Major were assigned a large multipurpose room and personnel to clean it out. Folding tables were brought in and placed along the walls. Ell went over to the command center and attached a linking chip to the secure military fiberoptic network.

While she was in there Allan said, "Amy's calling."

"Put her on."

"Ell, where are you?"

"Hmmm, not supposed to say, but I'm on a military

base in a safe location. Might not be home for a while though."

"Okay. I disconnected the power and then disassembled the chamber on your small lab table like you asked. It was full of water? I don't know if that's good or bad?"

Ell pumped her fist, then realized that Amy couldn't see it. "Great! That means we've successfully moved liquid from one chamber to another!"

As Ell arrived back in the multipurpose room a couple of Noncoms showed up with some civilians and pallets loaded with equipment.

Ell said, "Sorry Amy, gotta go."

Ell turned to the civilians and said, "Set them up on these tables," she looked at the pallets speculatively, "or are they designed to sit on the floor?"

The oldest of the civilians scratched his balding pate, "Lady, we've been shanghaied away from our jobs and sent down here to D.C. without any explanations and we're tired. We've worked well beyond our normal hours and our contracts don't specify time and a half or anything. It's time we got a little rest. We'll help you set up in the morning, but for now we need some down time."

Ell tilted her head as she eyed them, "We need your help now, minutes could count in lives. What would it take to get your cooperation?"

He barked a little laugh, "Lady, I mean Lieutenant, I spent some time in the military. I know all about the old hurry up and wait. I doubt very, very seriously that anything'll change if we sleep through the night and start fresh on this setup in the morning."

For a moment Ell wondered if she could brief them on the situation. She decided not. Working for PGR

Comm, they likely all had PGR connected AIs and could readily connect to the outside world and she doubted any of them had a security clearance. If they spread word on what was happening to the world in general… Ell's thoughts paused momentarily, *Would that be so bad? If the world in general knew what China was doing? Maybe not,* she decided, but *she* didn't have authority to disclose that information. She glanced up, "Allan, forward 5K to each of these men's personal accounts." She looked at the six men, "Please check your accounts, you should each find a deposit of $5,000. If you help me unstintingly tonight, I'll make another deposit of 10K in the morning."

They looked at her in startlement, then up at their HUDs, then back at her, then almost as one, they nodded. The older one grinned, "Unstintingly it is!"

One of the others stepped forward, "Are you *Ell* Donsaii, Lieutenant?"

Ell nodded.

"Oh my God," he beamed, "I'm so very, very proud just to meet you. What do you want us to do?"

"Start setting up the servers while I get you guys some food and coffee."

The men looked around, argued briefly and then started uncrating a pallet over by the far wall. Ell turned to the Sergeant assigned to help them set up the room. "We need food and coffee for these men."

He gave her a worried look. "Kitchen's closed this hour of the evening."

"It needs to be opened."

He slowly shook his head, "*I* can't make that happen."

"I need to speak to Colonel Whitt then."

He looked agitated, "Oh, you *don't* want to do that!"

She raised an eyebrow at him, then when he did nothing she looked up, "Allan, get Colonel Whitt on the line."

A moment later she heard Whitt's angry voice, "*What now?*"

"Sir, I need food, coffee and cots for the civilian crew that's helping with setup."

"Kitchen's closed and those civilians need to leave base to sleep. There's a hotel one mile from the gate."

"Sir, I really don't want to contact SecDef?"

~~~

Thirty minutes later a coffee cart rolled in. Thirty minutes after that, some unhappy looking kitchen crew showed up with a rolling cart loaded with MREs (Meals Ready to Eat). Ell looked at the MREs and turned to the staff sergeant who'd left the cart and already turned back to the door. "Sergeant!" Her sharp command voice brought the sergeant to a halt and to attention. "You need to provide something *much* better than MREs for this crew."

He turned slowly, "Colonel said MREs." he said slowly and with evident satisfaction.

Ell sighed and wondered where Major Geller was, he was supposed to be running interference on this kind of stuff. She tapped her foot, "Sergeant, I'll be happy to call Colonel Whitt if you want?"

He gulped, then shook his head. "I'll be back."

Ell said, "Allan, contact Major Geller."

"Yes Lieutenant?" Geller sounded sleepy and impatient.

"Major, I'm having to spend a *lot* of time getting cooperation from the local base personnel."

"Welcome to life as a Lieutenant, Lieutenant."

Ell took a deep breath. "Sir, I need to get this comm center set up. The success or failure of our response to the PRC may well depend on it. SecDef assigned me to do that and he assigned you to provide seniority so that I wouldn't have to fight all these little battles. Do I need to call and ask him to clarify your orders?"

There was a pause.

"I'll be there in a couple of minutes." His tone was surly, but when he appeared, he asked Ell what she needed and started commandeering local base personnel without further complaint.

Over the next several hours the PGR Comm personnel set up racks of servers and they plugged the chips Ell had brought into the chip sockets that covered the upper surface of each rack insert. The racks had their own CPU that directed connection of one chip to another so that an incoming signal on one chip could be cross connected to deliver an outgoing signal to another chip. That CPU used a disappointingly low powered AI though. It wouldn't have the intelligence to be able to sift messages and direct them appropriately upon the sender's request, it could only connect them if the incoming message had a correct address for the connection.

This wouldn't be a problem for PGR Comm's commercial use because incoming data streams would have headers directing them appropriately. Unfortunately, in the current situation, incoming messages *wouldn't* have correct addresses for their connection. They'd likely have voice requests to be connected to a certain officer or ship. For a job like that you needed a powerful AI... "Allan, can you connect to this server?"

"I can, but at present I'd have to reach it through the

civilian net, then connect through that to the secure military fiberoptic network and through it to the chip you installed in the command center, to the server. Military firewalls may block my access. It'd be better if I were connected directly to the server."

"Okay," Ell pulled her headband off and picked up one of the few pairs of PGR chips she still had. Most of the chips she had were only one end of a pair, the other end of which was presently out over the Pacific. She plugged one member of the pair she'd picked up into the empty USB socket on her headband and put the headband back on. Then she picked up the mate to the chip she'd just installed on her headband and carried it over to the rack. "Is there a best location?"

Allan had downloaded the circuit design for the rack from PGR Comm and said, "There's a USB port on the CPU itself right at the top of the rack."

Ell saw the slot and plugged the chip in, "Is that correct?"

"Yes," Allan responded, "a moment... Okay, I've inserted myself in the system and can now screen the data streams and make sure they are directed appropriately. I'll forward any issues I can't handle to you."

Ell set about helping the civilians plug chips into the boards and then set up another rack. Contacts started coming in from outlying chips that'd already been installed, first those at the Pentagon, then Admiral Larsson on his flight back to Hawaii, eventually from ships in the Pacific and then Okinawa and Taiwan. Allan was able to handle most of them though she had to run interference on a few. She specifically asked to be contacted as they hooked up their first submarine, because she thought it would be exciting to be the first to provide instant communication for a submarine at depth.

***

General Wang stepped into the room. "We're approved to proceed." He looked back and forth across the room. "Proceed with the satellite attacks at 10AM. That'll be the middle of the night in Washington so the Americans'll be sleepy and confused. By evening here we should have an accurate assessment of the status of any satellites they have that're still functioning. If their observation and control systems appear to be satisfactorily disrupted, we'll launch on Taiwan under cover of darkness here. As planned, go ahead and send out the slower cargo ships during the day, we'll call them back if we abort."

***

Just after midnight, a knock on his door awakened President Teller. "Sorry sir, but, as forecast, almost all of our Asian satellite assets began failing to respond. This began about thirty-five minutes ago. Of the five that initially continued to function, three more have gone down since then. We expect to have no space assets over that part of the world shortly. Beijing has issued a statement that they 'will no longer tolerate space based spying on their sovereign realm.'"

The President groaned as he sat up and put on his slippers. "Have they launched their invasion?

"Not yet."

Lieutenant

"How are we doing with shoring up our communications using the new chips?"

"The chips have only begun arriving in Okinawa and Taiwan. The three aircraft carriers have received allotments of chips and been able to successfully hook them into some systems.

***

A knock came on his door. Already awake because he'd felt the changes indicating his sub was surfacing, Captain Allred rolled over, "What is it?"

"Sir, we've received a VLF message to surface for a communication."

"Okay, I'll be there before we reach the top of the water."

Hardly able to stand the taste of his own mouth, he brushed his teeth and put on his coverall. To his astonishment, once they broke surface with an HF antenna they were queried as to their exact location and told to stand by for delivery of some "chips." Apparently, an aircraft carrier was within flight range. While awaiting the aircraft that would deliver the chips they were to continue at flank speed toward the western side of Taiwan.

An hour and a half later they were instructed to surface again. A jet dropped a package in the water that they picked up with their inflatable boat. The jet also dropped fuel tanks, apparently at its own extreme range. The package proved to be nothing but a chip with a USB jack on the end of it. The only other thing in the package was a set of actual *printed* instructions on how to jack the chip into the sub's main comm board in place of the auxiliary radio system and then to switch to that system and send a test message.

Allred clicked the mike button and said "Testing, testing, testing."

The voice of a young woman came back, "We read you five by five. Is this Captain Allred?" He thought the woman sounded very young. Was a brand new seaman handling communications with his sub?

"Yes." He said in an irritated tone.

"You may resume course and maintain a depth of your choosing. PACOM will be able to communicate with you at depth using this chip."

"That's ridiculous!" he said while cranking his hand to indicate to his crew to resume flank speed. "The board you had us install the chip on isn't hooked into the ELF system!"

"Um, sorry Captain. I meant to say you'd be able to communicate at optical data rates using this chip, even at depth. Please, try it out. I'm not sure what data systems you have but I'm turning you over to Admiral Larsson at PACOM now."

There was a click from the speaker before he could yell at the seaman for such a ridiculous statement. Then he heard Larsson's voice. "Larry?"

"Yes sir?"

"Are you at depth?"

"No sir." Allred was startled that the Admiral thought it was possible that they could speak at depth. ELF messages can be received at depth, but not sent and had too low a bandwidth for voice transmission.

Larsson said, "Ah damn it. I knew it was too good to be true."

"What's that sir?"

"That you could send and receive at depth. How far

down have you tried it?"

"Sir, I haven't tried it, but... we both know that it's just not possible."

"Oh. Well... try it, I'll stand by. I don't believe it either, but I've been told this is gonna work."

Allred raised his eyebrows and then motioned for a dive, saying, "Okay, we're going down. I'll try to keep speaking so you can tell when it cuts out. Where are you sir?"

"I'm just out over the eastern Pacific on a flight back to Hawaii from D.C., where are you?"

"We're still 20 nautical miles southeast of Taiwan, proceeding at flank speed into the Taiwan Strait as directed."

"Okay, in case you haven't been brought up to date since you surfaced to get the chip, the Chinese have shot down all our satellites over the PRC and western Pacific."

"What!" Ice flooded into Allred's veins.

"Yes. More'll come over the horizon to the Asian theater soon but they'll probably shoot those down too. We expect them to launch an invasion fleet toward Taiwan in the next few hours. They expect us to be blind, but if the chip you just installed actually works we'll be able to vector you to the best possible locations to discourage them."

"My God! Are we declaring war?"

"Perhaps. At present we're hoping that they'll lose their nerve if they realize that we aren't completely blind without our satellites. We expect you'll need to fire some warning shots though."

A tingle shot down Allred's spine when he saw the depth indicator read 70 meters, "Ramirez, are we trailing the buoyed antenna?" He realized as he asked the question that the comm system was switched to the auxiliary radio system that'd been unplugged to install the new chip. So, he wouldn't be picking up signals from the buoyed antenna anyway. In any case the buoyed antenna was for the ELF system which had too low a data rate for voice communication.

Lt. Ramirez looked up. "No sir."

"Are we in contact over hydrophone?"

Ramirez' eyebrows rose and he glanced at his board. After a momentary pause he said, "No sir."

Allred depressed the button on his mike, "Admiral?"

"Yes?"

"Uh, we're at a hundred meters depth, sir."

"Really! And you're not trailing an antenna or anything?

"No sir."

"My God! That's fantastic! Continue at full speed and position yourself half way between Taiwan and Quanzhou. Work on trying to hook data transmission to your auxiliary board. My plan at present is to use aerial observation to place you *precisely* in front of the PRC fleet and give you GPS coordinates to set off a few torpedoes just in front of them. You won't be the only sub there, Jim Knight and Al McDowell aren't far behind you in subs John Warner and Mississippi. Carriers Kennedy and Reagan are already close enough for a little bit of air support, but they'll be at extreme range. Okinawa has a lot of recon birds aloft to keep us up to date. If you get your data feeds set up correctly you should be able to download the stream from the UAV of your choice to see for yourself what's happening on the surface."

"Yes sir," Allred said, slumping back in his seat. His mind reeled as he came to grips with the fact that the rules of submarine warfare—the ones he'd worked so hard to learn over a long career—had just been blown out of the water by that little chip they'd installed. Head swimming he turned, "Ramirez, you been listening?"

"Yes sir." Ramirez' eyes were wide.

"Let's see what we can do about feeding data streams out of this aux board to our screens. Then talk to the people on the other end of the line and let's see what we can see from those recon feeds they claim they can deliver."

***

Captain Carson walked down the hall of the Taiwan ministry of Transportation and Communications. His guide took him to the office of a Mr. Zhang who was responsible for the submarine communication cables. Zhang's secretary apologized, "The PRC has disabled our communication satellites. Mr. Zhang must cancel your appointment. He's fully committed just dealing with the crisis."

Carson's guide began to back out of the office, saying "So sorry, I will help the Captain make another appointment."

Carson didn't move, even when his guide tugged at his elbow. "You must tell Mr. Zhang that I have been sent here expressly to help deal with this crisis. I'm carrying part of the solution with me!"

The secretary stared round eyed at him. "No! He told me that *no one* should interrupt him!"

Before the others comprehended his intention, Carson stepped to his left and opened the door to Zhang's inner office. Zhang, looking extremely flustered, was staring in horror at the screens on his desk while speaking frantically through his AI. Now both the guide and the secretary were plucking at Carson's elbows. The secretary spoke Chinese in a frantic tone that suggested she was calling the guards. Carson summoned his command voice and said, "Mr. Zhang! I've been sent by the United States to help you with this crisis, you've got to listen to what I have to say."

Zhang's eyes had widened when Carson opened the door. Now his eyebrows rose. He held up a finger to wait, said a few more words in Chinese over his AI, then said, "What?"

"The PRC has taken out our satellites as well. We're concerned that they'll cut the undersea cables next." Zhang's eyes widened again. *Surely*, Carson thought, *they must have considered the possibility?* He said, "I've brought equipment to provide an alternate method for communication if the cable's destroyed."

Zhang continued to stare a moment, then spoke to his AI in Chinese again. Carson wondered if he was calling security himself. Carson looked over his shoulder and saw that a couple of guards had appeared, but for now were simply standing there. Zhang's secretary wrung her hands and Carson's guide looked appalled. Carson turned back to Zhang and found that the small man had come around his desk and held out his hand to shake. Zhang said, "I am sorry I don't have much time. What do you have to offer?"

Carson said, "Obviously I can't replace your missing satellites, the PRC shot down the American satellites in this part of the world as well."

Zhang's eyes widened again.

"However, we suspect they may cut your undersea cables as well and we have a method to replace them at least temporarily. I'm sure you understand just how much worse your situation'll be if you're completely cut off from communication with the rest of the world?"

***

Colonel Ennis stepped up to the podium in the packed briefing room at Nellis UAV flight control. "Ladies and gentlemen! All the American and ROC satellites over the western Pacific and eastern Asia have gone down over the past few hours. The brass are sure the PRC did it, and in fact the PRC has just filed a protest against our 'invasion of their sovereign privacy through our constant and untenable satellite observation.' Most importantly however, intelligence believes that the PRC is about to invade Taiwan and other islands in the Taiwan Strait. At present, we and our UAVs represent the United States' only observation platform that'll provide real time information regarding what the PRC's doing. We need that info so Command can respond to this situation.

"Therefore we'll be flying constantly, even at night, using IR. Major Carlsson's working out a rotation schedule, but we're all going to be putting in long hours for the foreseeable future. Questions?"

A senior NCO stood, "Sir, how can we fly the birds or retrieve their images without a satellite link?"

Ennis ran his hand through his hair, "Yeah, though we're hoping their AIs will return them to base, we may have lost the two birds that were up when they shot down the satellites. This is classified Secret, but all of you are cleared and have need to know so I'm telling you now that we have a new system for communicating with the birds that doesn't rely on satellite communications. From now on we'll be flying everything with the new system and don't expect to lose any more planes unless the PRC shoots them down."

Ennis pointed to the same non-com who'd put his hand up before. "Sir, without the satellites, will the latency be low enough to fly the UAVs?"

Ennis barked a laugh. "You'll find this hard to believe, but talk to Apert there next to you. He's been using the new system already. Latency's as close to zero as we can measure, and data transmission's way up! You're actually going to be able to do your job better, not worse…"

***

Twilight crept over Quanzhou as Wang received the message he'd been waiting for. "Sir! We've confirmed that all of the American satellites over us have been destroyed. More are coming over the horizon, but Beijing Aerospace Command's confident they'll be able to deal with those as they come over.

Wang looked at his screens to confirm the status of his battle plan, then turned to his left, "Send the signal to detonate the charges on the fiberoptic cables for Okinawa and Taiwan. Then send test queries over the internet to determine whether the cables were indeed transected. Ping them regularly so we'll know if they repair the cable."

Turning to his right, he said, "They're blind. Launch the boats. Aircraft to stand by…"

***

Allan spoke in Ell's earpiece, "SecDef would like to speak to you."

"Put him on."

"Lieutenant?"

"Yes sir?"

"Are you meeting any resistance to setting up your comm center?"

"There was some at first sir, but I've extensively taken your name in vain. That pretty much smoothed it over."

The Secretary barked a laugh, "Good! I'm hearing that your comm center's succeeding in reconnecting our forces and giving us eyes in the sky again. Do you need any more help from me to make that work better?"

"No sir. We're currently set up to handle all the comm situations I can envision, the only significant issue is delivery and hook up of chips out on the sharp end. I can't really influence those issues."

"Okay, if you're caught up, I'd like your help with a different issue I'm hearing about?"

"Certainly sir."

"The people in the field are apparently suffering information overload. I imagine you're familiar with the issue? There's so much raw information available that they can't comprehend it fast enough to utilize it?"

"Yes sir."

"We have algorithms that sort satellite data into maps of friendly and opposing forces. Our people are used to that kind of info. Information from UAV surveillance has always been used to elaborate and refine satellite data, but now that we *only* have UAV surveillance our folks aren't doing very well mapping it usefully. Knowing you're some kind of math genius, I'm hoping you can do something to fix that issue?"

"Sir, I doubt that I can figure out how to incorporate UAV data into current mapping setups—which I'm not familiar with—as fast as I can create a new mapping paradigm that displays all the info I have access to. Would that be okay?"

"Lieutenant, almost anything you could give us would have to be better than the mess we've got at present, please do what you can."

"Sir, if I may make a suggestion?"

"Go."

"Sir, if I can produce clear maps, we might want to deliver them to the news services. The PRC watches our news. Seeing that we know exactly where their forces are might be pretty daunting?"

"Hah! That's a ballsy—excuse the metaphor in your case—idea. I'll need to get advice on that idea; just let me know when it's available."

***

Allred cursed continuously as he tried to comprehend the voluminous data from the recon flights. He'd positioned his sub in the Strait as directed and they were at "silent stations," trying to disappear into the sea. However, he felt like his head was going to explode any moment now! There were ships *everywhere*, many of them moving toward Taiwan, all at different rates. If there was a "fleet" there to attack, he couldn't recognize it. A hushed voice said, "Captain?"

"Yes?" He noted his heart beating faster with apprehension.

"Admiral Larsson's on the line."

"Okay," he said quietly, pointing to his AI headband to indicate he wanted the signal routed there.

He felt the eyes of the crew in the command center, a mixture of anxiety and anticipation on their faces. He looked up at his HUD, "Admiral?"

"Hello Larry. I just started looking at the feeds from our aerial recon, trying to understand what I'm looking at. There's a crap load of boats in the Taiwan Strait, and a lot of them seem to be heading toward Taiwan, but there sure as Hell isn't an obvious fleet to my eye. You doing any better than I am at sorting that mess out? Damned sure we don't want to *start* a war by shooting up some commercial shipping."

"Sorry Admiral, I've been gnashing my teeth, probably looking at the same imagery you are. I can't tell squat from the current nighttime infrared pictures. Boats everywhere, just like you say. Using the images from just before sunset I've figured out how to zoom in on some of the ships and identified some of the ones out in the middle as bulk carriers. Doing that one by one is taking *far* too long to be useful, but I've got crew doing it anyway. They're trying to figure out which of the boats we see on current infrared imagery can be cross identified with the warships from the daytime imagery. We don't have much experience with analyzing overhead imagery here in the sub. If there's a way to use shipboard AIS transponders to identify the vessels none of my people can figure it out." He heaved a big sigh, "Can't the *intel* people help us sort this mess out?"

"I've sent messages up to intel about it. We've been

using satellites to query shipboard transponders for decades and they've gotten dependent on that data. It's as if taking down our satellites put us back into the dark ages! The transponders can be queried from Taiwan, but only out to about 45 kilometers which doesn't help much. I've got some of my crew here at PACOM trying to zoom in and categorize them too and we'll try to get back to you. I'm about to touch base with the other sub captains and the carriers to see if they've got any ideas."

A young female voice broke into their conversation, "Admiral?"

"Yes." Larsson said irritably.

"I believe I can help, sir."

"You've been listening in on our conversation? Who the hell *are* you?!"

"Sir, this is Lieutenant Donsaii. I haven't been listening, but my AI's handling all communications through the PGR relay servers and it forwards problems to me. The idea was that I would troubleshoot comm issues, but my AI forwarded this one too because it's something the Secretary of Defense asked me if I could help solve."

"Donsaii!" Allred could almost hear the Admiral's blood boiling over the audio connection. *Who the Hell is Donsaii?* Allred wondered, *the name's familiar but...?*

"Yes sir."

"Your *personal* AI is handling this entire comm situation?"

"Um, yes sir, my AI's running on a supercomputer sir."

Sounding like someone having their words extracted one by one like teeth, the Admiral grated, "Okay... tell, us, your, idea, El Tee."

"Yes sir, I've gotten access to the UAV records for the past few days and had my AI backtrack through the recon images to follow each boat back to the PRC coast. We'd previously identified those ships as cargo or warship as well as by type a couple of days ago. I've just had current IR imagery that combines data from several UAVs put up on your displays. Let me know if you're getting it? PRC warships are designated in red and PRC cargo vessels in yellow. Non PRC vessels are green. Size of dot corresponds to size of vessel. If you hover over a dot, a window should open displaying details regarding the type of ship, armament, speed, plotted destination etc. The tails are proportional to their speed, the fine black lines are where they came from. The fine white lines point out eventual destinations as they'll intersect on Taiwan if the vessels don't change course. As you can see, at their present rates and vectors, most of the ships will converge at several locations near the west coast of Taiwan. Despite their different start times and speeds the warships will arrive semi-simultaneously off the coast of Taiwan at about 0300 local time. Cargo craft will arrive 2-3 hours later. Support aircraft intended to converge simultaneously with the naval warcraft would need to be launched shortly before 0200. In keeping with such a plan we haven't as yet identified significant air launches, though there are a few—probable surveillance craft—up."

"My God!" breathed the Captain as he took in a display that suddenly made sense.

Ell paused momentarily, then she said, "I'd also like to be sure you're aware all the undersea fiberoptic cables for Taiwan and Okinawa have been transected sometime in the past thirty minutes. Some communication has been restored using PGR chips, but technical challenges incorporating the chips have prevented complete restoration of services."

The Admiral said, "Lieutenant, get me SecDef for mission authorization. Allred, position yourself out in front of that middle collection of warships. Knight, McDowell, position yourselves in front of the northern and southern groups respectively.

"What I'm expecting from Command is that you'll be tasked to fire warning shots that'll make them aware just how exactly we know their locations—despite our satellite losses—so consider that in your mission planning. Be aware we expect eleven more attack subs to arrive in your area over the next 10 hours in case we need to do more than fire warning shots. That, in combination with our sudden ability to give you exact positioning data for their surface assets should let you make every torpedo count.

"Lieutenant, also forward your image analysis to the Admirals commanding the three carrier battle groups. They might be getting similar tasking."

"Yes sir. Might I also suggest that a question on this line, directed specifically to my name, would allow me, through my AI, to provide your Captains an exact GPS location and updated expected location at current course and speed for the ships at which the warning shots are to be fired. Truly exact positioning would, I'm sure, be more impressive to the opposing force?"

After a brief silence, Admiral Larsson said, "Okay, sub captains, you heard her, get updates right before you fire.

"Lieutenant..." there was a long pause, "*damn* glad you're on our side."

"Thank you sir."

Chapter Ten

General Wang noticed a stir of excitement among some of the men in the command center. He'd been contemplating leaving the command center for a nap as they were in a quiet phase while waiting for the naval craft to cross to Taiwan. So far everything had gone so well it made him nervous. Nonetheless, he wanted to be rested at the time of the actual invasion. The excited jabbering and pointing was occurring in the media observation group near the door so he decided to stop by their desk on the way out to his cot...

As Wang approached he saw someone had come up with a very nice display for the tactical map for the Taiwan Strait. It looked like it showed all their naval assets in red, and their cargo vessels in yellow. It showed their current locations and extended fine lines disclosed their eventual destinations. He leaned forward, focusing on it. "Excellent strategic display!" He looked around, "Who developed this?" To himself he was thinking, *I'll promote whoever it is to my staff; saying this makes it far easier to evaluate our status. It makes the board we've been using seemed clumsy.* He realized no one had answered him. He looked around at them; they were all nervously looking at one another. "Who?!" he demanded. Still no one answered so he focused on the man who sat behind the display.

That man stuttered, "S-s-sir! This's a feed from the

American news site CNN. They're reporting that we're about to invade Taiwan and are displaying this map detailing what they believe to be the location of our forces. We have no idea why they'd invent such a thing?"

Icicles drove into Wang's chest as he stared at the map. *Now* he noticed that the markings were in English. He turned and rapidly walked back across the room to stare at the main tactical display. On it markers for elements of his fleet made little jumping movements as their locations were updated. He knew where they were supposed to rendezvous, but the American news agency's map was much more elegant in the way it displayed the progress of *his* fleet. He looked back over his shoulder at the CNN map. It seemed similar, but tingles in his scalp greeted the thought that the CNN map might be more accurate and up to date. *How can this be?*

Wang turned to bellow at the Aerospace Command desk, "You've missed one of the American satellites! They're displaying the location of our fleet on their bái chī news services! Find it! The satellite probably belongs to one of their damned news corporations!"

The room paused for a moment of panic stricken silence, then chattering swept across it as Wang stalked to the Aerospace desk with murderous intent...

***

At CNN headquarters the announcer indicated the map. "This display of the Taiwan Strait has been provided to CNN by the White House itself. All American satellites, including CNN's, over the eastern

Pacific and China were destroyed at approximately midnight Eastern Standard Time. Statements from the People's Republic claimed the satellites were downed in order to stop Western spying on their sovereign territory. Of note, they also shot down communication satellites, not just observation satellites. White House press releases and" he waved at the screen, "this strategic feed suggest that the destruction of our satellites may actually have been a first blow in a war strategy intended to reclaim Taiwan, which the People's Republic has long asserted is simply a runaway part of its own country. It's unclear, however, how the White House has access to this constantly updating map of the Taiwan Strait which reportedly discloses the exact location of each of the Chinese naval assets. If, in fact, as claimed, all American satellites including military observation satellites are down, we have no idea how they're obtaining the information..."

***

"General Wang."

The general recognized the voice of the Chinese President in his earphone. "Yes?" the general responded irritably.

"The American news services are displaying a map that they claim shows our forces crossing the Taiwan Strait!"

"Yes sir. I've seen it."

"Well? Is it accurate?"

"Surprisingly so." Wang ground out.

"How?!" he paused, "How are they acquiring this information?"

"Exactly what I am asking Beijing Aerospace Command! They *claim* that they've taken down *all* the American and Taiwanese satellites, but that simply cannot be." He paused a moment, then said, "Unless one of our allies is providing them this information?"

"Could it be their planes?"

"Their planes send their data back by satellite. With the satellites out of commission, the planes would have to return and land and their information wouldn't be this current."

"Should we abort?"

"Absolutely not! They *can't* stop us!"

"My information says two of their Carrier Battle Groups are within range."

"Extreme range." The general said reassuringly. "Their planes can reach the theater, but can't loiter to acquire targets. The Taiwanese don't have the *strength* to stop us and the Americans are too *far away*. We'll have the island firmly in hand before the Americans arrive, never fear."

"Okay." the president said dubiously, then, "Wait, I have a call from the American President. I'll patch you in so you can hear what he has to say."

Moments later the two men listened to the recognizable sound of the American President's voice in the background with a translator's voice following in the foreground. The President didn't sound angry or emotional. The translator said, "We, the American People protest the destruction of billions of dollars' worth of our satellite technology. You have done this on the pretext of wanting your privacy without even a warning of your intent to do so. We demand compensation for the value of our satellite technology and negotiations regarding how the satellites of all countries may coexist. More importantly, we note that the obliteration of our satellites occurred concurrently with the destruction of the satellites of the Republic of China, a country which *should* have the right to observe its own part of the world under your privacy pretext. It's evident from the mobilization of your naval forces into the Taiwan Strait that the destruction of the satellites was actually just the first step of an invasion of the Republic of China. Your claim that the Republic of China is actually a part of the People's Republic of China is belied by the fact that you must use military force to obtain their cooperation.

"We the People of the United States of America hereby signal our intent to help the Republic of China defend itself against your aggression."

Wang heard the seething undertone of fury in his own President's response, "Americans have *no* right to interfere in internal affairs between the *People's* Republic of China and its own rebellious province which only *characterizes* itself as an independent Republic. Your vaunted military won't be able to significantly influence this internal disagreement without your space based spies." Wang silently applauded those words and felt gratified to see that his own President seemed to have more spine than he'd expected.

The American President responded enigmatically, "We're sorry to hear your response. We've deployed new technology that will provide us the ability to respond to your aggression without our satellites. In an effort to avoid bloodshed, we'll demonstrate that ability within the next sixty minutes. Goodbye."

***

Laurence E Dahners

Allred heard Admiral Larsson's voice in his earphone. "Okay sub commanders, we have Command authorization for the warning shots, alpha, hotel, delta, zulu, echo, foxtrot. Execute to achieve detonation 30 minutes from my mark... Mark."

Allred looked to his weapon's control officer and received a nod. He nodded back and shortly heard the deployment of the two torpedoes from their tubes. The fish dove below the thermocline in order to diminish their sonar profile and swam straight and true on their wire guidance using a speed that provided a very low sonar signature. They precisely located themselves in front of the designated PRC warships' courses—as provided by the RQ-7 loitering above, through Ell to the sub captains. The torpedoes paused at depth until a precisely calculated moment, then drove up to detonation depth.

***

Captain Lee dozed in his command chair on the bridge of his LST (Landing Ship, Tank), grateful for the relatively quiet seas that were allowing the embarked soldiers in his loading bays to transit the Strait without emptying their stomachs. A brilliant flash woke him and his eyes flashed wide to see a mountain of water rising in front of his bridge. Moments later the bow of his ship heaved up violently. Tremendous creaking indicated the strain placed on the frame of his landing ship. The top of the mountain of water blew open and water began pouring down out of the sky onto the upper works of the LST. Cursing he called out for damage reports while simultaneously demanding to be put in contact with Command.

***

"General Wang! Six underwater explosions have detonated, presumably torpedoes! They missed, but were very close and *exactly* off the bows of six of our ships! Some damage to the frame of three LSTs has occurred, with leakage into the cargo bays holding their armored vehicles! Two destroyers also have frame damage and some leaks."

Wang's heart sank as he saw the plots of the location of the six ships subjected to the warning shots. They consisted of two ships at the front of each of his three groups. The destroyers had not picked up any torpedoes on sonar. How had the warheads been delivered? Submarines seemed obvious—after all the American submarines were famous for their stealth—but how had their president been able to communicate with submarines so immediately *while* they were stealthy? By report, the detonations had occurred *precisely* off the bow of all six ships indicating precision placement in keeping with the Americans' damnable "smart weapons." But *how* would their submarines have known *where* his ships were with such precision? *And* known which ships were military assets rather than civilian or cargo?

It was a convincing demonstration of their understanding of his tactical plan and their ability to deliver devastating blows at will.

Radar on his missile boats had detected the first glimmer of American aircraft coming over the horizon.

Taiwan was launching aircraft as fast as they could.

The element of surprise was lost. For a moment he contemplated bulling through, but the defenders would have an incredible advantage from their apparent knowledge of the *exact locations* of his ships. Even if they only had three submarines, each could be carrying as many as fifty torpedoes. They'd just demonstrated they could take out a ship with *each* torpedo.

Or a hundred and fifty of his ships with three submarines.

If they actually had more submarines available...? His aerial assets should have readily been able to overcome the ROC's Air Force when the enemy didn't know where he was.

But with this evidence that the Americans could vector their forces precisely to each of his ships, it'd be a bloodbath, exactly what he'd been told to avoid. With a heavy heart he said, "Get me the President."

***

The CNN anchor looked up at the cameras. "We interrupt this broadcast with some good news. As you know the White House has been providing us a feed displaying the alarming naval deployments of the People's Republic of China into the Taiwan Strait. That feed has, over the past twenty minutes, disclosed that the PRC naval elements have stopped advancing and begun to withdraw. The PRC has just announced that they'd been conducting an 'unscheduled naval exercise' which has now been completed. Further they have apologized for not disclosing the nature of the events to the rest of the world more quickly and thus inciting so much tension.

"I believe that I can speak for the world as a whole when I say we'll all rest easier now.

"There were no further announcements regarding the obliteration of Western and ROC satellites earlier except to say that the PRC would be willing to negotiate reparations for the costs of the destruction of the existing satellites and consider some verifiable means to allow restoration of communication satellites, though not spy satellites, over their part of the world in the future."

***

A week had passed since the Chinese backed off. Ell sat in the PGR communication center wondering whether *anyone* remembered where she was. The civilians from PGR Comm had left the morning after, having completed their assigned setup task. Ell had, to their great delight, delivered the additional $10,000 to each of their accounts as promised. She and Major Geller were the only personnel assigned to the comm center. Now that the shouting had subsided, Colonel Whitt was no longer intimidated by Secretary Amundsen's admonitions. The Colonel said he didn't have any spare noncommissioned personnel to help watch over the comm center.

Major Geller felt shanghaied and abused. He spent most of his time trying to get assigned elsewhere.

The comm center didn't really need much in the way of maintenance, but Ell shuddered to think about what would happen to Pacific military communications if one of the chip racks failed for some reason, especially with no one present in the center to address the problem. She'd taken to sleeping on a cot in the comm center, stepping out only briefly for food and showers.

At least Colonel Whitt hadn't denied them food from the commissary. It wasn't all bad; things were so slow that Ell'd been able to plan out several experiments and order equipment delivered to her apartment back in Las Vegas.

"Allan, please contact Amy."

"Ell! Where are you now?!"

"Still in a hole somewhere on the East Coast. Does the sun still shine out there in the big world?"

"My God! What do they have you doing?"

"Right now I'm maintaining a comm center for the military. It's using my new chips."

"Really? Does it actually *need* someone there maintaining it?"

"Well, not really, unless it goes down, then they'll desperately need someone to fix it. That's what I'm here for."

"Crazy! Well what'cha need?"

"I'd like to have you arrange removal of the wall between my lab and that empty bedroom."

"What? Why?"

"I've ordered a bunch more equipment. There won't be room to set it all up in the current lab."

"Hah! Can do, but what if they permanently reassign you back east, wherever you are?"

"Well, we'll just have the wall restored when we have them remove all those doorways we had installed."

"Okaaay, you still have no idea what's going to happen next huh?"

Someone rapped on the doorway to the comm

center. "Nope. Hey someone's here. I've gotta go," Ell said. She turned to the door and came to her feet.

A Captain stood in the door, looking pinched. "Where's Major Geller's office?"

Ell shrugged, "Sir, I'm afraid he doesn't have an office, he works out of the comm center here."

"Where would I find him then?"

"I'm not sure sir. I can have my AI contact him if you'd like."

"I thought he was in charge of some kind of high tech comm center?"

"Yes sir."

"Well, where is that?"

"Sir, this is it."

His eyebrows drew together, "When's the new equipment coming in?"

"Sir, that's it," Ell said, pointing to the five racks sitting against the far wall.

The Captain blinked slowly. "Okay... please call him for me."

~~~

When Major Geller arrived, the Captain said, "Major, Captain Norris reporting for duty. I'm to relieve..." he looked up at the orders displayed on his HUD.

Geller whooped. "Finally!" He stepped forward holding his hand out to shake.

Norris said, "...a Lieutenant Ell Donsaii."

"God *damn* it!" Geller exclaimed, dropping his hand.

***

When Ell got back up to the real world on the

Laurence E Dahners

surface, it turned out that the driver who'd delivered Norris had waited for Ell in order to take her back to the Pentagon. She reported as directed to the Office of the Air Force Chief of Staff.

A Captain looked up when she knocked. She appeared to be shocked, "Lieutenant, what are you doing here in BDUs!"

"Sorry, Ma'am, I wasn't told what uniform to wear. I thought I was catching a flight back to Nellis."

"Oh my God! We're supposed to have you at the White House this afternoon for some kind of ceremony. Please tell me you have a dress uniform with you?"

"Yes Ma'am," she held up her duffel. "Where can I change?"

"You can't go to the White House wearing a uniform that's been wadded up in a duffel! Let's take it over to the Pentagon cleaners and get them to press it."

Ell smiled, "It isn't exactly wadded, but I take your point."

Captain Platt shepherded Ell around, getting her uniform pressed and then back to her office where Ell changed into her dress blues. "Oh my God! You look like a recruiting poster! How did you get such an exquisitely tailored uniform?"

Not wanting to say anything about how clothes just seemed to look good on her Ell said, "I took in a seam or two myself."

Platt said, "Wow! You'll have to teach me how to do that!"

Platt then took Ell to meet an official car that took Ell to the White House. The entire time Platt kept up a chatter about protocol for visiting the White House. She got in the car with Ell, still continuing her patter. Ell finally interrupted, "Do you know why I've been invited to the White House?"

Platt looked surprised, "No, don't you?"

Ell shrugged, "Well I have an invention that I would think they're wanting to incorporate into military communications, but I'm not sure why I'd need to meet the President for that? I'd expect the military brass would be making those decisions."

After stopping several times for security checks, they pulled up to a side entrance portico and got out. Platt consulted her HUD and said, "We're supposed to go to the Blue Room."

A White House staffer met them at the entrance, "Lieutenant Donsaii, right this way. Oh Goodness! We want you to wear your Medal of Honor!"

Ell ducked her head minutely, "Sorry, it's in storage at present. I *am* wearing my ribbon."

Platt exclaimed, "You won the Medal of Honor?!"

The staffer said in horror, "No one told you to bring it?"

To Platt, Ell said, "Yes Ma'am." She turned to the staffer, "I'm sorry Ma'am, no one told me until this morning that I was expected at the White House."

The staffer put her hand to her brow as if she'd developed a headache. She almost moaned, "I suppose they wanted to keep it a surprise!" She turned and looked down the hall, "Jimmy!" A young man stopped and looked questioningly at her, "See if you can scare up a Medal of Honor. I think they keep one or two for impending ceremonies." The young man nodded and started purposefully down the hall. He returned shortly with a Medal of Honor in its display case.

Platt helped Ell put the Medal around her neck, then Ell was directed to a room filled with military brass. When they stepped in, Platt said, "Oh-oh, lotta gold leaf in here!" She turned to Ell and said, "Just keep calm. We'll stand over here and fade into the woodwork."

Ell did as recommended, but moments after they entered Admiral Larsson spotted her and started their way. Ell's stomach tightened with some apprehension, thinking he might begin another confrontation. Instead, he stopped in front of her, came to attention, glanced down at the medal around her neck and gave her a dress formation salute.

Nonplussed to be receiving yet another indoor salute, Ell returned it.

The Admiral said, "Lieutenant, I owe you a heartfelt apology and my sincere gratitude. My attitude toward you during the recent crisis was inexcusable; born out of years of exhibiting a lack of respect for junior officers who've not yet earned it. In your case my low regard was unfounded and unacceptable. I've reviewed the actions for which you were awarded that Medal and I'm truly humbled by the bravery you've shown." He raised an eyebrow and gave a little grin, "Your tolerance of my bad behavior is typical of the forbearance I've heard that you offer others with my tendencies.

"Much, much more, I appreciate the fact that you provided my command the means to pull its irons out of the fire without loss of life, to say nothing of the fact that you successfully averted a war. I thank you from the bottom of my heart."

Platt gazed in astonishment as Ell, apparently calmly, said, "Thank you Admiral. I'm fully aware we were all under a great deal of stress."

Platt's eyebrows remained high as a number of other senior officers including the Chairman of the Joint Chiefs of Staff came over, each saluting the young woman in their turn, then offering congratulations.

At one point, when none of the brass were speaking to Ell, Platt leaned near and whispered, "*What* did you do?!" but before Ell could respond, the Secretary of Defense came over to offer his own congratulations.

Then they were all asked to remove their AI equipment before being herded into the Blue Room. Once they were seated the President spoke briefly to the entire assembly. "The people in this room deserve our Nation's public congratulations as well as the Nation's thanks for their roles in averting a war in the Straits of Taiwan. Unfortunately, a public announcement of your roles and a celebration of your achievements would further damage our shaky relationship with the People's Republic. But, even if I cannot do so publicly, I at least intend to hold this closed door ceremony. I'm sorry about requiring you leave your AIs, with their attendant cameras out of the room, but I want there to be no chance this ceremony might be recorded and become verifiably public."

The president began calling some of the senior officers to the podium to present them with Distinguished Service Medals for their roles in the crisis, finishing with Admiral Larsson. Because Distinguished Service Medals were typically given to senior officers, Ell wondered why she was there. Perhaps the President intended to speak to her about incorporating PGR chips into the military after the ceremony?

Then, to her surprise, the President said, "Lieutenant Donsaii, if you'd approach the podium?"

Platt's eyes were wide as she watched the young Lieutenant gracefully rise and approach the President without apparent apprehension. Platt couldn't know Ell was taking long slow breaths to stay out of the zone.

She strode to the podium with her usual uncannily

graceful coordination. It looked as if she approached the President every day. Teller said, "Lieutenant, I have two items for you. First, I hear through the grapevine that your junior rank served as a significant impediment during your attempts to accomplish some of the tasks recently set before you by your Commander in Chief. Therefore I would like to replace those single gold bars," he opened a box, "with these paired silver ones." The President displayed a set of Air Force captain's bars to the room. "Now it's my understanding that I haven't promoted you far enough to have prevented some of the obstructionism you recently encountered at the hands of officers superior in rank to yourself," he smiled, "however, apparently even the Commander in Chief is constrained from jumping an officer too many grades in a time of peace."

He turned back to the room, "I'm not sure everyone in the room's aware that this young lady is the one who developed the theory for and worked out the construction of the communication chips that saved our bacon when the satellites went down? But here she is, nineteen years old and in this past week, arguably the most important person in our world. Thus, Captain Donsaii, I'd like to add a medal to your collection of Presidentially awarded symbols of your Nation's appreciation. It seems to me that your Medal of Honor is lonely." He turned to the room, "Don't you think it would look better with the Presidential Medal of Freedom accompanying it?" The room surged to its feet in applause as he lifted a medal out of its box and hung the ribbon around her neck. As he did so he said in a low voice, "Please stay here after the ceremony, I'd like to speak to you about how best to utilize your talents in the service of your country?"

"Yes sir."

A session of all around hand shaking and congratulations followed. At some point Ell noticed the President had left the room and wondered if she was supposed to have followed him, but then a staffer came and guided her quietly away to the Oval Office. While she and Platt waited outside, Platt pinned on her Captain's bars. Then Ell was admitted, though Platt was instructed to wait outside.

President Teller and Secretary Amundsen were seated in comfortable chairs with another man Ell didn't recognize. To her surprise they all rose to their feet when she entered. The President extended his hand and she shook it as he murmured, "Captain, so good of you to come."

Nonplussed, Ell thought to herself that he was acting as if she had some choice but to obey her "Commander in Chief."

Teller turned and said, "Of course you know Secretary Amundsen and perhaps you recognize my Science Advisor, Doctor Horton?"

~~~

As Ell shook their hands Horton stared at the young woman, finding it difficult to reconcile this pretty, college-freshman-aged girl, with the Donsaii who'd turned the physics world upside down. He shook his head, reminding himself that attractive women *could* be highly intelligent, bemused that the old stereotype was confounding him even when he should know better.

They all sat and a staffer brought coffee. When Ell didn't want coffee he promptly produced a Coke per her request. President Teller steepled his fingers and looked at Ell over them, "Doctor Horton tells me that you are likely the most brilliant scientific mind since Albert Einstein. He's been chiding our military commanders" the President grinned at Amundsen, "for utilizing your incredible talent to fly UAVs."

Ell had blushed, "I'm sure *that's* not correct. I just got lucky that I managed to find a map that does actually fit a 5th dimension to quantum results. I was even luckier finding a physical means to build the PGR chips based on that math."

Horton chuckled, "Maybe Einstein was lucky that $E=MC^2$ worked out too?"

Secretary Amundsen interjected, "I must say, I *am* embarrassed that we failed to recognize her potential despite her graduation from the Air Force Academy in only two years and her notification to us that we were entitled to royalty free use of her new PGR communication chips. Apparently, whoever received that notice didn't recognize the chips' value and simply filed the notice. Do you mind if I ask what kind of royalties you receive on that invention?"

Quietly Ell said, "Two point one billion dollars."

The three men's eyes widened. The science adviser said "You sold it for two billion dollars?!"

Again quietly Ell said, "No sir, that's the minimum annual royalty."

"My God!" the President said, also in a quiet voice. "How can it be worth so much?"

"Sir, it should replace *all* forms of communication over the next one to two decades. It's far cheaper than laying fiberoptic cable, has much higher data rates than radio, is uninterruptible, uninterceptable and undetectable. I'd strongly recommend that your administration give some thought to minimizing the economic upheaval it's going to cause in the communication industry as it supplants all broadcast radio, cell phone technology and hard wired communications."

President Teller's eyes widened in alarm, then he produced a wry grin. "Crap! Just when I've been thinking of you as a solution, it turns out you're another *problem*?!"

"Yes sir." Ell said apologetically.

The three men, some of the most powerful people in the world, looked at one another in a mixture of consternation and amusement. The President narrowed his eyes at Ell, "You aren't about to create even more upheaval with some other technology are you?"

Abashedly, Ell said, "I'm afraid that appears to be likely, sir."

Dr. Horton exclaimed, "What kind of technology?!"

"Sir, I only have a minimally functional prototype at present and it's unclear whether this technology can be matured sufficiently to be broadly useful, but it seems likely that it'll heavily impact current satellite technology. In view of current patent law, I'm sure you can understand why I wouldn't want to fully divulge its nature without a non-disclosure agreement in place?"

Horton guffawed, then grinned at the other two men, "Someday I'm going to tell my grandkids about the day a nineteen year old told the President of the United States she wouldn't talk to him unless he signed an NDA!"

Teller shook his head ruefully, "Somehow I don't think this will be the last interesting story you'll have. Tell you what, Chip, you sign a non-disclosure agreement with her, learn what it's all about and then decide if and when *I* need to know about it.

"All that aside," the President continued, "we still

have the initial issue we set this meeting up to discuss. Captain Donsaii, it is my belief that your talents are wasted as a soldier. Do you agree?"

Ell tilted her head, "Not wasted perhaps, but it *is* plausible that they could be utilized more fully."

This time Secretary Amundsen laughed, "Politely put. I suppose that my idea of setting you up with your own Air Force funded research lab wouldn't be full utilization either?"

Ell slowly shook her head. "My military obligation would be up before it really got going."

The President said, "How would *you* suggest we use your talents? For whatever time you still owe on your military commitment?"

"Yes sir, that'd be twenty one months." She looked up at the ceiling a moment to collect her thoughts. "If I were you, I'd again release me from active duty—like I was released to go to grad school. You could then hold the twenty one months that I owe in reserve against a time when you *do* need my talents, such as they may be, for a particular problem. In the meantime I'd be free to continue my research at a more rapid pace; if I'm lucky, bringing more useful products to fruition. Like the PGR chips, such products will probably be disruptive in the short term, but helpful in the long run."

The three men looked at one another. Horton said, "And you'd do what? Set up your own private research lab somewhere?"

"Yes sir, but I'd also like to go back to grad school. I have a yearning to be around brilliant people my own age. I'm hoping to work it out so I still get to work on what *I* want to work on."

Horton barked a laugh, "I imagine you could, but what professor would take you as a graduate student?

He or she wouldn't be able to teach you anything."

"Oh no, that's not true sir, I have a *lot* to learn from experienced investigators, though I take your point that they might not want someone with my notoriety assigned to them." She shrugged, "I was intending to use an alias anyway since I fear the Chinese or others might make more attempts to kidnap me. With an alias and a disguise I hope to work with a group that'll treat me like any other researcher, rather than thinking of me as the weird kid who got lucky."

The meeting degenerated at that point as Ell had to explain the multiple kidnapping attempts made on her so far. Eventually President Teller sat back and said, "Well, *we* might not have recognized her talents, but it would certainly appear that the PRC did!" He stood, "I'm late for my next meeting. My decision is that we *shall* release her from active duty, pending a need for her services. Lean on the Witness Protection people to provide her with another identity as she's requested and let her do what she does best, however she wants to do it." He paused, tilting his head as if wondering if he'd failed to consider something, then gave a sharp nod, "Make it happen gentlemen."

Horton shepherded Ell to an empty office where Platt again had to wait. Ell pulled up the non-disclosure agreement she'd obtained from Dr. Smythe and Allan modified it to fit the current situation. Horton printed two copies and they both signed them.

Horton said, "So, tell me."

"Well you know my math postulates a microscopic fifth dimension through which quantum entangled particles are attached to one another?"

Horton nodded.

"It appears that it's possible to open a portal from

one location in our universe to another location in our universe through that fifth dimension. I have *some* evidence that material objects can pass through such a portal."

Horton's eyebrows climbed high, "I'd call bullshit if it weren't for the fact that I'd have said the same thing about your PGR chips. Do you have any physical evidence that you can do this, or only a theory?"

"Yes sir, I've opened some microscopic holes through which gas and liquid have successfully traveled, but those were very preliminary experiments."

"My God!" Horton leaned back in his chair and cradled his head in his hands. "Are you thinking that people can travel through such portals?"

"Sir, I have no idea as yet. The process does require a great deal of power to energize it and theory would predict that power requirements would increase rapidly with portal size. There may be side effects from the waste energy released in the area. These may make it impractical to transfer large objects or people. But I mentioned satellites earlier because an ability to transfer even small quantities of liquid or gas to an orbital facility could have a huge impact on space satellites or stations."

"Oh Geez!" Horton ran his hands through his hair. "Can you keep me up to date on developments with this?"

Ell looked at him calmly, "Sir, I don't believe that this kind of information can be trusted to email. If you'll let me provide you with a PGR chip so I can be certain of the security of the communication?"

Horton frowned, "Huh? Oh! You mean a chip for which you'd have the paired member so no one could intercept?"

"Yes sir. Then I could send you an e-mail telling you I had information for you. You could unplug your AI and attach the chip to your AI headband and we could have a secure conversation."

Horton's eyebrows drew together, "Okay..." he cleared his throat, "I can see I need to give more thought to the security implications of your chips."

Chapter Eleven

Ell didn't have her disguise or her security team in D.C. so she caught a military flight back to Nellis. She called Steve in transit so her security team could meet her as usual when she left Nellis proper. "Steve, I have news too. I'll be leaving Las Vegas so I'd like to meet with the team when I get back to talk to them about it?"

"Okay... Amy too?"

"Oh, yes please."

~~~

Amy and all ten of Ell's security team crowded the living room of Ell's apartment. Amy'd laid out corn chips, salsa and beer. Ell was initially pleased to see her team showing restraint regarding the beer, but then noticed that their mood seemed... somber? She tried teasing Barrett, "Big B, why is it you always seem to be assigned in rotation with Mary? You and her going sweet on me?"

Barrett stared at her somewhat apprehensively, "Uh, no Ma'am. It's just uh, worked out that way. If it's a problem I can ask Steve to work on rotating the assignments more?" He raised his eyebrows.

Ell quickly said, "Sorry, no, no, I was just busting your chops a little."

Ell worried even more about what had them down. She pondered it a little. She wondered if she had some form of Asperger's syndrome. Something mild that still left her out of touch with what was bothering these folks she worked with. Or was it just normal boss-employee standoffishness? Finally she waved her hands to get the attention of the group, "So we've got some serious stuff to talk about." Ell raised her eyebrows and the room fell silent.

Everyone's eyes fixed on her. They all had the round eyed look of someone waiting for truly bad news. "I've been released temporarily from my commitment to the Air Force so I'll be leaving Las Vegas. I'm not sure where I'll be going, but I expect that I'll be heading back to North Carolina," she shrugged, "at least temporarily."

You *couldn't* have cut the silence with a knife. Ell's heart sank, *something was seriously wrong,* she thought.

She cleared her throat, "Personally, I'm hoping that you'll all be willing to come with me, wherever I wind up going. But, of course that'll have to be up to you. I'm concerned because many of you seem kind of down in the dumps? If there's something I'm doing as your employer that's making you unhappy, please let me know. If you want to leave, we can work out some kind of severance package..." Her voice broke.

They stared at her like deer in headlights.

She thought about how she'd become so fond of them. Even though, in order to preserve the notion that they weren't known to one another, she rarely spoke to them in public, they often talked to one another in her apartment. She'd gotten so used to seeing them hanging around her that their mere presence was comforting. She was going to feel terrible if a lot of them quit...

Then Randy did a little fist pump, "All right!" He turned and glared at Steve, "You had us all worried for nothing!"

Ell turned to Steve who reddened, "Sorry Ms. Donsaii, I got the impression from your call that you were letting us all go. I tried to let the group down easy by giving them some warning." He dropped his gaze embarrassedly to the floor.

Ell raised her hands to her cheeks, "Oh! Heck no! I *love* you guys! It's so comforting to know that you're always there, ready to protect me! I'm worried that about the time the Chinese finally stop hassling me, some other groups are gonna step up!"

A cheer went up in the room. Amy raised her glass, "A toast... To the best boss *ever*!"

They all raised their glasses and Ell felt her anxiety melt away. The atmosphere became party-like and Ell made it a point to go around and talk to each member of the team one on one. Just before they broke up Ell buttonholed Steve and Amy and said, "I think we should go somewhere for a little R&R? Maybe Amy could reserve us a house on the beach in Florida for a week? A place where we could assume no one'd find me and we could all relax together. I was *really* worried about our morale there and feeling that I should have done something to boost our *esprit de corps* a long time ago."

Steve rubbed his chin. "I'm a little worried that too casual a relationship might undermine their sense of duty to you. But, on the other hand," he looked away and his voice got raspy, "if they love you like they will if they spend much time with you, they might have even more motivation to do their utmost."

Ell rolled her eyes and grinned, "Well I don't know about all that, but let's try to set it up between now and Christmas. I hope to be busy again come January."

***

Nuñez and Chief Milton were looking up into the comm bay of one of the MQ-9s discussing the progress of refitting the UAVs with the PGR chips when they heard crisp footsteps approaching from behind. Nuñez glanced back, then to Milton's surprise dropped his hands to his sides, came to attention and did an about face. As Milton turned, Nuñez fired off the sharpest salute Milton'd ever seen him produce. Expecting to find a general behind him Milton was bemused to find Lieutenant, no Captain! Donsaii standing there, a big grin on her face. He saluted too, trying to render his sharpest as well.

Donsaii saluted back "Chief, Sarge," she nodded to each man. "I believe you owe me a beer?" She smirked at them.

"Yes Ma'am!" Milton's normally taciturn face beamed. "Word is you saved our ass in the Pacific? That where those Captain's bars came from?"

"Yep." She grinned, "'Unofficially.' Couldn't 'a done it without you two. Thanks! In celebration I'm throwing a little party at The Flight Risk Friday at 1830 hrs. You able to buy me my beers then?"

"Yes Ma'am." They replied in unison.

"Good, 'cause that's my last day, I'm getting discharged. Hate to have to come back and haunt you for my beers after I'm a civilian again."

They looked at one another.

"See you then." She turned to go, then stopped to toss something to each of them. "Here's the other part of our bet."

Milton looked down into his palm where a key chip for a Ford rested. Wide-eyed he said, "Ma'am? You can't do this!"

She grinned, "Sure I can Chief, we're in Nevada and I lost a wager."

"But... a car? That's too much!"

She frowned, "Yeah, probably." Then she grinned, "But I really appreciated your help. Those chips are bringing me more money than I can spend. I'll be a civilian soon, so I can do things that are too much if I want to can't I?" She mock glared at him, "It *is* still a free country, isn't it?"

***

The Flight Risk was packed. Ell'd invited everyone she knew from Nellis and it looked like every last one of them must have taken her up on the offer. The free drinks were flowing freely as Ell had an open tab for anyone else in the bar too. Nuñez and Milton approached her, each carrying a beer. When they held them out Ell raised her eyebrows, "Gentlemen, I'm disappointed in you! You *do* know I'm not old enough to drink don't you?"

They looked at one another, then back at her, "Really?"

"Really," she grinned, "but I'll take a Coke?" she raised an eyebrow.

They laughed, "We'll have to drink these beers ourselves first!"

Sasson nudged her elbow, "Hey, last time we were interrupted before I could properly demonstrate the finer points of pool to you! You ready to be humiliated?"

Ell moved her head to look over both of his

shoulders, "Where's your army?"

"Oh ho!" he crowed, "It's on! I'll rack the balls."

Ell was speaking to Axen when Sasson said, "You want to lag for the break?"

Ell wondered how hard she should play this game of pool. But she wanted to speak to Axen a moment longer so she said, "No, you go ahead and break."

Sasson's break was heralded by an explosive "Crack!" and he crowed as a ball dropped. "I'm about to school an Olympic athlete on the finer points of a game!"

Ell raised an eyebrow and leaned on her cue as she watched him put in five balls, talking smack with each one.

When he stymied himself he turned to her, "Stick that in your pipe!" he chortled. "Knowing the user's manuals backward and forward ain't going to save you this time."

A small group had gathered to watch by then, drawn in by Sasson's noisy patter. Axen called out, "I wouldn't piss her off Lieutenant. If I recall, last time she was in this bar she sent a dude to prison with a broken wrist."

"Hah, she's got to win this one by putting balls in, not by hitting people with her pool cue!"

Ell peered down the length of the cue Sasson had handed her. It was straight.

He said cheerfully, "Checking the cue isn't going to help. This is a game of *skill*."

She grinned at him, then without a word she ran the table.

By the time she'd dropped the sixth ball, nudges and whispers had brought the focus of attention of most of the people in that end of the bar onto her. Ball after ball had dropped. All falling perfectly into the centers of their pockets, even on hard cuts and bank shots. Ell gave him a little bow and handed him the cue stick, "Thank you for the game," she said gravely. She turned to an open mouthed Nuñez, "I'm *really* ready for that Coke now."

A susurrus of conversation washed over a room that'd grown quiet while she played, Axen called out, "If I were you, Sasson, I'd stop challenging her."

Sasson grinned and shook his red face, "You'd think I'd have learned by now."

<u>Epilogue</u>

Amy and "Raquel" walked past Randy and Steve as they entered Tres Locos for a last session of dancing. Ell and her security team were heading back to North Carolina the next day. Amy would stay a few days longer to supervise the packing of Ell's research gear by the van lines and negotiate the remodeling of the team's apartments back to their original state with the building's owners. Neither Amy nor Ell had strong ties to Vegas, but they both felt a little wistful about leaving their favorite bar.

Ell went directly to her favorite taqueria for her usual grande burrito. While in line she heard a familiar voice.

"Raquel?"

Ell turned, "Dan! How are you doing?"

"Good! Hey, you're using more than one word at a time!"

Ell shrugged.

"Nooo! Back down to none! Hey, I'd love to dance with you again, I have fond memories."

"Okay, let me eat my burrito."

Dan raised an eyebrow as he looked at the huge burrito she'd just taken from the vendor, "Careful how much you eat! I'm planning to give you a workout."

~~~

As Amy and Ell ate they saw Dan out on the floor doing his freestyle routine and occasionally waving to Ell to come join him. After they finished eating both Amy and Ell got up and walked out to the area on the huge floor where the freestylers were doing their thing. Dan smiled at Ell as she walked out and he imitated her stride as she walked out to the floor, though he only marched in place. As Ell approached she began walking in time to the music and slowing so she was soon marching in place like he was. As before, he then threw in some little moves starting with a pumping of his right arm which she imitated. He changed the footwork and began making turns which she followed. Dan, entranced with her graceful coordination, again wondered whether she could somehow read his mind and therefore knew what he was about to do, or just followed so fast that he couldn't tell she was lagging him. He led her in more and more complex moves without losing her at all, then sped up his rhythm, delighted as she easily kept up. Finally he did a front flip, but to his disappointment she didn't flip with him. He raised his eyebrows at her.

She shrugged at him lifting her own eyebrows. He reached out his hands and she took them, easily following his tug to spin into a cuddle. They began swing dancing and, following the Tres Locos tradition, Dan steered Ell out to circle around the periphery of the big floor.

~~~

Amy continued freestyling herself as she watched them moving around. She looked around at other people in the bar, noting that many of them were already watching Dan and Ell. Looking back at the floor she saw several other couples doing more intricate routines, but slight missteps, slipped grips and bobbles produced a certain inelegance in their movements. Amy shook her head, though Dan and Ell weren't doing anything terribly complex, the grace and beauty of their movements drew eyes to them.

~~~

Dan's eyebrows rose as he made an attempt to lead Raquel into a Lindy Flip. She somehow started to follow yet stopped him and bobbed back from the move so gracefully that he felt sure the little dip they made would have appeared choreographed to anyone watching. Every turn they made flowed so smoothly, he felt like he'd been dancing with the girl forever! Why couldn't it be this way with other women?

The song drew to a close and he tried to get her to stay on the floor for another.

She leaned close and said, "Thirsty."

Dan grinned at her, "Back to one word at a time?"

She grinned back, shrugged and turned to walk off the floor. He admired her as she walked away. He shook his head. *Even just walking she displays that simple, supple grace.* It wasn't that her hips swung suggestively, just that every motion seemed perfect, catlike, harmonized. *Oh well maybe she'll dance again in a bit?*

~~~

Despite the grande burrito she'd eaten Ell still felt hungry so she headed back over to the tiendas to get some nachos. On her way there she saw Cody who'd first taught her to swing dance. Cody had his eyes on Ell despite the fact that Connie, his school dance partner, was standing next to him with a possessive hand on his arm. He lifted his hand to give Ell a little wave, but Connie said something sharply to him and he dropped his hand. Ell gave him a friendly little wave back and continued over to the taqueria she liked, somehow feeling Connie's eyes burning into her back. She wondered why Connie disliked her so. It wasn't as if she'd tried to horn in on Connie and Cody's relationship.

When Ell returned to the table Dan was sitting there with Amy. He grinned up at her, then eyed her plate. "You're *still* hungry?!"

Ell raised an eyebrow, then nodded with a grin, but said nothing. She waved at the nachos indicating they should help themselves. Dan and Amy both had a couple of nachos.

Dan said, "If you don't explode, would you like to dance again after your nachos?"

Ell nodded.

Dan rolled his eyes and turned to Amy. "Does she carry on these word or less conversations with everyone, or is it just me?"

Amy raised one eyebrow and dropped the other as if concentrating on a serious question. After a pause she narrowed her eyes and said, "Nope, just you."

He looked at Ell whose lips were pursed around the straw in her Coke. Her eyes sparkled at him.

Then Connie led Cody out onto the floor. They began a very complex and athletic routine they'd been working on in class. It was exciting and almost looked dangerous. Fascinated, Ell couldn't take her eyes off them.

As they left the floor when the song finished, Connie pulled Cody directly past Ell's table like she had the last time they'd been at Tres Locos. Ell continued to clap as they approached, but Connie glared at her as she approached and just before she passed she sneered and said, "You'll *never* be able to dance like that."

Cody leaned down and said quietly, "Don't listen to her, she loves being a bitch like this!" Connie tugged at his wrist but he resisted and said, "I'll be back, I hope you'll dance with me?"

Ell shook her head minutely. "I'm leaving town, you should save your friendship with Connie."

Connie said imperiously, "Come on Cody. She's *just* a pretender. She can't *really* dance."

Cody frowned but acquiesced to being led away.

Ell found Dan's eyes wide on her. "What?"

"You're leaving?"

Ell shrugged and nodded.

"And you're not going to show that girl what you can really do?!"

Ell snorted, wrinkled her nose and shook her head.

His eyebrows rose, "You're gonna just let that 'pretender' and 'can't dance' crap stand?"

Ell narrowed her eyes.

Amy put her hand on Ell's forearm, "Come on. Show her what you can do! We're *all* dying to see." Amy's eyes flicked briefly over toward where Steve and Randy sat trying not to look their way. "Besides, we're leaving town, you'd just as well leave a mark behind."

Ell leaned close to Amy's ear. "But then no one else'll ask me to dance."

Amy grinned, then leaned close herself, "Dan's staked you out so they probably aren't going to ask anyway, go ahead and go out in a blaze of glory."

Ell said quietly, "It might ruin your chance for a dance too."

Amy rolled her eyes, "Don't worry about that, I want to *see* it!"

Ell's eyes focused a moment in the distance, then she turned to Dan. "Okay."

"Great!" He started to rise but she had her hand on his arm.

"I don't have much stamina so we have to be done in three minutes okay?"

"Sure." Again he would have risen, but she still held his arm.

"Wait until another fast song starts, start with swing and finish with breakdancing?"

His eyes moved up to the left as he considered. "Okay."

She bent to suck on her straw again, grinning up at him.

~~~

They waited through another slow song, but when a fast one started Dan stood eagerly, holding out a hand. "Raquel?"

She makes the simple act of standing into a work of art, he thought. As they walked out to the floor he realized she'd taken off her boots.

Soon they were swing dancing with the elegance she always seemed to bring to it. As they spun through several pretzels she said, "Faster."

He raised his brows and complied. He twirled her and she said, "We can do some of those flips you've been trying to get me to do."

He hadn't tried to do a Lindy Flip at this speed before and wasn't sure if it actually *could* be done, but he tried it. As he swung her into it he worried about whether he'd be able to catch her if it went wrong. But it didn't go wrong! It went perfectly, as did an "around the world," a "frog," a "cannonball," and a "back flip!"

Dan knew he'd have goose bumps if he weren't working so hard. Doing these elements with other girls was a physical struggle with a sense of danger, even at lower speeds. Doing them with Raquel seemed effortless and somehow completely controlled despite the speed they were dancing.

Her hands pulled free from his, she moonwalked away from him, but then he found her following him like they'd started when they first met. So he boosted the complexity of his standing "toprock" moves more and more, amazed as she followed his moves effortlessly. As they danced he noticed that everyone else on the dance floor had stopped to watch them. Briefly he wondered if she'd freak out and quit like she had before.

He shrugged and dropped to the floor to begin a windmill, as he leapt back to his feet she dropped to windmill herself. His eyes narrowed as he realized she was perfectly copying his own personal style of windmill.

She was back on her feet! He dropped to helicopter and leapt back up to see her dropping for a perfect copy of his helicopter too. He did a backflip, so did she! He did a front flip and she was right with him! The song was reaching its ending so he skipped and did a round off into a series of back handsprings across the dance floor.

Out of the corner of his eye he realized she was tumbling beside him, so that they were performing handsprings in perfect synchrony. When he landed she came down slightly after he did and he realized that *she'd* finished with a double! *Holy crap!* Instead of landing and stopping like he had, she bounded backward from her landing to go back across the floor the other way.

Her first turn was a standard handspring, next she bounded two flips without touching her hands down!

As Dan watched dumbfounded, the next flip she twisted as well as tumbling end over end without touching down on her hands, then did another double and landed perfectly on her feet, throwing her hands up like a gymnast! She grinned at him.

The room exploded in applause, people surging to their feet, having just seen something they'd never seen before! Dan narrowed his eyes, there was something different about her nose! Suddenly, she reached up and grasped her hair, tugging on it... it came off—a wig! The hair underneath was short and reddish blond. She looked different, yet familiar.

My God! I've been dancing with Ell Donsaii! he thought, scalp prickling.

She took a deep sweeping bow and strode off the floor. *Holy shit!* he thought. *No wonder she could do any dance move I ever thought of!*

~~~

As Ell walked to the table where Amy sat, she passed near an open mouthed Connie and winked at her with a grin. She picked up her boots, quickly stamped them on and headed for the exit. Dan trotted out after her, but by the time he got there, she was nowhere in sight.

The End

Lieutenant

Hope you liked the book!

Try the next in the series, Rocket (an Ell Donsaii story #4)

To find other books by the author try Laury.Dahners.com/stories.html

Author's Afterword

This is a comment on the "science" in this science fiction novel. I've always been partial to science fiction that posed a "what if" question. Not everything in the story has to be scientifically possible, but you suspend your disbelief regarding one or two things that aren't thought to be possible. Then you ask, what if something (such as faster than light travel) were possible, how might that change our world? Each of the Ell Donsaii stories asks at least one such question.

"Lieutenant" asks, what if some genius worked out a way to used quantum entangled molecules to send faster than light messages through another dimension? How might that affect the way our world works? Considering the enormous impact of improved internet communication on our world, there's little doubt that such quantum based communication would result in further changes of almost unimaginable potency.

Laurence E Dahners

Acknowledgements

I would like to acknowledge the editing and advice of Gail Gilman, Elene Trull and Nora Dahners, each of whom significantly improved this story.

Made in the USA
Middletown, DE
07 December 2018